Elwell Stephen Otis

The Indian question

Elwell Stephen Otis

The Indian question

ISBN/EAN: 9783337056803

Printed in Europe, USA, Canada, Australia, Japan

Cover: Foto ©Andreas Hilbeck / pixelio.de

More available books at **www.hansebooks.com**

THE

INDIAN QUESTION.

BY

ELWELL S. OTIS,

LIEUT.-COLONEL U. S. ARMY.

———◆———

NEW YORK:

SHELDON AND COMPANY,

No. 8 MURRAY STREET.

1878.

CONTENTS.

THE INDIAN QUESTION.

CHAPTER I.

HAS OUR INDIAN POPULATION DECREASED?

THE long established belief, that the Indian population of the United States is rapidly disappearing, and that the time is not far distant when it will become so insignificant in size, that it will cease to give annoyance to the Government, has scarcely received contradiction until within the past ten years. Among a large portion of our citizens an opinion still widely prevails, that the Indian tribes which formerly roamed over the country east of the Mississippi River, have almost ceased to exist. We are occasionally informed of the sad fate of the nations of the former North-West Territory, or possibly, of the advance in civilization which those small remnants of the Iroquois, and Cherokee nations which still remain with us have reached. The State of Delaware is about to place in his final resting place its only red native, while the summer visitors at Nantucket are shown the grave of the last representative of the original proprietors of the soil of that island.

The generation last past, were more firmly convinced of this alarming decay, than the people of the present. President Jackson found humanity weeping over the fact, and that fact was known to every succeeding President until the Mexican cession of territory partly replenished the loss.   More than forty years ago the artist Catlin hastened to the far west, "to lend a hand to the dying nations" and to snatch "from a hasty oblivion what could be saved for the benefit of posterity."   In the official documents with which we are now furnished, we learn that this decay has been, in some instances, arrested, and that a few of the Indian nations are actually increasing in numbers.   Yet we are asked to believe, that the Indian population of to-day is surprisingly small, when compared with that which existed at the beginning of the seventeenth century.

The reliable data upon which this belief is based cannot be discovered.   Many of the reports of the French, and indeed of the Jesuit fathers, in regard to our early native population, appear as romantic as the Spanish accounts of the population of the West Indies and of Mexico. We can as readily believe, that the Emperor Montezuma controlled a force of three millions of fighting men, or that Hispaniola contained a population of one million of souls when discovered by Columbus, or that the Spaniards destroyed within thirty-eight years the lives of fifteen millions of the inhabitants of the New World, or that the Spanish Jesuits in Mexico, in the space of twenty years brought nine millions of converts to the faith of Rome, as to place confidence in the ingenious stories which deceived the ministers of the fourteenth Louis.

And yet the current literature of a very recent time spread abroad these reports as historical truths, and added thereto unsupported statements of marvellous invention. We are told that the Six Nations of New York numbered at one time upwards of sixty thousand ; that more than two hundred thousand Indians subsisted upon the fish drawn from the Columbia River, and the game taken in its vicinity ; that the missionaries on the California coast happily governed seventy thousand Christian converts, and that forty years ago the country watered by the Mississippi and the Missouri Rivers, and their tributaries, contained an Indian population of four hundred thousand souls.

These, and similar fictions, in reference to population, have often arisen from the statements made by Indians themselves to the early missionaries, and to those whites who mingled with them for the purposes of trade. Nearly every tribe, however small, boasts of its former importance. They all have their brilliant traditions. An apparently well informed Tuscaroran will to-day place the population of his tribe, before its removal to the State of New York, at ten thousand. In the latter part of the seventeenth century, the Sioux nation was supposed to number forty thousand, but in the year eighteen hundred and fifty-two the Rev. Mr. Riggs estimated their number at twenty-five thousand; and during this interval of time, the nation probably received an almost constant numerical increase. These estimates were partially based upon Indian reports, and almost entirely so, as far as the early French writers were concerned.

Many fictitious accounts were spread abroad by the early Canadian voyagers, and gained more or less credence. Their desire to magnify the dangers attending their journeys into the interior of the Continent, influenced them to enter the field of romance in their descriptions; and their residence upon the extended plains of the west, and their exciting labors upon its magnificent rivers and broad lakes, so enlarged their imaginations, that it was impossible for them to confine their statements to the strict limits of truth.

The received impression of a former numerous Indian population, has been supported by historical mention of frequent Indian wars, in which the Colonies and the United States Government have been engaged. History often satisfies itself by informing us that the Indians "were defeated with great slaughter," or it occasionally relates that in certain engagements, the power of certain nations was forever broken. It seldom gives numbers or losses.

Mention of exceeding great mortality from pestilence, also gives strength to this impression regarding population. Vigorous nations are supposed to be reduced to insignificant proportions ; and indeed this supposition has more to sustain it than the supposed destruction in battle.

The amount of Indian literature, as it is termed, still in existence, is very great. The number of authors who have exclusively treated of the Aborigines of the United States, and of the southern portion of the Dominion of Canada, may be counted by hundreds. Surely during the last three centuries these Indians have not been neglected by historians and chroniclers.

Congress appropriated and paid about eighty thousand dollars for the labor of collecting and digesting "such statistics, and materials, as would illustrate the habits, present condition, and future prospects, of the Indian tribes of the United States," and received its information, I believe, in six large volumes.

For several years, ethnology has been endeavoring to discover the origin, and peculiar characteristics of the aboriginal race, and has been enthusiastically assisted by skillful toilers in the various branches of science. Yet with all the research necessarily given to the collection of this mass of historical and scientific literature, the fact that the original Indian population of our territory has ever been extremely scanty, except possibly, within the valley of the Columbia, has but recently been discovered. An enumeration of this entire early population, either relatively or approximately, has not been attempted. It would be considered very rash to assert that it is nearly, if not quite as numerous as at the time of the first successful colonization upon our eastern border, especially since such a statement would conflict with that "curious fact, that savages waste away before modern civilization." Such a statement would directly oppose the received opinion and understood experience of the past century. We are told that the New Zealanders, the Australians, the Hottentots of South Africa, and the Moors of Barbary, are vanishing; "that the Tasmanians have vanished;" that many of the nations of the North American Continent have ceased to exist, and that the red men are doomed to disappear. But with the light which documentary history, and published correspondence of a private nature, have thrown upon the former condition of the aborigines, their slight punishments at the hands of the whites, their subsequent wanderings, and the varying political or social organizations, in which they were included; from a careful consideration of their habits of life, and the extent of country required to subsist them, the assertion that this population has not diminished to any considerable extent, could be maintained with a fair degree of plausibility, even if it could not be supported by convincing argument. I am of the opinion, that upon our own territory it has scarcely decreased during the past two and one-half centuries,—if it can be considered to embrace both the full and mixed bloods, whether within or without present tribal relations. Or, to make the statement more clear and emphatic, I believe that the Indian population of the United States, as shown by the ninth census, differs very little numerically from the actual existing Indian population of the seventeenth century.

The Smithsonian publication upon "Systems of Consanguinity," prepared by the Honorable L. H. Morgan, of New York, traces the migration of the United States Indians from the valley of the Columbia river. It suggests the probable courses, or routes of migration, followed by those Indians who passed to the east of the Rocky Moun-

tains, and sub-divides them into two great families of nations, called respectively, the Dakotan, and Algonkin families. The Mobilian Indians of the South are attached to
the Dakotan branch. The Indians west of the Rocky
Mountains are classified as the Columbia, Shoshonee and
Apache families of nations, and the village Indians.

More than one hundred distinct nations are mentioned,
and the leading characteristics and recent movements of
many are discussed. Mr. Morgan's conclusions are generally accepted by the scientific world, and I am not aware
that any attempt has been made to overthrow them.

His work furnishes the only comprehensive history of
our Indian race yet prepared, and at the same time, it
gives much valuable information concerning its present
condition.

Many of the statements regarding population are necessarily based upon the opinion of others, for reliable
statistics cannot always be obtained, and therefore in some
cases his estimates of numbers are placed at too high a
figure. Numerical losses, which many of the nations have
sustained during the past two centuries, are also evidently
exaggerated.

He however discovers to us many of the lost tribes
living in new localities, and still within their former tribal
organizations. He follows the remnants of once powerful
nations, and finds them incorporated with kindred people
of other tribes, or existing as small bands under new appel-
lations. He has undoubtedly put an end to the wild
statements regarding Indian population which have been
so universal, both in this country and Europe, during the
last quarter of a century, and which cannot be better
illustrated than by quoting the language of Sir John
Richardson, recorded in the report of his journey from
Montreal to the mouth of the Mackenzie River. He says
of the Crees and Chippeways : " They are identified as a

nation with the Algonkin, and Leni-Lenape, or Delawares, who once owned the whole country east of the Mississippi, as far south as Carolina, but who, blighted by the precocious expansion of the Anglo-Saxon colonists, have dwindled down to a few remnants of mixed blood."

A great many of the facts which Mr. Morgan presents in his work, are supported either by Indian tradition, or by information acquired within the present century. The character and numbers of those Indians inhabiting the interior of the former Louisiana territory, were almost entirely unknown until the expedition of Lewis and Clarke, in eighteen hundred 'and four and five, passed through the heart of that country. It is true, that for a long time previous to that date, the fur trade was actively conducted by many private individuals, and also by partnership enterprises ; but those who communicated with the Indians in the prosecution of that business, furnished little information upon which reliance could be placed. The factors of the great American fur companies were about to enter the regions watered by the Missouri and its tributaries. These men were shrewd, and intelligent, yet undoubtedly in many instances very imaginative, but they were competent to make important inquiries, and to arrive at seemingly satisfactory conclusions ; and through them, much of our knowledge respecting the Indians with whom they communicated has been derived. They often varied materially in their conclusions upon the same subject, and as to population they differed widely. Indeed the same individual was constantly changing his views, or at least his report of estimates, when giving, upon different occasions, the population of those tribes with whom he was most intimately connected.

We possessed knowledge of the Indians of the Pacific coast at an earlier date, although meagre, and from very questionable sources. Long before the beginning of the present century, citizens of foreign nations were engaged in trading along that coast. In seventeen hundred and ninety, more than twenty vessels, part of which were owned in Boston, were solely occupied in that business. The natives were supposed to be very numerous from the confused accounts which sailors rendered. Little that was reliable could be obtained, until Lewis and Clarke reported their discoveries upon the Columbia. Bonneville in eighteen hundred and thirty-three added materially to the stock of information, in the report of his journeyings among, and at the bases of the Rocky Mountains. Lewis and Clarke found thirty-four distinct tribes, or nations, along the above mentioned river, but Bonneville ascertained that the population to the west of the mountains and south of that river, was exceedingly sparse.

On the coast of Lower California, missionaries had settled as early as sixteen hundred and ninety-eight, and missions were extended to the north, under the auspices of the Jesuit, the Franciscan, and the Dominican orders. They exerted considerable influence over that native population, numbering some thirty thousand souls, and dwelling between the forty-second parallel of latitude and the southern point of the peninsula, and from the Sierras and the Colorado River to the ocean.

The Indians of New Mexico, who have so long plundered the extensive region between the Colorado of the West and the forks of the Colorado of Texas, are increasing in population. Crafty and warlike, they have for three centuries held the territory over which they roam, against the white man. They drove out from that country the Spaniard, and the Mexican, and have successfully resisted, until very recently, the attempts of the American troops to place them in subjection. The number of Mexican captives among them attest their success, and their utter inability to understand the binding force of treaty stipulations is apparent from the frequency with which they have made and broken faith with their neighbors— the Pueblos.

The Comanches of to-day, differ little from their ancestors of the seventeenth century, who robbed and murdered the inhabitants of the Mexican border, and who even then mingled with their own wild rites and superstitions a barbarous imitation of the mass. Those who entertained La Salle on his voyage down the Mississippi River, would doubtless compare favorably with their descendants, who are now puzzling the agents of government in their endeavors to invent some method of treatment which will secure their willing obedience. They should, from their long contact with European civilization, be very much wasted in numbers, but they are obstinate, and set natural law at defiance. They refuse "to melt away as ice and snow do at the approach of summer," and insist upon perpetuating and increasing their species.

The population of the Missouri and prairie nations is undoubtedly smaller than formerly. As a rule, strong Indian nations increase, and those which are weak, diminish. The Ojibways, the Sioux and the Crows, are stronger now than ever, while the Poncas, the Omahas and the Missourias are represented by feeble communities. Many causes produce this result. Frequent hostilities between powerful and weak organizations, as between the Sioux and Poncas, or the Sioux and Pawnees, make constant drains upon the population of the weaker, which is not replenished by natural increase. These weaker organizations, hemmed in as they sometimes are, within a small section of country, are often without sufficient means of subsistence ; or from continued residence in the same locality, without change of camp, they invite by their filthy condition the ravages of disease.

There is also an attraction for the young men of the

1*

weaker tribes to join with stronger societies; and for this reason, the agents in the Indian territory have great difficulty in keeping intact some of the smaller bands. The Yanktons and Yanktonais are largely represented in the hostile Sioux camp, and the Delawares, who wandered into the State of Texas, resisted all attempts of the Government to unite them with their own people. These causes have affected the Indians of the Platte and Arkansas countries, who, though probably in diminished numbers, are not by any means as depleted as commonly represented.

The Pawnees, who formerly roamed the arid plains south of, and along the Platte River, have been reported within the past forty years, to number ten thousand, but are now reduced to about twenty-five hundred. In the days of their highest glory, four thousand warriors defended a nation twenty thousand strong.

A little reflection would show how utterly incorrect any such enumeration must be. An Indian population of twenty thousand, which totally neglects agriculture, and is deprived of the fruits of the earth, would require a herd of at least one hundred thousand buffaloes for its subsistence. Twenty or thirty thousand must be annually slaughtered, and a great number retained for increase; and one million of acres of those nearly barren plains would hardly nourish them, even if economically herded. How many millions of acres it would require to sustain a sufficient quantity of buffalo to subsist twenty thousand Indians, when the customs of the Indians and the habits of the buffalo are properly considered, is a problem exceedingly difficult of solution.

It has been said, that it requires six thousand acres of land to support an Indian who follows strictly the hunter's avocation, and the assertion can be stoutly maintained.

The territory embraced within the present boundaries of the United States contains about twenty-three hundred millions of acres, and our estimated native population, Alaska included, is three hundred and eighty-three thousand ; hence, the area of land in acres is six thousand times as great as the number of our Indians. Scatter this population throughout the country, and give to each person his three miles square of land, would it be unreasonable to suppose that the game would be exhausted in a series of years, if that alone was depended upon for food ?

The great majority of the native population which inhabited that portion of our territory now known as the plains and mountain districts of the west, subsisted on the products of the chase. They were not agriculturists. There are but few streams in that region from which fish could be procured. That population must therefore have been extremely scanty, and the stories of the early traders in regard to their numbers do not contain an element of truth. To this day the size of the wandering tribes is not known. Agents make wild estimates, based upon the statements of half-breed interpreters, or of whites long resident at their agencies, and whose convictions depend entirely upon their feelings.

The estimates are embodied in their reports, and they refer to them in succeeding years as being probably correct. The thirty-five thousand Indians heretofore reported as inhabiting Nevada, Utah and portions of Idaho, Arizona and California, dwindle to eight thousand upon actual count ; and when a correct census of tribes in other localities is taken, a great falling off in numbers will result.

Indians, when obliged to subsist on the game of the country, generally separate into small communities, and never remain in the same place for any length of time except during the winter months. Large encampments can be maintained only where the buffalo are plenty. In certain seasons of the year when the buffalo appear, the small communities unite in large camps which break up and divide after the pursuit of the buffalo is ended.   It is common to see small bands of five, ten, twenty or thirty lodges roaming the plains, or to see them encamped on the bank of a stream where wood and water are abundant.

In a section of country where the native population was great, the traveller would almost daily encounter these small bands ; but published accounts of journeys made forty years ago in the heart of our western territory show us that it was possible to pass from the Wind River Mountains nearly to the mouth of the Platte, without meeting a single Indian.   The larger rivers of Colorado, of Utah, and of southern Idaho were explored about the same time, and but very few native inhabitants discovered.   The Yellowstone River and its tributaries were descended with comparative safety though the cunning and hostile Crow warrior was a dangerous enemy to meet.

The territory between the Mississippi and Missouri Rivers was, upon its first discovery, under the sway of the Sioux, and allied nations, to whom reference has already been made.   They were even then pressing back adjoining tribes.   Migration to the east had ceased, and the tendency of movement was in a westerly direction.   The Crees were leaving the Lake Superior region and looking for a new home towards the setting sun.   The Chippewas were endeavoring to wrest the banks of the Mississippi from the Santee Sioux, and they in turn were crowding on their Teton brethren.   The latter were engaged in fixing the boundary line of the Crows and Blackfeet along the base of the great mountain range, and the Columbia River nations had found an eastern barrier, beyond which they found it impossible to advance.

As our information of the territory beyond the Mississippi River—the greater portion of which is still unreclaimed, and much of the same still unexplored—has been obtained during the present century, our knowledge in regard to what is considered its native Indian population is very incomplete. The aborigines who inhabited the country east of that river, even those roaming along its banks, were visited by whites more than two hundred years ago. It is essentially the last mentioned population which is supposed to be so fearfully wasted ; for, it has been made to contend with a vigorous Europeon civilization, which was constantly encroaching upon it, as it moved slowly to the westward. Erroneous opinions now entertained of a large native population during the early colonial period, and the positive knowledge of to-day, of the insignificance of the present existing population which has descended from the aboriginal tribes and nations, brings the conclusion of the great decay.

As it is impossible, with all the carefully prepared data furnished during the past ten years, to make a correct estimate of the number of Indians now within the limits of the United States, it is apparent that it would be difficult to even approximately approach the strength of the eastern Indians in the beginning of the seventeenth century, if we alone rely upon recorded opinions, which vary so materially that we can not escape the conviction that many of them had not the slightest foundation upon which to rest.

This is not to be wondered at ; for should we consult government official statistics of a recent date, we would be involved in confusion. We there find that in eighteen hundred and twenty-two, an Indian population of four hundred and fifty-seven thousand is reported. In eighteen hundred and thirty, that population numbered three hundred and thirteen thousand. In eighteen hundred and forty, it was four hundred thousand, and in eighteen hundred and fifty-five three hundred and fifty thousand. We therefore discover a loss between the years eighteen hundred and twenty-two, and eighteen hundred and thirty, of one hundred and forty-four thousand ; and between the years eighteen hundred and thirty, and eighteen hundred and forty, a gain of eighty-seven thousand, which is followed by a loss of fifty thousand in the succeeding five years. But the official reports of the War Department during this time, show the estimated population of the eastern Indians, and we can consider the estimates nearly reliable. In eighteen hundred and twenty-two, before Government had put in operation the policy of Indian removal to the West, the eastern Indians were said to number one hundred and twenty thousand. In eighteen hundred and thirty-eight, the Commissioner of Indian Affairs reported, that the total number of Indians with whom treaty stipulations had been made for their removal to the west of the Mississippi River, was one hundred thousand, of whom eighty-one thousand had then emigrated. Treaties had not been made with Indians living without the tribal relation, nor even with all those within the same. There were about twenty thousand Indians not included in the report, so that the figures of eighteen hundred and thirty-eight agreed with the estimates of eighteen hundred and twenty-two. The plan of removal and the expense attending it obliged the War Department to know the number of individuals who passed the Mississippi River under the provisions of treaties, and the most of those reported probably entered the new Indian country. The thirty-nine thousand still remaining were much scattered—many of them living in the populous States of the East. It was comparatively easy to enumerate them. The number in the north-west could not be determined with as much accuracy, but they were well known, and not over-estimated to any great extent. It is safe therefore to consider that the population of the eastern Indians in the year eighteen hundred and twenty-two was one hundred and twenty thousand. This is the earliest reliable enumeration that I am able to obtain. From this date until the present time, the eastern Indians can be followed in their migrations. The policy of removal beyond the Mississippi River, once inaugurated, was pursued through several successive administrations, and in eighteen hundred and fifty-three, the Secretary of the Interior announced that but eighteen thousand of the aborigines remained east of that river. The announcement must be taken with a grain of allowance, for the ninth census reports thirty thousand in that portion of the country. Of the ninety thousand removed, about sixty thousand are under the care of the Government within the present Indian territory, and a large part of the remainder might be discovered after diligent search.

But it is sufficient for our purpose, if it is admitted that the former population of the eastern Indian nations has not, within the past half century, met with any great numerical decrease. During the remainder of the discussion upon the subject, it becomes unnecessary to refer to very recent dates, except when an attempt is made to trace the movements of particular nations or tribes, and to discover their strength at different periods.

The question which presents itself, therefore, may be briefly stated as follows, viz :—Did that portion of our territory lying east of the Mississippi River contain an Indian population numbering more than one hundred and twenty thousand at the time of European colonization ?

Thirty-five years ago, the historian Bancroft, after a careful examination of authorities, placed the eastern Indian population in the first half of the seventeenth century, at one hundred and eighty thousand souls. His enumeration, he remarks, approaches and perhaps exceeds a just estimate of the number then existing, and if we examine official statistics, some of which are now generally accessible, we are led to conclude that many of his estimates are too large. Historians of particular nations however, writing at more recent dates, intimate that he has placed at too low a figure the past population of nations whose deeds they were endeavoring to commemorate, but produce little authority to overthrow his calculations. Bancroft allows a past population of ninety thousand to the Algonkin family of nations, and a like number to the Dakotan division. His conclusions in regard to the strength of the latter branch are probably more nearly correct than his estimate of the size of the former. In one of the early French reports, transmitted to the home government in seventeen hundred and thirty-six, an enumeration of all Indians claimed by that kingdom, as connected with the government of Canada, is attempted. We find that the total number of Indians capable of bearing arms, and inhabiting the country lying along the St. Lawrence and Ottawa Rivers ; from thence west throughout the entire lake region to Lake Winnipeg ; thence south along the Mississippi River, sufficiently distant to include by an eastern line the former Cherokee country ; thence north to Lake Ontario, including part of the Five Nations, was placed at fifteen thousand eight hundred and seventy-five warriors. Two thousand of the Sioux nation are embraced in the calculation, and might be excluded. Supposing therefore, that every five inhabitants could furnish one warrior, a fair proportion, we shall have within the territory above described less than seventy thousand Aborigines. Deduct from this number the ten thousand Indians of the Huron and Algonkin nations, dwelling north of the present United States boundary, and less than sixty thousand remain ; and by making a further deduction of seven thousand one hundred warriors, or thirty-five thousand inhabitants, which this French report credits to the Cherokee and Iroquois nations, we find that the entire population of all the Algonkin nations west of the Blue Ridge, and Alleghany Mountains, was placed at less than thirty-five thousand souls. To the east of these mountain ranges, the Algonkin population was little larger, as we shall hereafter attempt to show, although it occupied the entire Atlantic coast from the thirty-fourth parallel of latitude to our northern limit of territory.

Sir William Johnston, who was in charge of the great American Indian Department, reported officially in seventeen hundred and sixty-three, the fighting strength of those Indians inhabiting the State of New York and northern Pennsylvania, and of all that territory included within the present United States lying north of the Ohio River, and between the western boundaries of the States above mentioned and the Mississippi River. He reports twenty-one hundred and fifty warriors among the Six Nations, and their allies living upon the Susquehanna, and nine thousand one hundred and twenty among the remaining nations. This fixes the number of Indian inhabitants within that territory at fifty-six thousand.

The Six Nations composed of the former Iroquois, and the Tuscaroras who joined them in the year seventeen hundred and thirteen, are credited with a population of nine thousand seven hundred and fifty. Bancroft gives as the numerical strength of the Iroquois in the seventeenth century, ten thousand people, and to the Tuscaroras seven thousand. If he is correct, and Sir William Johnston's report is reliable, the Tuscaroras had lost more than six thousand of their number. This cannot be possible. Their former condition has been romantically portrayed, and their former importance overestimated. They were undoubtedly much reduced before they removed to the north, but their fifteen villages in Carolina were not as populous as generally supposed. If they were not larger than the villages of Cherokees they could not have contained more than thirty-six hundred inhabitants. Sir William Johnston finds upwards of nine thousand of the Five Nations proper, excluding those bands which had already removed from them. Bancroft's estimate of their former strength can not therefore be exaggerated. He is strongly supported by French and English authorities, dating from the middle of the seventeenth century.

A French report of sixteen hundred and sixty-six contains an account of nine Iroquois nations of small numbers, and Greenhalgh, who visited the Five Nations in the year sixteen hundred and seventy-seven, admits that they were able to muster twenty-one hundred and fifty warriors. They attained their greatest strength about the middle of the seventeenth century, at the time of the establishment of the French missions among the Onondagas and Cayugas. The Senecas were then friendly to the French arms, and they were known to include within their organization fully one-half of the entire population of the Five Nations. The earliest missionaries among them do not estimate the number of the Seneca warriors above twelve hundred.

We have more correct, and more complete information regarding the Iroquois, than of any other portion of our early Indian population. They had pushed their conquests over the native race in every direction. Their war cry had been heard from the New England coast to the Wabash, and from Virginia far into the interior of Canada. They had reduced a score of nations to submission, and the resolutions adopted at their council fires might be enforced in far distant regions. The important geographical position which they occupied, their strength and determination, made them arbiters of the future of the French and English colonies. They did more to arrest French extension of empire in the north, than all other human causes combined. Of them Governor Dongan said in sixteen hundred and eighty-seven, "The five Indian nations are the most warlike people in America, and are a bulwark between us and the French and all other Indians. They go as far as the South sea, the North-west passage and Florida to war. New England, in its last war with the Indians had been ruined, had not Sir Edmund Andros sent some of those nations to their assistance ; and indeed they are so considerable that all the Indians in these parts of America are tributary to them."

In the same year the French send to Europe their complaints, and demand the destruction of the Iroquois. They say that war against the latter is absolutely necessary to prevent a general rebellion of the savages, which would bring ruin upon trade, and extermination upon the colonies. "An exterminating war will be a merit in the sight of God, and for the glory of the King ; for it will assist to establish the faith in the west, and the King will have an empire from the mouth of the Saint Lawrence to the mouth of the Mississippi."

Louis listened to the complaint, and directed that a force be put in motion sufficiently strong to subdue the Iroquois warriors, which were placed at two thousand strong. He further directed that the captives should be sent to France for use in his galleys.

It seems incredible, that so small a nation could sweep over such an extent of our northern territory, and hold in subjection a large number of the inhabitants, who were of the same race and of equal advancement. If the country between the Ohio and the lakes was as populous as many early reports represent it, those small wandering bands of the Iroquois, which were frequently absent from their villages on the war path, could not have escaped destruction. The Miamis and Illinois were allied, and they boasted of large landed possessions. Had they been in any considerable number, the Iroquois could not have wrested from them and retained their territory.

It is extremely probable, that between our northern coast States and the Mississippi, the Indians located near

the shores of the lakes and along the banks of the larger
rivers, and did not penetrate the interior except in pursuit
of food. That even there they were guided by the water
courses ; for, prior to the introduction of the horse among
them, their movements must have been slow and tedious,
and they could not with safety separate themselves from
water. It is extremely probable, that their villages were
considered as permanently fixed, for without the horse or
some other beast of burden, any movement would have
been attended with great labor.

These conclusions are supported by the experience of
intelligent whites who could judge from observation. If
they are correct, do not the incidents connected with the
journeys of La Salle and the French Jesuits convince us
of the insignificance of the Indian population ? The
return of La Salle from the centre of the present State of
Illinois to Canada, along the rivers and lakes, and in the
winter, when Indians are collected in large bodies, and
the wanderings of those men who absented themselves
from his expedition, show that the country which he was
exploring was almost without population. Joliet emerged
from the mouth of the Wisconsin, and directed his canoe
down the Mississippi when that river was replenished with
the waters which the season of Spring bestows, and was
borne for many days upon its swift current, without detect-
ing any indications that the vast wilderness was inhabited
by man. From the mouth of the Wisconsin to the mouth
of the Ohio, he saw no Indians save a small band of the
Illinois. Hennepin, in his journey to the north, reports
and undoubtedly had, a different experience, although his
enemies assert that his statements bear the stamp of falsity.
The reader, after properly weighing these accounts, can
not escape the inference, that the great bulk of the Indian
population was in the north along the chain of lakes, and
that the country immediately south, extending we might

say, to the territory of the Southern Indians, could hardly
be considered inhabited. I am of the opinion therefore
that Sir William Johnston's estimate of numbers, mentioned on a preceding page, is large, and that the whole
north-west to the Mississippi boundary, did not even contain a population of thirty-five thousand.

A great difficulty is met when we attempt an enumeration of the Algonkins of the coast. Romance and history
have been artfully or unconsciously blended, and it almost
appears to us that the first white settlers were men of ex-
traordinary mould and surprising prowess, who forcibly
beat back into the wilderness the hordes of savages which
had determined upon their annihilation. In New England,
the great Captain Standish slew and spared not, until the
voice of the good Robinson was heard from across the
waters, deprecating the deeds of blood, and recommending
in their stead earnest Christian efforts for conversion. The
European emigrants of to-day, who are located upon our
Western plains, and whom the shadow of a passing Indian
affrights, can herein find examples worthy of emulation ;
but it would be very mortifying to them to discover how
degenerate they are when compared with the lion-hearted
giants who preceded them in their journeyings, two and
one half centuries ago. We learn that two men prevented
by their efforts, the destruction of the English settlements.
—Miles Standish and John Eliot. The former by the application of physical force spread terror among the natives,
and the latter, who as early as sixteen hundred and twenty-
eight, was deliberating upon the possibility of bringing the
heathen under the power of the Gospel, shortly thereafter
entered upon his mission, and subdued the savage passions
of members of contiguous tribes. Standish enforced submission through fear of speedy retaliatory punishment. Eliot
counselled obedience to the teachings of Christ, and taught
the brotherhood of man. These two men averted impend-

ing ruin. Without the one, our Pilgrim Fathers and their children would have been destroyed ; and without the example and labors of the other, which were attended with beneficent results, the English settlers would have been driven by King Philip and his warriors, into the sea.

Such conclusions may reflect great credit upon our ancestors and exhibit in us a proper filial appreciation of merit. But in attempting to reconcile the contemporaneous testimony of the past, one can not escape the belief, that the number of the straggling, naked savages of New England, has been magnified above all proportions. The Indians were unfriendly to the whites and retired at their approach. They left it to their Penobscot friend to extend the hospitalities of their country, in that memorable brief speech of welcome. We can not understand how an isolated, wasted, and famishing colony numbering but fifty souls, could become so firmly fixed upon the New England shore, that the hostile natives could not dislodge it ; nor how one hundred persons, composed of men, women and children, could penetrate the country to the Connecticut River, and in the midst of savage neighbors, separate and successfully found, Hartford, Springfield, and Wethers-field. I am unable to determine whether Captain Mason with his eighty men, slew one hundred and eighty, or seven hundred of the Pequods, in that battle which broke the power of the Pequod nation.

Nor is one able to obtain any satisfactory information regarding the numbers of the Indians of New England in sixteen hundred and seventy-five, at the breaking out of King Philip's war. When eminent historians vary so materially in their estimates of its white population at that time, how can any similarity of well matured opinions regarding Indians be expected. History is very undecided upon the entire subject of population. New England may have contained one hundred and twenty thousand whites,

as Marshall avers, or only fifty-five thousand, as Bancroft
maintains. The latter however introduces sufficient circumstantial evidence in support of his position to convince
the general reader. Now it is very strange, that when
statements concerning the white settlers are so irreconcilable, there should be unanimity of opinion in respect to
the Indian. Marshall, Bancroft, and Trumbull place the
number of Philip's warriors at three thousand, and the
entire native fighting force was assembled under his command, except the Praying Indians, the Mohegans, and a
portion of the Abenekis. He also drew from Eastern New
York, as far as the land of the Mohawks. Bancroft says
of this war, "More than six hundred men, chiefly young
men, the flower of the country, of whom any mother might
have been proud, perished in the field. Of the able bodied
men in the country, one in twenty had fallen." From this
we infer, that out of a population of fifty-five thousand
whites, twelve thousand were capable of bearing arms.
Apply the same rule in proportion to the Indians, and we
find that three thousand warriors could be secured from a
population of less than fourteen thousand. But how has
it been ascertained that Philip controlled a force of three
thousand men ? They were never seen and counted.
They never met the whites in a general engagement.
They fought in small numbers and depended upon surprise. The same band could attack at different points
thirty or forty miles distant, within twenty-four hours.
In less than one week it could pillage and murder on the
Connecticut River and on the Eastern coast. How then
could the number of his warriors be known ? Were the reports of the armed men opposing them received ? They
would be remarkable for uncertainty. Was the estimated
strength of the tribes of Indians in hostility considered ?
Correctness could not be attained in such computation.
New Hampshire and Western Massachusetts must have

counted, as do now our Western Indian census-gatherers, for Connecticut in the days of the elder Winthrop, but forty years before the war of Philip, claimed four thousand native warriors. How then could the number be determined ? The difficulty seems to be settled by the assertion that, " between two and three thousand were killed or ' submitted.' " To one acquainted with the modes of Indian warfare, and who naturally supposes that the Indians made the act of submission through their chiefs and representatives, and were not individually present at the time of its consummation, the assertion is very unsatisfactory.

But it might be well to ascertain the size of this Eastern population at a more recent date. One century later, Governor Tryon of New York made report and expressed himself as follows : " The Indians who formerly possessed Nassau and Long Island, and that part of New York below Albany, are reduced to a small number, and are so dispersed that no account can be taken of them. They have generally been denominated river Indians, and have about three hundred fighting men. The tribes of Indians within the Province of Massachusetts, and the colonies of Connecticut and Rhode Island, are in similar circumstances with the river Indians, and the Stockbridges living on the eastern border of New York, are in number about three hundred. The Indians near Montreal, and on the St. Lawrence number about thirty-five hundred." What became of the thirty or forty thousand Indians of New England, whom fifty millions of acres could not support ? Did a single century destroy them and their descendants ? We are told that many perished in King Philip's war ; that many fled to the French in Canada, and some to their brothers on the Hudson. That many died during the war from starvation and exposure is undoubtedly the case, although Indians have great tena-

city of life, and are not easily overcome by the ills of the
flesh. A few fled to the friendly French country, and
but few, else they did not cease their flight until they put
the St. Lawrence between them and their enemies. The
rest of course decayed, and with astonishing rapidity ; for it
is doubtful if three thousand Indians could be found within
all New England, at the time when Governor Tryon wrote.

A careful consideration of the habits of the New England Indians in sixteen hundred, and the conditions which
climate and the scarcity of large game imposed upon people following their modes of life, outweighs the unconsidered statements of Europeans who early visited them,
when an attempt is made to approximately determine
population. Some of the nations rudely cultivated the
soil, and grew their winter's supply of corn ; but the
majority of them depended upon the chase, and the supply of fish which the streams abundantly yielded. Game
was scarce and the territory limited, and they must have
settled on the banks of rivers, or the shore of the ocean,
for the purpose of obtaining their support. The sparse
population found in such localities, except along the coast
of Connecticut and Rhode Island, dispels our ideas of
great numbers. The climate was rigorous, and the win-
ters long and severe. The exposures to which the Indian
children were submitted, and the hardships which adults
were compelled to endure, together with the consequences
of tribal hostilities, prevented numerical increase. If New
England ever contained twenty thousand natives, it was
densely populated when compared with other portions of
our eastern territory. At the time the Puritans landed on
its coast, the Indians, wasted by pestilence, were too feeble
to make resistance, although of unfriendly disposition.
Disease must have visited the interior and rendered them
likewise weak, or the tribes could soon have gathered to
drive off the invader.

Of the Indians of eastern New York, Long Island and New Jersey, the Dutch left few accounts ; for they were not interested in their condition, unless they possessed valuable articles of trade. Prescott remarks, that " the French missionaries took up their dwelling among the Indians without protection ; they sought martyrdom: the Spaniard came as the knight-errant, the Dutch came for money, and the Saxon for a home." The Dutch trade, first confined to its Indian Company, was finally thrown open to all of the inhabitants. They resembled some of the individuals with whom the West is now peopled, who leave their morality and Christianity in their eastern residences, with the intention of returning, and assuming former social and spiritual relations after the acquisition of fortunes. They mingled familiarly with the natives, and drove sharp bargains. Such conduct naturally produced unpleasant consequences, and terminated in strifes, which the valorous Dutch maintained with loss to their opponents. They relate, that in some of their engagements, they slew as many as eighty Indian warriors. During the forty years they retained possession of New Netherlands, the Indian population decreased. Before their arrival, the Leni-Lenape, and kindred people of the Hudson, had their masters in the Five Nations of New York, and could not have been numerous. The Delawares alone were able to make a formidable show of strength, and of them we shall speak hereafter.

The Algonkins, to the south of the Dutch provinces, were scattered and found in feeble bands, as far as the country of the celebrated Powhattan Confederacy. Its capital at Richmond, Virginia, the home of its distinguished chief, consisting in sixteen hundred and seven of twelve lodges, gave law to the numerous people of the confederated tribes, who had acquired a dislike for the whites, as their coast had been plundered by the slave-

traders for nearly a century. In the heart of this unfriendly nation, and but a short distance from its capital,
one hundred Europeans planted a settlement, and were so
reduced in a few months by famine and sickness, that but
fifty remained alive. Of this fifty, but five able-bodied
men remained to guard the defences, and still they held
their post secure against the natives. The losses were replenished from the old world, only to be reduced by
desertion and disease. In sixteen hundred and ten, the
colony numbered but sixty souls, and "these were so feeble and dejected that if relief had been delayed but ten
days longer, they all must have utterly perished." While
this colony bravely maintained its position, the Indian
tribes plotted for its destruction. Its wanderers in search
of food were cruelly murdered.

The relentless savages hung upon their footsteps if they
emerged from their palisades. In the meantime, Captain
John Smith, with twenty sturdy followers, attempted an
exploration of the land, and was unsuccessful, only because
his little army separated into independent columns, which
were overpowered by their enemies. He made a subsequent attempt, and reached the mouth of the Susquehanna
River, from whence he returned in triumph to Jamestown.
During this expedition, Smith met many Indian tribes
which he vanquished and reduced to submission, and
then sought their friendship and alliance. Upon the
arrival of Lord Delaware, the condition of the colony commenced to improve, and to increase in numbers. It
grew to seven hundred men, extended itself, and drove
back the Indians, whose lands it forcibly appropriated.
From sixteen hundred and seven to the time of Rolfe's
marriage in sixteen hundred and fourteen, the native
population warred against the intruder, but without success. Its numbers were great, and the warriors could be
counted by thousands. Within sixty miles of Jamestown,

there were five thousand Indians, and the banks of the Potomac, Rappahannock, and other large rivers of Virginia, were thickly populated.

Such and similar accounts, history records as truth, and permits the reader to reconcile the inconsistencies as best he can. History proceeds in its deception, and not only receives within its elastic folds, the unrestrained statements of imaginative persons, which posterity has preserved, and which the evidences of circumstances overthrow, but it so presents supposed statistical facts, as to give color to those statements, and the deception can not be detected, unless a careful analysis is made.

Immediately following the narration of the Indian outbreak of Virginia, in sixteen hundred and twenty-two, is given the number of the white inhabitants of the colony. The London Company sent out nine thousand people, and still the population in the year above mentioned was but eighteen hundred persons. Bancroft however speaks more guardedly, and says, " A year after the massacre there still remained two thousand five hundred men ; the total number of the emigrants had exceeded four thousand." These figures must be in a great part, matter of conjecture. A loss of six thousand in the colony in fifteen years, could not be accounted for, except on the supposition that the action of the Indians produced it. A loss of fifteen hundred could be mostly attributed to natural causes. The colony extended itself upon the lands lying along the rivers, where the deadly miasma would rapidly diminish its numbers. The first three years' experience at Jamestown, show what destruction the diseases of that climate can accomplish upon emigrants from a healthy European country.

A candid examination of events convinces us that Virginia contained but few of the aboriginal race, even if the extended territory necessary for Indian subsistence is unconsidered.   Forty or fifty sick men, within rude fortifications of hasty construction, (and we can imagine them extremely rude, if we take into consideration the character of the first Virginia immigrants,) could not maintain their position against hundreds of hostile savages for successive months, notwithstanding the latter had only weapons of their own manufacture.   Days and nights of painful watching and waiting depress the spirits of the most determined, precedes despair, which is followed in turn by submission to what seems an inevitable destiny.   Neither could eighteen hundred, nor twenty-five hundred men furnish needful protection to the settlements of Virginia, and at the same time exterminate, drive out, or subdue, a numerous native race, furnished with fire-arms of as good pattern as they themselves possessed.   That the Indians had many European arms when the war inaugurated by Powhattan's successor was waged, has been placed upon record as a fact ; and that they obtained them in trade with the whites as early as sixteen hundred and seventeen, appears evident from the prohibition contained in our first colonial intercourse law, issued by Governor Argal, in which it was forbidden to "any person to traffic privately with the Indians, or teach them the use of fire-arms, under the pain of death."

We might descend in Virginia history, through the administration of Governor Jeffreys, and discover many accounts, equally as marvelous and as difficult of comprehension, if the belief in a numerous Indian population is entertained.   We intend no disparagement therefore to the memory of the great Powhattan Confederacy, when we state our conviction that it never contained ten thousand individuals.   It would be to its credit rather to place its numbers at a lower figure, and to represent it as too weak and scattered to resist the feeble attempts of the whites during the early years of colonization, or to allay the fears which seized it at the approach of the Mohawk warrior.

To the Southern nations, namely, the Gulf nations, and the Cherokees, Bancroft allows at the beginning of the seventeenth century a population of fifty thousand, and says, that since that time their population has increased. Early information regarding them is very meagre. The Spanish and French missionaries in Florida and Georgia knew little· of the interior. Some of the statements might be as worthy of belief as the sad story of the extinct Hatteras tribe, which in the days of Sir Walter Raleigh had twenty thousand people, and lost all but one hundred of them in a century and a half. De Soto, in his expedition along the Southern coast, from Tampa Bay to the Mississippi River, during fifteen hundred thirty-nine and forty, found a number of small Indian villages, and quite a city upon the site which Mobile now occupies ; but he did not penetrate into the interior of the continent. At the beginning of the eighteenth century, when French colonization in the South was begun, the wars between the Choctaws and the Chickasaws had produced deadly enmity between the representatives of those nations, and the Chickasaws excluded the French from their territory. The Spanish priests in Florida had gathered the Indians of the peninsula into towns and villages, and were endeavoring to impart to them the benefits of a European civilization ; but they were confined in their labors to a small section of the Spanish possession. When hostilities between the English and Spanish colonies broke out, it was possible for Carolina to summon one thousand Indian warriors to its assistance, and Florida could count its native allies by hundreds. It was possible for the French to call twelve hundred Choctaw warriors to aid in the proposed chastisement of the proud Chickasaw nation, and that nation was able to resist the invasion, and to drive back the combined force. It would seem then, that the Southern portion of our territory, east of the Mississippi River, had a large native population, and that Bancroft's estimate is not an exaggeration. Within this section, if anywhere, the presence of great numbers would be expected. Here a warm and genial climate protected infancy, and gave comfort to the sick. A luxuriant soil returned an abundant harvest of corn for the seed carelessly planted, and nourished a great abundance of game. Winter did not compel a summer's labor on the part of the inhabitants, and famine and frost had no victims.

Thus have we hurriedly considered the Indians who roamed over the eastern portion of our territory, and briefly noted the suggestions which arise in the mind, in regard to their strength. When we study their habits of life, and the relation which they sustained to the French, English, and Spanish colonies, does it not seem that Bancroft might have made a great reduction in his estimate of one hundred and eighty thousand, and supported it with equal consistency? If to the Algonkin nations there should be allowed for population, sixty thousand, and to the Dakotan nations, after deducting the Sioux tribes which voluntarily crossed the Mississippi, sixty-five thousand, would the estimate appear to be too greatly reduced? Upon such a basis, the population of the Algonkin family west of the Alleghany Mountains could be placed at twenty-five or thirty thousand; and the nations of that family east of the same at thirty thousand; the Five Nations of New York, and the Tuscaroras, at thirteen thousand, and those of the Gulf, with the Cherokee included, at fifty thousand.

We will again recur to the eastern Indian population of eighteen hundred and twenty-two, which we know to have been about one hundred and twenty thousand, and ask how supposed great losses in numbers can be accounted for. We wish to discover the causes of this great decline or decay of population, and ascertain how effective they have been in producing supposed results. Any definite determination is of course impossible, but many long existing fallacies may be exploded. The mere presence of the European does not produce a miraculous blighting effect upon Indians. The white man's food does not instantaneously kill, nor does it shorten their span of life. On the contrary, they thrive admirably upon it, and the wild tribes of to-day which government is feeding, furnish sufficient proof of the fact. The European injures them, because he limits the hunting grounds, and assists to destroy the game, their chief subsistence. Distress and famine may follow, unless they remove into the wilderness, or become tillers of the soil and depend upon the earth for nourishment.

But it may be said that the European brought pestilence. Undoubtedly he is responsible in a certain degree for its frequent recurrence, but the results of its ravages were apparent when he reached the American shore. Indians never attained that purity and simplicity of living which defies disease, and European intercourse was not necessary to originate it among them. Those contagious and infectious diseases, which medical skill has partially placed under its control, and which occasionally visit white communities, are particularly severe upon our Indian race. During the year eighteen hundred and seventy-three one-ninth of the Santee Sioux of Nebraska died of small pox. That contagion swept away great numbers in eighteen hundred and thirty-two. It will never be known how serious have been the consequences of communicated maladies, or pestilence in its varied forms, to the aborigines; but that they have been sufficient to prevent much increase in population, or to periodically cut off increased population, can be believed. The plagues of Europe appeared to have almost depopulated sections of country. Towns and cities were scourged, until the remaining inhabitants seemingly constituted but a small fraction of former numbers ; yet a few years of ordinary health and prosperity restored the wasted strength, and brought society to the condition attained before it was visited by malignant disease. So with our native stock ; pestilence has sought it, and destroyed the accumulated increase of favorable periods. A few strong nations are brought low, while others escape, and in a short time the united population is found to vary little from that of a preceding century.

Another supposed cause of Indian numerical decrease is war. As a rule, distinct races of men, when brought in contact, contend for the possession of territory. Antipathies of race add energy and cruelty to hostilities, which continue until terminated by the submission, removal, or extinction, of one or the other of the combatants.

Impressed with this fact, which universal history supports, and which the philanthropist ascribes to the moral weakness, depravity, or degeneracy of humanity, and not to natural law, we think of the poor Indian as forcibly driven from his home through great tribulations and slaughter, and bemoaning in his present exile, departed glory and past importance. Or, remembering the unchristian contention of the Christian colonies settled within the land, and the base uses which they made of Indians as allies, we are prepared to believe, upon slight investigation, that great destruction of Indian life ensued. We forget, that before the European undertook the task of native subjection, or before he attempted to give direction to the impulse of savage passion, the Indian nations were engaged against each other in open, relentless wars. —Irving, in speaking of the traditions concerning the contests between the Sioux and Cheyennes, remarks, that "there appears to be a tendency to extinction among all

2*

the savage nations, and this tendency was in operation long before the advent of the white man." Iroquois and Huron, Mohawk and Mohegan, Choctaw and Chickasaw, Pawnee and Crow, Chippewa and Sioux, were arrayed against each other in uncompromising hostility. Tribes were constantly provoking each other's enmity, and severing the rude national organizations.

New combinations or affiliations were continually being made, and small bands were being scattered never to be re-collected. The entire population, uncivilized, unsettled, and divided against itself, expended its surplus energy in violation of moral law, in deeds of atrocity and blood. At the approach of the European, it was necessary to combine. As he slowly but steadily advanced from the ocean shore toward the interior, firmly grasping in his progress the hereditary possessions of the Indians, the latter were obliged to force him to retreat, or else to retire before him. The situation compelled a healing of long nourished animosities, in order that they might unite for the struggle. "The advent of the white man" therefore, arrested "the tendency to extinction," which was in operation before his arrival.

What now, we ask, was the result of this struggle upon Indian population ? Did it produce a greater reduction than the natural increase would be likely to supply ? Or, to give a broader signification to the question, we will ask whether or not the battles between the whites and Indians, and the battles between the opposing colonists in which Indian aid was employed, materially reduced our native population ? The question admits of considerable discussion, because of the dearth of accounts, or rather positive, historical statement. We will refer to particular instances, in order to show how erroneous prevailing opinions are, in regard to the destruction of Indian life consequent upon European interference. The Cherokee nation for instance.

is understood to have received fearful punishment at the hands of the whites, upon three different occasions :—in seventeen hundred and sixty-one, in seventeen hundred and seventy-nine and in seventeen hundred and eighty. The injuries received in seventeen hundred and sixty-one are generally stated to have been an overwhelming defeat, the destruction of the middle settlement, and the wasting of the country to such an extent that the nation sued for peace, which it obtained by the ratification of a treaty. Loss of life must have been slight, or the speedy recuperation which followed would have been impossible. In the engagements of seventeen hundred seventy-eight and nine, the Cherokee loss is thus stated, in a communication written by Jefferson addressed to Gen. Washington : " The damage done them was killing half a dozen, burning eleven towns, twenty thousand bushels of corn, and taking so many goods as sold for twenty-five thousand pounds." Referring to the last mentioned punishment, Jefferson thus describes it in a letter dated February 17th, 1781 : " The militia of this State and North Carolina penetrated into the Cherokee country, burned almost every town they had, amounting to about one thousand houses in the whole, destroyed fifty thousand bushels of grain, killed twenty-nine and took seventeen prisoners." From these reports it appears that the Cherokees lost but thirty-five of their people in two invasions which devastated their country.

In seventeen hundred and seventy-nine, General Sullivan, in command of a body of troops numbering four thousand, undertook to chastise the Six Nations of New York. He was but slightly resisted at Chemung and Newton and found their villages deserted. After destroying their abodes, their fruit orchards and stores of grain, he retreated.

Here were two powerful and warlike nations, which could not be forced into regular engagements when even their country was invaded, and houses destroyed ; but after the manner of Indians, they retired at the approach of armed bodies, ready doubtless to strike, when they thought success might be obtained without much danger to themselves.

But how did the French and English allies conduct themselves, and did they make attacks or resist those of the enemy, in honorable warfare ? Montcalm's Indians were useful when concealed by timber, or rude breastworks, and they delighted to slaughter a conquered and unarmed foe. Sir William Johnston with his thousand Iroquois, might have furnished substantial aid to Amherst, in the progress of his march to Montreal, had he sooner joined him, but could do little after that city was invested. The French, who controlled the entire native population of the North and West, except the Six Nations of New York, strengthened the small garrison at Fort Du Quesne with a large body of Indians, who deserted at the approach of the English, and without waiting to contest the position. Upon the capture of the fort, the Indians, from the lakes to the Ohio, transferred allegiance to the British crown. In seventeen hundred and fifty-nine, the French garrison at Niagara, deserted by its Indian allies, found itself too weak to make resistance, and was obliged to capitulate.

Such instances might be multiplied ; but the foregoing recitals sufficiently illustrate the peculiarities of Indian warfare, and direct attention to the fact which is intended to be presented, namely that our engagements with Indians have not materially reduced them. In the long desultory war between the New England colonies, and the French of Canada, and their native allies, which continued from sixteen hundred and eighty-nine, until seventeen hundred and twenty-six, with only the temporary suspensions produced by the treaties of Ryswick and Utrecht, very few Indians were slain, though many white people were butchered. The French sent small expeditions, consisting of not more than five hundred men into the heart of the Iroquois country, and compelled declaration of future peace ; but those Indians characterized as that perfidious " people from whose promises we have nothing to expect but murder and treason," broke faith upon the withdrawal of force, and renewed allegiance upon a new invasion.   In sixteen hundred and eighty-eight, eight hundred Seneca warriors, "skillful in the use of the gun, and all well armed," assisted by the Governor of New York, attempted to drive off a French force which had landed on the southern shore of Lake Ontario, and although they are reported as having fought valorously, appear to have been easily scattered without suffering sufficient loss to make the battle memorable.   The former influence and advancement of the extinct Natchez nation, was glowingly described by early travelers, and its fame was spread abroad throughout Europe.   Montesquieu thus speaks of its customs in his Spirit of Laws :—" Their chief disposes of the goods of all his subjects, and obliges them to work and toil according to his pleasure.   He has power like that of the Grand Signior, and they cannot even refuse him their heads. One would imagine that this is the great Sesostris."   The destruction of such an important nation by war, would furnish support to an argument that the whites caused great loss of life among the native race.   But when the position and relations of this Natchez band dignified by the name of nation, to surrounding Indians is considered, its importance dwindles into insignificance.   It was destroyed, but few of its people were killed.   They were scattered, and sought asylums with other nations, with which they remained.   Their misfortunes were not the result of open determined hostilities on their part.   They were surprised by the French and Choctaws, and defeated before they could prepare for resistance, and like the Tuscaroras in Carolina, they were unable to escape their fate.

Our national expeditions against Indians, from the foundation of the Government to the present day, have not resulted in serious Indian casualties, except in two or three instances. Such a statement appears rash, in view of the fact, that during the first six years of our national existence, the western frontier was in a state of constant alarm ; and more than ten millions of dollars were expended in attempts to conquer a peace. The victories of Wayne led to an adjustment of difficulties, but did not put an end to the labors of foreign emissaries, who, as President Adams intimates in one of his messages to Congress, were engaged in attempts to excite the native population to continued hostilities. Their labor finally ceased some time after the ratification of the treaty of Grenville, and an almost uninterrupted quiet was maintained until eighteen hundred and twelve. President Jefferson, in his first message, speaks of the improved condition of the Indians, and their increasing numbers ; and in his third message, he is pleased to call attention to their advancement in civilization. The war of eighteen hundred and twelve again brought the Indians in opposition to the federal armies. Great Britain, says President Madison, turned the savages against us in every possible quarter. While the policy of the United States invariably recommended "and promoted civilization among that wretched portion of the human race, and was making exertions to persuade them from taking either side in the war, the enemy has not scrupled to call to his aid their ruthless ferocity, armed with the horrors of those instruments of torture which are known to spare neither age nor sex." The war was of short duration. The ninth article of the treaty of eighteen hundred and fourteen, between Great Britain and the United States, restored the Indians to all the possessions, rights and privileges which they enjoyed, or were entitled to, in the year eighteen hundred and eleven.

Those in the Northwest probably suffered more from starvation, after they were abandoned by Great Britain, than during the war, from the bullet of the enemy.

Since eighteen hundred and twelve, the Black-Hawk and Seminole wars, among our Indian disturbances, alone seem vested with importance. The latter, prosecuted for seven years at a reported expense of thirty million of dollars, is said to have reduced the Seminole population from five thousand to three hundred. The most reliable accounts, however, seem to place the number of the Seminole warriors, at the breaking out of that war, at about seven hundred, of whom a considerable portion were escaped African slaves. The three hundred supposed to have remained, have increased to twenty-four hundred, as present statistics show—an increase too rapid to be easily comprehended.

The Indian loss in battle with the whites, since seventeen hundred and eighty-nine, might fairly be placed at about six thousand—certainly not above eight thousand. Both Harmer and St. Clair were defeated and routed at a cost, to the Indians engaged, of not more than two hundred men. Their defeat by Wayne could not have taken from them more than three or four hundred warriors, even if one-fifth of their fighting force fell. Still our Indian engagements have produced sufficient political excitement to make and unmake Presidents, and have governed popular favor, to a certain extent, in the bestowal of its praises. "Who killed Tecumseh ?" It is as difficult to make intelligent reply to the inquiry, as to ascertain whether or not Generals Coffee and Jackson destroyed in battle one thousand of the Creek nation.

Our expeditions have, for the most part, been either unsuccessful, or have terminated without the accomplishment of desired results. The difficulty has not been found to exist in the incapacity of the white man to cope with this opponent, when brought face to face, but in his inability to force the latter to openly contend with him. Indians cannot be driven into engagements, unless they are able to overwhelm the enemy by numbers, or to maintain great advantage by reason of concealed or covered positions ; and then only when a safe retreat is possible. If surrounded, they can make desperate defence to avoid death or captivity. The natural instinct of self-preservation will, in such an event, give them the courage of despair. Yet they are not wanting in individual bravery.

It is their inability to cement force, and to unite in that concert of action, wherein the constituent parts are supported and propelled by each other, that renders them powerless before a well organized and well disciplined foe. Their past success has been mainly due to their cunning and deceit. They depend for conquest upon treachery and surprise. Their butcheries at Montreal, in New England, New York, Virginia, Carolina, on the Mississippi, and more recently in our central States, and in the Northwest, all alike seem to show that they possess these iniquitous qualities, and in so remarkable a degree, that they might almost be considered characteristics of their race. In the exercise of these qualities the European has not shown himself a match for the native. He has seldom been able to anticipate him in fraud, or to detect him, until after the injury contemplated was received. He has generally found him an enemy, who disappeared the moment a blow was struck, and who was ever present when vigilance was allowed to sleep. The former hath slain his thousands, but the latter his ten thousands. Such has thus far been the result of the long contest between these antagonists.

The subject of past population admits of another method of consideration. If the strength of distinct Indian nations at different periods can be ascertained, or to present the matter in its most simple form, if we can determine approximately the strength of certain nations at the time when our earliest information regarding them was obtained, and at the present day, we can decide with a considerable degree of accuracy, the effect which European communication has produced.   In following an individual people with such an object in view, it will be necessary in some instances, to search for scattered bands, broken from what we know as the original organization ; also to seek out persons who have united with kindred or alien tribes, either from accident, marriage, or from other causes.

Take as an example the Delaware nation, which is supposed by many to have been once great and powerful.   It has been in direct contact with the Europeans and their descendants for the last two hundred and fifty years.   It has always occupied the border of civilization, and retired slowly before its advance.   It is the nation which first experienced the Quaker Indian policy of government, and to which William Penn announced the truth of the unity of man.   With it, the colonies made many treaties, and our statute books record nineteen, which the several senates have duly ratified and confirmed.   To it " Ministers Plenipotentiary " were sent nearly a century ago, to enter into " a treaty of alliance offensive and defensive," and it was counseled to unite its energies, become the head of a great confederacy, and demand representation in Congress. These ministers made promises which would now be considered very difficult to fulfill.   They promised to open a brisk trade with the Delawares, and to furnish them with " an intelligent, candid agent, with an adequate salary ; one more influenced by the love of his country, and a constant attention to the duties of his department by promoting the common interest, than the sinister purposes of converting and bending all the duties of his office to his private emolument."   The agent was found and forwarded, but how long, through personal suffering, and vicarious sacrifice, he maintained his position, is unknown.

Now, what was the condition and strength of the Delawares, and what section of country did they occupy, when first known to the whites ? They roamed over New Jersey and eastern Pennsylvania. They had been conquered by the Iroquois and remained tributary to them. Their strength could not therefore have been above three or four thousand, and as their national organization had been sundered, the bonds which held them together had been weakened, and the work of disintegration, ever since active among them, was even then in progress. For sixty years before the arrival of Penn, the English, Dutch and Swedes had been trading with them, and undoubtedly wrought demoralization. The coming of the Friends pushed them back to the Susquehanna, and subsequently they retired beyond the Alleghanies to the head waters of the Ohio. They became the allies of the French, and took an active part in the long continued border warfare, which was terminated by the treaty of Paris in seventeen hundred and sixty-three. At this date Sir William Johnston reports the number of their warriors at six hundred. They served the English in the Revolutionary war, and after its termination made peace with the United States and settled in Ohio. From thence they were removed to Missouri, thence to Kansas, thence to the Cherokee country, where they still remain. Those of them occupying the reservation in the Indian Territory number, at the present time, a little more than one thousand.

This people therefore seem, upon casual examination, to have experienced a loss of population in two and one-half centuries, of from fifty to seventy-five per cent ; but when we look carefully into their history we shall discover, that a large portion of the loss has either been absorbed by the white race, or has served to increase the strength of other Indian nations. In their movements to the west they travelled in straggling bands, and some of their population remained permanently behind. Penn﹣sylvania has a few representatives, known and denominated as Indians, and also a few inhabitants slightly tinged with the blood of the native. Many of the Delawares, through the labors of Moravian missionaries, became Christians, and separated themselves from their heathen brethren. Some of the latter joined the hostile Indians to the north and west, and others wandered to distant portions of the country. As early as seventeen hundred and ninety-three, a small band had passed beyond the Mississippi, and obtained permission of the Spanish Governor to occupy territory. Under the treaty of eighteen hundred and eighteen, by which the Delawares agreed to enter Missouri, only a portion left the State of Ohio ; the remnant remained until eighteen hundred and thirty. Under stipulation of more recent treaties, the United States has offered them citizenship, and given them lands in severalty. These constant changes of place, joined to the influences which have been brought to bear upon this nation, have scattered it far and wide. Its people may be found on the Susquehanna River, and in Central Texas. It is but a few years since the government endeavored to induce two or three hundred of them to sever their connection with the Southern Indians, and join their relations in Kansas. They may now be found with the Kiowas and Comanches, and can recite the traditions of their ancestors, who came from the shore of the great ocean of the East. The nation has nearly disappeared, but the descendants of its former representatives are numerous.

The Delawares have been selected to illustrate the subject under discussion, because they are commonly referred to as well nigh extinct, by those who endeavor to maintain the theory, that our former Indian population has been

rapidly disappearing. We wish now to make a brief statement in regard to other nations which are still comparatively numerous, in order to show that they have increased
with as much rapidity as the smaller nations have declined.
The Cherokees, for instance, number more than thirty
thousand, and eighteen thousand of them are living upon
their reservation in the Indian Territory.   In eighteen
hundred and twenty-seven, the statistics of the War Department placed their numbers at thirteen thousand five
hundred and sixty-seven.   They have probably doubled
their population within the past century.   The Creeks,
Choctaws and Chickasaws have also largely increased, but
not in an equal ratio.   The Ottawas and Chippewas number
more than twenty thousand, while the Six Nations of New
York seem to have neither increased nor diminished in
population since first known.   There are nearly seven
thousand of them within the United States, and probably
from three to five thousand within the Dominion of Canada,
all living within the tribal relation.   A few have withdrawn
from their people, and are pursuing their interests in the
paths of civilized life.

    Should each particular Indian nation of the United
States be traced in its movements, from the time it was
first known to the Europeans to the present day ; should
its decrease by sickness and famine be carefully weighed
and estimated ; should its casualties in the conflicts with
the white intruder be reasonably determined, and its natural increase properly considered, the investigation would
lead to the conclusion, that loss in population in particular
instances, is balanced by a corresponding gain among the
more important Indian organizations.

    As already stated, many of the feebler nations have
declined, while the majority of those which were strong
have received accessions and increased.   The total of the
present native population differs little numerically, from

that which existed when the whites began their first en-croachments.

We have been forced to this belief by an examination of authorities, and a consideration of attendant circumstances. It may be carried to an erroneous extent, but if it is conceded that the Indians, instead of wasting away before a vigorous practical civilization, in some mysterious manner, have only been affected by direct physical causes, which have not been sufficient to produce a remarkable diminution in numbers, our chief purpose in this chapter will be attained. We merely wished to point out the fact, which the events of the past conclusively establish, that the Indians are not likely to soon decay and disappear from our midst, but are destined to remain with us for many future generations. The existence of the former Eastern nations, in increased numbers, after their experience with the white man during two hundred and forty years, makes that fact too plain for contradiction.

How are the United States affected by this peculiar race ? Evidently, a long continued care and control, on the part of the general government, must be expected. What the nature and extent of the supervision should be, seems to be now as little understood as it was fifty years ago. The opinions of eminent men upon this subject vary wildly. The great Indian problem is not yet solved. Its difficulties are as puzzling as ever. Past experience furnishes no definite rule to guide future conduct. It is therefore unsatisfactory, or new combinations of circumstances have arisen which require different action. We intend to glance at the past and shall attempt to discover some of its teachings. We shall endeavor to ascertain why former and existing methods have not produced desired results, and why the Indian cannot be speedily brought into the path of civilization, and into the marvelous light of Christianity.

CHAPTER II.

COLONIAL INDIAN POLICY.

NATIONAL legislation reflects the condition and sentiments of a people. Laws prescribed by kingly decree,
or enacted by popular assemblage, alike indicate the limit
of intellectual and political advancement which a nation
has reached. But it is when we study the foreign policy
of a government that we ascertain with certainty the extent
of its true development in morality and Christian civilization ; for we find embraced therein its knowledge of natural law, and can discover in many instances how far
selfish interest is controlled by a sense of justice in the
determination of positive human right.

The policy pursued by European governments towards
the aborigines of the American continent, furnishes a very
faithful representation of European opinion, concerning
responsibilities under the law of nature, as applicable to
national action. It shows how that law was understood.
Its frequent modifications mark in a certain degree the
rapid advancement of Europe, in a knowledge of the correct relation of prerogative and privilege, and an understanding of those absolute rights which belong to every
individual of the human race of whatever name or tongue.

The Spaniards began their conquests and colonization
in the new world at too early a period. Then the will of
God directed the destruction of idolaters and barbarians,
unless they submitted at once to Christian dictation. The
teachings of Peter the Hermit and St. Bernard were not
yet forgotten. The Vicegerent of Christ gave to Spain

and Portugal all the heathen for an inheritance, and the uttermost parts of the earth for possessions. To them, the Indians were but property to be used and expended as public and private gain. The best educated opinion of the Christian world permitted the enslavement and wanton destruction of the Indian race. The latter had no rights nor immunities which received recognition, and theologians recommended slavery as necessary to conversion. The maxim of Las Casas that " God forbids us to do evil that good may come of it," was still a meaningless precept.

Neither were France and England one whit in advance. The commission from Henry the Seventh to the Cabots, by which they were authorized to seek out and occupy the countries of the heathen and infidels, is prepared in the spirit which moved the Spanish Knight, when he took formal possession of the Pacific Coast and the islands therein, and all the lands embracing it, in the names of the Castilian sovereigns " whose it was and should be, as long as the world endures, and until the final day of judgment of all mankind."

A single century wrought a great change. Absolute monarchy, built upon the power wrested from the feudal lords, had been compelled to limit its pretensions. Society had made intellectual progress, and was morally improved. As it expended its physical force in the cause of individual freedom, its mental powers were employed in an endeavor to determine the absolute and relative rights of man. The elements of society were analyzed, the duties arising from the condition of citizen discussed, and the ultimate sources of positive law beginning to be ascertained.

But not yet was individual liberty understood. The divine prerogative of kings was only giving way before the tyranny of majorities. Superstition and the spirit of intolerance were not yet overcome. Still an energetic progressive religion and a practical advancing intelligence, were earnestly at work, and even while the elder Winthrop declared that "Majistracy is certainly an appointment from God," Roger Williams announced a new theory of government. In things temporal, said Williams, the voice of the majority must rule, but in things spiritual, we are responsible only to God. For the Indians, Williams claimed the same freedom of action that Europeans enjoyed. They were the original proprietors of the soil, and were at liberty to retain or dispose of their possessions, notwithstanding the meaning and intent of royal charters.

Williams, however, heralded a political doctrine which was not comprehended until a later generation, although society was fast becoming prepared for its partial reception. Yet at the commencement of successful colonization upon our Eastern coast, European sentiment had so far advanced as to recognize the aborigines as a portion of the human family, and as such, within the pale of that great law of nature which was then being discussed. Pretexts were found to excuse invasion, appropriation, and settlement of country. The Protestant based his conduct upon the natural right of the oppressed to seek a home where the worship of God could be enjoyed without persecution ; or in the demand of an overcrowded home population ; or in the expressed wish of extending the benefits of civilization. The Roman Catholic justified his encroachments by pleading that he sought conversion of the heathen to the true religion. The English confessedly came to improve their worldly condition ; the French, for the eternal welfare of their newly found brethren. The action of the respective governments seemingly supported these pretensions, for while England made no effort to improve the native, Louis the Thirteenth directed by charter, that strong endeavors should be made for his conversion and civilization, and expended the royal revenue in that laudable work.

But although the enlightened opinion of that day maintained that certain rights and privileges belonged to the Indian race, they were not considered to be of sufficient importance to receive recognition on the part of European governments, when determining the questions which arose in regard to the extent of their American possessions. As between those governments, conceded discovery, followed by occupation, gave indisputable title to country and exclusive control of the Indian population which inhabited it.

This principle was early established ; but when it was sought to be applied, the question of extent of country which priority of discovery and coast occupation carried with it, could not be pacifically determined, and gave rise to the wars which followed. France beyond the St. Lawrence, Spain in the Floridas, and England between the mouth of the Kennebeck River and the thirty-third degree of latitude, were at liberty to act towards the Indian tribes and nations within those respective limits as pleased them.

The course pursued by France and Spain need not be referred to. It is only necessary to examine the action of Great Britain towards the Indians, and the conditions she imposed upon them ; for the policy which she and her colonies inaugurated and developed, was, in all its essential features, adopted by our own government.

The political status which she fixed remains unchanged to the present time. A recent Supreme Court decision, defining the estate of the Menomonees in the land which they occupy, would have been rendered by a court of the colonial days upon a like presentation of facts, because then, as one of the royal governors reported, " purchases from the Indian nations, as of their aboriginal right, have never been held to be a legal title in this province ; the maxim obtaining here as in England, that the King is the fountain of all real property, and that from this source all

3

real titles are to be derived:" and Chief Justice Marshall said in one of his earlier decisions, that the United States gained title by conquest, and "conquest gives a title which the courts of the conqueror cannot deny, whatever the private and speculative opinions of individuals may be."

As this government adhered to the English common law, so did it perpetuate the English Indian policy, which it has extended by congressional act over all the territory since acquired, whether by conquest or by purchase. In fact, the Indian population was unconditionally transferred with the land which it occupied, except in a single instance, and the exception may be found in the treaty of eighteen hundred and three under which Louisiana was obtained. Its sixth article stipulated, that the United States "should execute such treaties and articles as may have been agreed between Spain and the tribes and nations of Indians, until by mutual consent of the Indians and the United States, other suitable articles shall have been agreed upon."

It is true that in some of our treaties with foreign powers, the contracting parties stipulated to permit mutual trade between their citizens and the Indian population inhabiting the territorial borders, and that that population might freely pass and repass the boundary-line with their peltries and ordinary goods without the payment of duty. It is true, that in our treaties of 1848 and 1853 with Mexico, we promised to protect the Mexican border from the incursions of the Indian tribes, and agreed not to place them in such parts of the new territory as would allow them to prey upon or remove into Mexico. Still, nothing can be found in any treaty, with the single exception above given, which binds this government to recognize the Indians as political or organized communities, or which compels it to follow any particular course of treatment, or administer on their behalf any prescribed code of laws. In our first treaty of peace with Great Britain, by which the latter yielded all claims to the country as far as the Mississippi River, not a single stipulation appears in regard to the aboriginal inhabitants, and when they were received they were considered to be in the same situation, as far as their legal status was concerned, as the nation by which they were surrendered, had placed them.

In order therefore to arrive at a correct knowledge of the Indian policy adopted and pursued by the general government, and to understand fully how that policy was developed, it is necessary to glance at the action of the colonies, and also at the action of the several states after the declaration of rights and during confederation. It will be perceived that it was the result of circumstances, and naturally grew out of the relation of the two races upon the coast.

In the beginning of the 17th century, the country claimed by Great Britain on the American continent, was considered crown land, and the natives inhabiting it were recognized as the lawful occupants of the soil, whose right of possession might be extinguished by purchase.

The charters under which settlements were first successfully made, were construed as vesting in the grantees the estate which the crown possessed in the lands therein conveyed, and the exclusive right to secure by purchase the Indian rights of occupancy. They also impliedly transferred to the grantees sole control of the native population dwelling within their respective grants, and allowed them to fix upon it by practice and law, such regulations as they deemed desirable—the parent government only demanding that such action on the part of the colonies should be dictated by kindness and moderation. The colonies were weak and the native tribes surrounding them were, by comparison, numerically strong. In the intercourse which followed, the latter compelled the former to recognize their rude political organizations, and to make treaties of amity, and leagues offensive and defensive, with their chiefs and principal men, in accordance with native custom. Thus, these tribes were looked upon as *quasi* free and independent communities, with full control of their internal affairs. Because of their strength and repeatedly threatened concert of action, it became of the first importance to the colonies, that friendly relations with them should be maintained ; and, as a measure of safety, the people allowed their general councils and assemblies to exercise supervision in matters in which they and the Indians were mutually concerned. Laws were enacted placing trade with the Indians under restrictions, and confining it to citizens residing within the jurisdiction of the colonies which respectively created those laws. Private parties could only make purchase of Indian lands under express statute, or by special executive permission, and treaties under which possession of tracts of country were relinquished were oftentimes made.

In all the colonies Indian intercourse laws were passed, which received amendment as abuses were perceived which required correction. In some, the system of confining trade to agents legally licensed was inaugurated, while in others, legitimate traffic was confined within certain limits.

As early as sixteen hundred and seventeen, Virginia had her intercourse law, which forbade any person to traffic privately with the Indians, or teach them the use of fire-arms, under pain of death. But this law was without its counterpart in the severity of the penalties which it imposed, and was made before Virginia had obtained her first legislative assembly. The following passed by the General Council of Martha's Vineyard in sixteen hundred and seventy-two, is more in consonance with the better popular sentiment of those early times, and shows what the evils were which required correction :

"Ordered, that if any person shall be accused by any, either Indian or any other person whatsoever, to have sold or furnished any Indian with wine, liquor or strong drink, he shall purge himself by oath, or shall pay for such offense after the rate of five shillings per pint for every quantity so sold.

"Ordered, that no person whatsoever, not inhabiting within this jurisdiction, shall directly or indirectly, either by himself or any one, trade with any Indian or Indians, within this jurisdiction, on penalty of paying forty pounds for twenty shillings trade."

The Georgia Company published an intercourse law upon its first attempt at settlement, and allowed only those of its people to traffic with the Indians, who should lawfully obtain license, and in most of the colonies, strong efforts were made to prevent private or indiscriminate trade between the white and the native population.

Generally the act of extinguishing the Indian land title was discharged by the highest colonial authority, and was commonly effected by purchase under treaty. Lord Baltimore, the Rhode Island immigrants, Penn and Oglethorpe purchased before settlement was undertaken, thereby recognizing in their first transactions the native right of possession. As early as sixteen hundred and forty, the Plymouth Colony acquired a large tract of land from the surrounding tribes, and the treaty under which the acquisition was made is in expression and character of sentiment remarkably like those which our own government has entered into within the memory of the present generation. Even then a reservation was set apart which should become the home of the grantees and should belong to them and their children forever.

In New York, the Dutch not only purchased but forcibly appropriated. To perfect their title to the Island of Manhattan, involved an expenditure of twenty-four dollars ; but this seems to be an exceptional case of liberality on their part. The Western Indian Company maintained sole control of the province for a few years, and the business of that corporation was ostensibly conducted to accumulate money, and not to confer benefits or extend civilization. Afterwards, when trade was thrown open to all the inhabitants, much trouble arose because, as expressed by one of the better citizens, of the familiarity practiced by the whites towards the natives, in order to induce traffic, and because of the unfair means used by private parties to obtain possession of Indian lands. In sixteen hundred and sixty-four, when Carteret conquered the provinces, and also concluded a treaty of peace with the Iroquois at Albany, Indian affairs were in a very loose and unsettled condition. The English Governor introduced but few regulations, for in sixteen hundred and seventy every man within the province "who desired to trade for furs had liberty to do so," and liberty was also given to the planters to find out and buy lands of the Indians wherever it pleased them best, and purchases so made were subsequently confirmed by grant.

Here as in all of the royal provinces, measures for the pacification, and for the protection of the Indians from the frauds perpetrated by private individuals, were less stringent than in the colonies. Revenue here became the great object of government, and that course of action was adopted which promised desirable and immediate results. Freedom in trade was finally abridged, and the trader obliged to pay a tariff which was regulated in accordance with the amount of his business. The Governor entered the list of competitors for Indian products, and offered " seven pounds of powder or as much lead as a man could carry, for a beaver." At the same time, the tribes maintained their independence, and the Indian right of possession to the soil was mostly secured by treaty, and became unincumbered government land. The consideration given in the exchange was generally insignificant, and the reported transactions lead one to infer, that the government matched its citizens in making sharp and profitable bargains. In sixteen hundred and eighty-three, the Cayugas and Onondagas transferred to the Governor General of New York all their land lying on the Susquehanna River, and received therefor a piece of cloth, two blankets, two guns, three kettles, four coats, fifty pounds of lead, and twenty-five pounds of powder.

The laxity which characterized Indian affairs in New York may be attributed to several causes. It virtually became a royal province upon the termination of Dutch rule, and the new government was more desirous to draw therefrom a large revenue, than to promote the welfare of the inhabitants. The system which had sprung up under the Dutch, and which was the growth of forty years of intercourse, and calculated to produce the most satisfactory results when considered in a pecuniary point of view, was continued with but few modifications, and the Dutch who remained in the province after conquest, maintained former relations with those of the native race with whom they came in contact.

The Iroquois alone of all the neighboring Indian nations, were sufficient in strength to cause serious apprehension in the event of hostilities, and they adhered to the Dutch, and subsequently to the English interest, and opposed French encroachments within their territory. Only two of the tribes, the Cayugas and Senecas, could, during the seventeenth century, be induced to assume the condition of neutrality in the continued contests of the whites ; but steadily remained the enemies of the French, although sometimes compelled to sue for peace.

About the middle of the eighteenth century, the French, despairing of success in the attempts to forcibly

reduce the Six Nations to a situation of permanent submission, endeavored to divide them, and the Abbe Picquet
was sent to accomplish the task. He succeeded in draw-
ing off some three or four hundred families, the heads of
which took the oath of allegiance at Montreal ; but the
majority of the Six Nations continued to be the friends of
the English, until the termination of our Revolutionary
War. These Indians therefore, who were at war with the
French, and were the deadly foes of the Hurons and their
Canadian allies, were not likely to break with the Dutch
or English, to whom they looked for aid in case of northern invasion. It was not as necessary then, that this
province should so completely supervise, or carefully restrict trade and intercourse between its Indians and citizens, as it was for Massachusetts, Connecticut, or Pennsylvania.

Yet even in New York our national Indian treatment
is foreshadowed. The almost yearly grand councils at its
capital, between the Governor and the distinguished
Sachems, when the covenant chain was brightened and
former promises renewed, was oftentimes attended by
sale of territory, and by arrangements for continued trade.
Then, the tribal organization was recognized, and the
tribes were bound by the action of their chiefs. In the
treaties of amity and alliance, the Governor promised to
assist them against the French ; and in sixteen hundred
and eighty-five, Louis the Fourteenth complained to the
English King that the Governor of New York had offered
troops to the Iroquois.

In fact the Six Nations possessed about the same attributes of sovereignty which have until very recently been
conceded to the separate Indian bands of our time.
They were free to live in accordance with their custom and
independently control themselves, and they were also at
liberty to adopt such a policy towards all Europeans as

best suited themselves, provided it did not prejudice the English claim. They had not to be sure as complete powers as were ascribed to the New England nations by the Governor-General of Canada, shortly after the publication of the treaty of Utrecht ; for then in response to remonstrances from the Colonies, he asserted that those nations were free and independent, and made war or peace at their pleasure. But they were considered to possess that freedom which released them from responsibility to the provincial law, unless bound by treaty stipulations, except that they could not dispose of the government's reversionary interest in the land in which they had the right of permanent occupancy, and could not inflict injury upon the king's subjects. The individual members of those nations held the same anomalous legal status that the members of the Western tribes now hold. They were neither citizens, nor aliens ; neither subjects, nor rulers ; neither slaves, nor freemen.

The time extending from the first permanently established settlement on our coast, to the declaration of independence on the part of the colonies in seventeen hundred and seventy-six, may for present purposes be divided into three periods. The first, commencing about sixteen hundred and seven, when the English planted Jamestown and the French Port Royal and Quebec, and ending in sixteen hundred and eighty-six when King James abrogated the New England charter, the second terminating with the treaty of Paris in seventeen hundred and sixty-three, and the third continuing through the thirteen subsequent years.

In the foregoing hasty review, sufficient reference has been made to the earliest colonial days to ascertain what political condition was first imposed upon the Indian race, and to show that it was the natural result of attendant circumstances. In attempting to discover whether this

3*

peculiar legal status was general, we have casually referred
to more recent action on the part of some of the colonies,
and have instanced the conduct of Georgia, which was
established after the New England charter was annulled.

But we wish now to briefly allude to the situation
occupied by the Indian nations, and the important part
which they took during the long struggle between the
European powers for continental supremacy and American
territory, which actively began in this country at the close
of the seventeenth century, and only actually terminated
on the cession to Great Britain of New France and the
Floridas.

Soon after the accession of James the Second, it was
determined to place New England under a single royal
Governor, and Sir Edmund Andros became its " Captain
General and Vice Admiral." In sixteen hundred and
eighty-eight it was considered necessary to place New
York and the Jerseys under the administration of Andros,
in order to unite the colonies against France, which had
made threatening demonstrations along the whole northern
borders, and taken possession of Lake Champlain. Under
this new arrangement the Indian nations maintained their
distinctive organizations, with the same exclusive privilege
of control, but they were brought in closer relations with
Great Britain, whose king they commenced to consider
their real protector and ally. The destruction of the new
government and the imprisonment of Andros, was succeeded after a short interval, by royal Governors in the
separate provinces, and the relations of the Indians to the
home authority continued.

The Indian nations have now become most important
communities, and their alliance is anxiously sought for by
the representatives of the European powers. The French
Governor, through the missionaries of the Church, is able
to influence the greater portion of them ; and by skillful

direction, is able, with the small Canadian population and with the slight aid furnished from Europe, to constantly threaten and harass the English colonies.

The Home Government, though anxious for supremacy in America, neglect in their negotiations of peace the interests of their colonies. The splendid victories of Eugene and of Marlborough, which made glorious the reign of Queen Anne, and gave her ministers the opportunity of determining French control in Canada, brought no relief ; for nothing was demanded from France but Acadie, with its vague and undecided boundaries. The war continued with few interruptions until seventeen hundred and twenty-six, when the honest statesmanship of Sir Robert Walpole, and the pacific policy of Cardinal Fleury, brought quiet to France and England, and enabled her colonies to enjoy a season of repose.

During this war at the North, the Southern colonies also experienced trials ; but more successful in their negotiations with the Indian population than their Northern brethren, were enabled to conquer a peace and drive off the power of Spain. But both France and England are vigorously pushing their interests in the New World. The latter extends her settlement inland, and in the South, she divides the royal province of Carolina, and undertakes the settlement of Georgia. The former, having transferred her Mobile colony to New Orleans in seventeen hundred and twenty-two, is engaged in perfecting her asserted right to the Mississippi valley, and in strengthening her Canadian frontier.

The English declaration of war against Spain, in seventeen hundred and thirty nine, again brought the North American representatives of the three great European nations in deadly conflict. France in alliance with, and actively assisted by all of the Indians of Eastern Canada, determined to make the conquest of New England, and

Spain, having secured the services of the Southern Indians, united them with her regular troops, and resolved to make good her Florida claim ; while Great Britain calculated, not only upon the conquest of Canada and Florida, but upon the expulsion of France from the entire Western continent.

Nothing was accomplished by the war, for the treaty of Aix la Chapelle placed the parties in regard to territory in their former condition, and still left boundaries unadjusted. France had now extended her settlements up the Mississippi towards the great lakes, and she determined to unite them to her Canadian possession, and consequently to fix the Alleghany range of mountains as Great Britain's boundary, while the latter claimed indefinitely to the west. Canada and Louisiana became a single royal province under the name of New France, and its Governor exercised control from Cape Breton to the mouth of the Mississippi River. He proposed to connect the settlements by a chain of forts, and to exclude the English trade from all that territory.

In seventeen hundred and fifty, the fort at Pittsburgh was established, and the English in that section of country were seized and removed therefrom.

The exorbitant demands of the French Governor were stoutly resisted, but the position of the Indians, and the negotiations favorable to France, into which they had entered, assured him that he could successfully execute his undertaking. New France, with a white population of fifty two thousand, was deemed sufficiently strong to resist the available strength of the English Colonies, whose inhabitants numbered more than one million. The events of the few subsequent years proved the correctness of this assumption. The Indians along the entire frontier, from Quebec to Georgia, with the exception of the Six Nations of New York and the Cherokees, rendered willing aid to the

French, and the Cherokees were finally prevailed upon to join the great alliance.

The middle colonies were unable to act offensively, or indeed to defend their exposed settlements. The results of the great struggle might have been very different, had Great Britain failed to send troops to the assistance of her colonies, or had France been enabled to spare a like number to reinforce her Canadian army. But the latter had work for all her forces in Europe. England's prime minister announced his war policy in the brief expression that "America must be conquered in Germany," and the signal victory at Rosbach presaged the success of the English colonies. Spain joined France too late in the war to enable her to retrieve disaster and soon the treaty of Paris was executed, by which Great Britain obtained undisputed possession of all that territory extending from the coast to the Mississippi River, and from the Gulf of Mexico to the extreme Northern limit of the continent.

In all of these contests the Indians were active participants. Their barbarous warfare against the defenceless, and the savage cruelties which they invariably practiced, embittered the animosities of opposing colonies and provinces. For a century they held the balance of power, and interest dictated that all possible efforts should be made to secure their alliance and friendship. Both England and France were ready at any time to forgive past injuries and enter into league with any portion of them. Their demands were granted if practicable, and their vanity was gratified in being ostensibly treated as free and independent nations, which gave and received at their option, and the actions of which were alone controlled by their national promises.

From the commencement of intercourse between the white and Indian races, to the termination of the French and English war, the Indians occupied, first the position of hostility to the European, and secondly, that of allies to one or the other of the contending European powers. In either position, they were able to obtain many concessions, and generally to retain their freedom. customs and organizations. Their employment was fighting, as it will always be as long as they remain within uncivilized tribal relations, in which individual reputation or importance depends upon deeds of cruelty. They retarded immigration, impeded colonization, prolonged colonial contests, and apparently checked American growth and development. It is possible that they *signally* checked development; yet it is difficult to make good such an assertion, when the results which their presence and actions produced are properly considered. Their threatening attitude frequently compelled the separate colonies to forget internal dissensions and to unite for protection. It also at times caused partial confederations of colonies, in which a knowledge of the correct principles of representative government was acquired. In fine, it may be said that their conduct had a most beneficial effect upon their declared enemies, as it assisted to destroy discord among those of the same colony who were influenced by varying interests; as it taught the people the necessity of maintaining a firm policy, and of submitting themselves to a rigid code of laws; as it forced rival colonies into league and friendship, producing an intermingling of communities and an interchange of ideas and sentiments; as it gave rise to frequent assemblages of representatives of different provinces, in which affairs of general importance were discussed, and unity of action determined upon; as it was the cause of bringing into existence confederations of equal and distinct political bodies, in which our own system of government was devised and developed.

The New England confederation which was formed in sixteen hundred and forty-three and terminated only with the amendment of its charter, took into consideration all those matters which were of common concern, and left the internal affairs of each colony to the management of the colony itself.

It was, says Trumbull, "A union of great consequence. It made the colonies formidable to the Dutch and Indians, and respectable to their French neighbors. It was one of the principal means of the preservation of its colonies during the civil wars of England, the source of mutual defence in King Philip's war, of service in civilizing the Indians, and propagating the gospel among them."

But this union was not only of importance because of its material strength, and its power of defence.

Its general councils were schools for theoretical and practical political instruction. They ascertained and were able to define the relation and responsibility of the individual to his colonial government, and the duties of the respective colonies under the compact. They enlarged the field of political science, and taught the people the elements of civil and constitutional liberty. The existence of such organizations, and the purposes of their formation, almost forces the conclusion that the Indians furnished most important, though unwilling aid, in American growth and development. Had they quietly yielded to the demands of the whites, or neglected to make forcible opposition, it is not unreasonable to suppose that some of the colonies would have been ruined by factious and partisan conduct ; that in some cases, neighboring colonies would have been arrayed against each other to determine questions of property and rule, and that all would have been less successful in maintaining social order, and have made less progress in determining the true principles of constitutional government.

It is interesting to note how these early existing and proposed confederations viewed the whole subject of Indian affairs. We find that the same general course of treatment was then pursued towards the Indians that our first Congress inaugurated, and that they occupied about the same political relations in respect to colonial authority, that they now do to the United States. In those early days the superior authority assumed control of all Indian affairs ; and if colonies united, that control passed to the confederated authority, and the opinion finally became well nigh universal, that those affairs should be placed under the supervision and management of a representative body, composed of delegates from the several colonies.

At that assemblage of commissioners in New York in seventeen hundred and fifty-four, in which all the colonies north of Virginia were represented, it was decided to make petition for the passage of an act by Parliament, which would authorize the formation of a Grand Council, consisting of delegates from the several colonial legislatures to be presided over by a President General, who should receive appointment from the crown. Among the powers which it was thought proper that this council should exercise, was that of regulating Indian matters, and it was proposed "That the President General with the advice of the Grand Council, hold, or direct all Indian treaties in which the general interest of the colonies may be concerned, and make peace, or declare war with Indian nations. That they make such laws as they judge necessary for regulating all Indian trade. That they make all purchases from the Indians for the crown, of lands not now within the bounds of particular colonies, or that shall not be within their bounds when some of them are reduced to more convenient dimensions." That they make settlements on such purchase by granting "land in the King's name."

In what does the control which the United States Government exercises over the Indian population differ from that which it was thought necessary that this pro-

posed council should possess ?   In nothing of importance,
except that the former assumes to regulate the entire Indian population within its boundaries, even that portion
living within the limits of organized states.

The short period of thirteen years, during which Great
Britain had undisputed possession of the eastern half of
this continent, needs but a passing glance.   The tribes and
nations roaming between the Alleghanies and the Mississippi, and also those in Canada, entered into treaties of
peace with her officers immediately upon the expulsion of
the French.   The King of England had, in sixteen hundred
and seventy-three, issued a proclamation, forbidding Governors in North America to grant lands westward of the
sources of the rivers falling into the Atlantic, and the western plains and valleys had no white population, except the
few French inhabitants who remained after the termination of the war.   The colonial and proprietary governments, had given place to royal provinces, and the Crown
took immediate control of its American possessions.   The
Indian department was organized, and the Indians placed
under the supervision of superintendents.   Sir William
Johnston, superintendent and chief agent, received a salary of one thousand pounds, and was assisted by four dep-
uties, under whose directions smiths and armorers labored
to instruct the Indians in the arts of civilized life, and to
prepare them to follow peaceful pursuits.   Great Britain
expended twelve thousand dollars yearly in maintaining
what was then termed the Indian Department.

Treaties were occasionally made by which the Indian title
to land was extinguished.   One of the most important of
these was that which was concluded at Fort Stanwix, in
seventeen hundred and sixty-eight, between Sir William
Johnston, acting as commissioner for Great Britain, and
the Five Nations, together with the Shawnees, Delawares,
Mingoes of the Ohio, and other dependent tribes.   By this

treaty the territory south of the Ohio River, and that eastward of a line extending from Fort Pitt to the east branch of the Susquehannna River, thence north to Fort Stanwix, was conveyed to Great Britain in consideration of fifty-two thousand dollars, and a number of presents of trifling value.

The course which Great Britain at this time pursued, in recognizing tribal relations and national organizations ; in acquiring by treaty such land as increasing settlements demanded, and quietly removing the Indians to the westward ; in adopting a system which brought the whole native population under its supervision, and in extending to it the means of instruction in order to induce individual and social improvement, is so like the course which this government first adopted as to make it apparent that our early Indian policy was borrowed, or that it was the continuation of the policy which had been developed under British rule.

Upon the commencement of hostilities between Great Britain and the provinces, the Indian nations again became important communities, and were considered a desired element of strength in the threatened contest. Their actions were carefully watched by both parties, and their alliance eagerly sought. Great Britain had the advantage in the negotiations which were attempted, because she, from the first, had determined to crush rebellion, and intended to employ every available means for that purpose ; whereas the Americans, even after the initiative battle in New England, and after the appointment of Washington to the chief military command, had not given up all expectation of reconciliation with the Home Government, and still pursued a vacillating course. Great Britain had already sent her commissioners to the Six Nations of New York, and to the Cherokees and Creeks, and Governor Dunmore of Virginia had dispatched an agent to the tribes upon the Ohio.

The Continental Congress, undecided as yet as to what treatment should be adopted towards the Indians, finally concluded to station agents among the different nations, in order to conciliate their friendship, and induce them to remain neutral. The action taken under this decision resulted in entire failure. During the summer of seventeen hundred and seventy-five, the chiefs of the Six Nations met the British authorities at Montreal, and pledged their support. Subsequently, the Creeks and Cherokees joined the alliance, and the latter, in seventeen hundred and seventy-six, put forth their strongest efforts to destroy the border settlements of the Southern States. The Ohio tribes, though favorable to the British interest, were too much divided to accomplish or undertake any important operations.

Congress labored under another difficulty, which even the declared determination to conquer political freedom did not remove. Composed of delegates from governments absolutely independent of each other, and which were only temporarily united for successful resistance, it was confined to the consideration of measures deemed necessary for the common defence.

Indian affairs therefore could remain but a short time under its supervision, and no policy intended to be lasting could be inaugurated. Besides, the several States within their respective limits, claimed to have succeeded to the sovereignty which Great Britain formerly possessed, and the limits of that sovereignty had not been determined. It was enough to know, that, within their united boundaries all territory to the Mississippi was embraced, and that therefore, the entire Indian population was subject to State jurisdiction.

Some of the States early proclaimed this asserted right to govern the Indian population both by legislative acts and by constitutions. They also claimed the fee of the

lands which the Indians occupied. Virginia declared her
title to such lands, and in seventeen hundred and seventy-
nine denied the power of the native race to sell any portion
of her territory. New York in its constitution of seventeen hundred and seventy-seven, "Ordained that no purchase or contracts for the sale of land," within the limits
of that State, to which Indians were parties, should be
binding upon the Indians or deemed valid unless made by
the consent of its Legislature. The Articles of Confederation signed in seventeen hundred and seventy-eight, recognized this affirmed right of State government within conceded State boundaries, and the ninth article of that instrument stipulated, that, "The United States in Congress assembled, shall also have the sole and exclusive right
and power of regulating the trade, and managing all affairs
with the Indians not members of any of the States," provided that the legislative right of any of the States within
its own limits, be not infringed or violated.

But territory of great extent was in dispute. Some of
the original charters under which the States claimed,
granted all country between certain parallels of latitude
from ocean to ocean, or vaguely defined the western limits
of the grants. The same territory was, in some instances,
supposed to be conveyed by different charters, and therefore conflicting State claims arose. Massachusetts, Connecticut, New York, Pennsylvania, Virginia, North and
South Carolina, and Georgia asserted title to lands west
of the Alleghany range of mountains. New Hampshire,
Rhode Island, New Jersey, Delaware and Maryland had
nothing upon which to base any such demand ; and the
Pennsylvania grant made in sixteen hundred and eighty-
one, did not extend beyond the eighty-first degree of
longitude.

This question of disputed territory furnished the chief
objection to the ratification of the Articles of Confedera-

tion. New Jersey demanded that United States commissioners should settle the western boundaries of the States, while Maryland declined to ratify the articles until the western lands were transferred to the general government.

Yet even while these conflicting claims remained undecided, the United States assumed control of the Indian population beyond the settlements. Within a few months after the Articles of Confederation were agreed upon by Congress, a treaty was made with the Delaware nation by which all territorial rights granted it by former treaties were confirmed. The vexed question of boundaries was however approaching a satisfactory determination. New York, in seventeen hundred and eighty, instructed her congressional delegates to cede her claims to all lands west of such boundary as appeared to them proper, and in the following year Virginia relinquished her interest to the territory north and west of the Ohio. Connecticut and Massachusetts made cession of their western lands in seventeen hundred and eighty-four and five. In seventeen hundred and eighty-seven, seventeen hundred and eighty-nine, and eighteen hundred and two, South Carolina, North Carolina and Georgia respectively yielded the land in dispute to which they had laid claim, and the General Government possessed entire unquestioned control of an extended public domain.

After the lands north of the Ohio had been relinquished by the States, Congress passed the Ordinance of seventeen hundred and eighty-seven, under the provisions of which the North-west Territorial Government was created, and which has been a guide in all legislation under which territorial governments have since been established.

In this important ordinance the United States promised, that the utmost good faith should be observed towards the Indians, and that their lands and property should never be taken from them without their consent.

The policy here announced apparently guided the action of Government in all its treaties which it made with Indian nations, before and after the ratification of the Articles of Confederation and subsequent to March, seventeen hundred and eighty-nine, when the constitution became operative.

Those first entered into, in which " Ministers Plenipotentiary " acted in behalf of the United States, were made to establish peaceful relations between the contracting parties, to efface the memories of injuries inflicted upon each other while the Indians were in alliance with Great Britain, and to determine and declare territorial boundaries. By the stipulations of those which followed, land was sold, or exchanged, and trade and intercourse were placed within certain regulations.

The Six Nations conveyed their entire interest in the lands situated west of the States of New York and Pennsylvania. The Delawares and confederated nations gave up their claims to all lands near the Pennsylvania line, and accepted instead a large tract within the present State of Ohio. The Cherokees agreed to abridge the limits of their country, maintain a perpetual peace, and live under United States protection. Nearly every important nation dwelling between the State borders and the Mississippi River were brought into negotiations with the General Government and placed under treaty covenants. Mutual aid and support were promised, extradition articles were agreed upon, and a commercial code established ; or to speak with more definiteness, the Indians, in consideration of peace with and the protection of the United States, and in consideration of the promise of the latter to maintain them in the quiet possession of certain tracts of country, and to restrain the whites from entering thereon, and in further consideration of a very small expenditure of money in their behalf, and the opening of trade with them under the management only of persons legally licensed, engaged to refrain from hostilities against the people of the United States, and to turn over to the General Government any of their members who should rob or murder any of its citizens.

Such was the tenor of most of the treaties made by the Confederation. It did not have negotiations with Indian nations residing within the conceded limits of a State, further than to establish friendly relations, and to extinguish the Indian title to land outside of acknowledged State boundaries, and to such small tracts within the same as were needed for general purposes. It recognized the Indian nations as distinct and independent political communities, lawfully possessing the soil because of the right secured by immemorial occupancy, and placed only those restrictions upon them which irresistible necessity compelled.

They could not convey the fee of the land, nor hold foreign intercourse. In all other respects, they were at liberty to conduct themselves as they pleased and could live under their own barbarous laws and be guided by their customs. Politically, they held the same relation to the Confederation which they at first held to the colonies, and subsequently to Great Britain. The policy which the first civilized governments adopted towards them remained in all essential features unchanged during a period of time embracing nearly two centuries. It was dictated by circumstances. A continuance of like circumstances prolonged and developed it, and made it the only feasible practical policy which could be followed. It was conciliatory, and at the same time economical, and was best calculated to check savage violence, and give at the least expense possession of the coveted hunting grounds.

While its main features remained unchanged, slight modifications were occasionally introduced for the purpose of removing causes of complaint—the principal of which were overreaching individual action on the part of the

whites—and during the existence of the Confederation, individual intercourse between citizens and Indians were
placed under most stringent legal restraint.   The policy
as thus developed, was in favor when our constitution was
adopted, and received recognition in that instrument.

CHAPTER III.

INDIAN POLICY OF UNITED STATES GOVERN-
MENT.

THE Confederation had performed a great amount of labor in the settlement of State boundaries, in the extinguishment of Indian land title, and in the establishment of treaty relations with the Indian nations.

All State boundaries were satisfactorily adjusted, with the exceptions of North Carolina and Georgia. The Indian title to more than one hundred millions of acres had been purchased, opening for settlement one half as much country as is contained within the limits of the thirteen original States. A judicious policy for disposing of those lands, and establishing governments therein, had been devised and put in operation, and population was moving rapidly to the westward, and appropriating the fertile soil along the Ohio River.

The Iroquois and Cherokees alone of the important Indian communities, remained within State jurisdiction, and the territory over which they exercised control had been determined and defined in treaties.

The constitution made all existing treaties binding upon the new Government, and declared them to be "the supreme law of the land." It also gave to Congress authority to regulate trade and intercourse with the Indian tribes, and conferred upon the Executive and Senate the power to make and ratify Indian treaties. In fine, it confirmed and continued the relations which had existed between the treaty Indians and the Government under the

Confederation, and pointed out a course of action which might be followed in future negotiations.

It virtually took from State management the Indian population within State limits, for Congress and the treaty-making power could, by the exercise of the authority which the constitution conferred, entirely destroy State supervision.

State control over that population remained absolute, as long as there was no action on the part of the United States ; but, as soon as the latter prescribed commercial relations, all conflicting State laws became nugatory. When the latter, and the tribal representatives of that population, entered into treaties, State jurisdiction was compelled to conform to the stipulations of those treaties.

The States owned, and never relinquished the ultimate fee in the soil which the Indians rightfully occupied ; but this only became an interest in possession after the Indians had willingly removed. This remote interest, depending upon a contingency which might require centuries for determination, could not be destroyed by the General Government, although the latter was under no obligations to extinguish the right of occupancy, in opposition to the occupants' wish. In every other respect, the Indian population and the soil upon which it dwelt, could at any time be placed under the control and disposition of the United States. Whatever agreements the United States and those Indian nations might enter into relative to laws for government, whether civil or criminal, regarding regulations for conducting trade, or in reference to abandonment or continued possession of territory, were obligatory upon State authority, " any thing in the constitution, or laws of any State to the contrary notwithstanding."

Did the constitution confer upon the Executive and Senate, the power to make all negotiations with the Indian nations other than those which regulated trade or commerce ? The question has received much discussion, and has apparently been decided by recent opinion as expressed in legislation in the negative. Early opinion however was explicit upon this point. Congress, in seventeen hundred and ninety-three, declared that all purchases of land from Indians must be by treaty entered into pursuant to the constitution ; and a similar declaration is contained in our first Indian intercourse law passed nearly three years previous to that time.

For three-quarters of a century, the legislative branch of the Government evidently considered, that contracts with Indian nations could only be made through the formalities of treaties. The House of Representatives has, to be sure, frequently asserted that the action of the President and Senate could not compel it to make appropriations in order to carry out Indian treaty provisions. In eighteen hundred and twenty-seven, representatives in Congress as strenuously declared, that the constitution vested in them a discretionary power in all matters of appropriation, as they did in eighteen hundred and sixty-six ; for then they claimed that they could negative a treaty by refusing to grant the means to make it effective. They then also claimed the right to deliberate upon the legality of the treaty itself, and upon the wisdom or feasibility of its provisions, else they could not act understandingly in the performance of a constitutional duty. But this asserted right upon the part of the House of Representatives, applied not only to Indian treaties, but to all treaties of whatever nature, which Government might enter into. It was early proclaimed, and involved a question of prerogative and privilege between the Senate and House, which still remains unsettled. It was earnestly discussed when the British treaty of seventeen hundred and ninety-four was under consideration. The President and Senate insisted that the power to make treaties was an important act of sovereignty, which the constitution conferred upon the Executive, and when the President exercised that power, and executed a treaty, it became, upon ratification by the Senate, the supreme law of the land, and as such was paramount to the laws of the United States, and could not be set aside by legislation. It was also insisted, that the constitution made no distinction between treaties with foreign nations and with Indian tribes, and that all treaties should be made by the President and then submitted to the Senate for approval; that when this rule was followed, and a treaty made and approved which involved the expenditure of money, the necessary appropriation should at once be made, or the national faith would be violated. The House replied by resolution and declared, "that it is the constitutional right and duty of the House of Representatives in all cases of treaty, to deliberate upon the expediency of carrying such treaty into effect, and to determine and act therein as in their judgment may be best for the public good."

The question again arose when the terms of the treaty of eighteen hundred and fourteen were under discussion, and as formerly, a compromise was effected, under which the required appropriation was made, but a settlement of the constitutional points involved could not be accomplished. The House maintained, that prior to the execution and ratification of a treaty which demanded an expenditure to carry it into effect, the Executive should obtain the sanction of Congress through an appropriation. This course was followed by President Monroe, and was generally approved and believed to be in strict conformity to the constitution. Had it been continued by succeeding Presidents, it is doubtful if the provisions contained in the Indian appropriation act of eighteen hundred and seventy-one, forbidding the recognition of Indian nations or tribes as independent powers, with whom the United States may contract by treaty, would have received congressional support.

In all the early discussions upon the treaty-making power, the Indian communities were conceded to be as free and independent as the nations of Europe, in so far as the possession of treaty rights was concerned. President Adams, in his message of eighteen hundred and twenty eight, remarks, that "at the establishment of the Federal Government under the present constitution, the principle was adopted of considering them as foreign and independent powers, and also as proprietors of lands. As independent powers we negotiated with them by treaties; as proprietors, we purchased of them all the land which we could prevail upon them to sell; as brethren of the human race, rude and ignorant, we endeavored to bring them to the knowledge of religion and of letters."

The judicial branch of the Government sustained the view above expressed in regard to the independence of the native communities, and the celebrated case of Worcester against the State of Georgia, decided in eighteen hundred and thirty-two, was supposed to set the matter at rest. The Supreme Court held, that the constitution placed the Indian nations among those powers capable of making treaties, and of maintaining the relations of war and peace, and that therefore the President and Senate could, under the treaty-making power, enter into compacts with them as with foreign nations.

But the provisions of the act of eighteen hundred and seventy-one, to which reference has been made, do not imply that the President and Senate had not the constitutional right to treat with the Indian nations. On the contrary, they concede that that right existed, and was legally exercised, by declaring : "That nothing herein contained shall be construed to invalidate, or impair the obligations of any treaty heretofore lawfully made and ratified, with

any such Indian nation or tribe." For the acknowledged
existence of Indian treaties "lawfully made and ratified,"
certainly necessitated the recognition of a power having
the legal capacity to make and ratify them ; and, as they
had all been made and ratified by the Executive and Senate, those branches of the Government necessarily possessed the requisite authority to make and ratify them.   If
therefore Congress should admit, that the United States
ever lawfully made and ratified Indian treaties, it must
likewise admit that they became such through the exercise
of the power which the constitution conferred upon the
Executive and Senate, since that power could not be derived from any other source.

Only two conclusions can be drawn from the provisions
of this congressional act.   Either that the condition and
importance of the Indian nations have undergone such a
change since the adoption of the constitution, that they
have ceased in fact to retain sufficient of the attributes of
sovereignty to be competent to enter into treaties, or that
the constitution never recognized them as nations, capable
of contracting with the United States by treaty.

Any other inference would make it appear that Congress had attempted by legislation to take away from the
executive branch of the Government the power which the
constitution has conferred upon it.

Of the two stated conclusions possible to be reached,
the first would seem to be the correct one ; because of the
virtual admission in the act that treaties with the Indians
had been lawfully made and confirmed ; and the provisions which have been quoted would therefore naturally
imply that Indian tribes with which the United States
have heretofore entered into treaties, and which have been
considered independent communities, have at last become
so insignificant or so dependent, that they are no longer
qualified to maintain national relations, nor to act other-

wise than as the United States may choose to direct ; and therefore they shall not hereafter be acknowledged as independent communities, but the departments of the Government shall henceforth recognize their actual condition, and be guided accordingly in all future transactions in which they shall be parties. If it is an absolute fact that the Indian tribes within our territories have lost the essential elements of independence, if they have surrendered or bartered away the right of self-government, if they have become disintegrated or widely separated, they are in no sense national organizations, and have not any longer the power to bind themselves by treaty, nor to impose treaty obligations upon the United States.

If such fact does exist, it would appear that Congress has the constitutional right to discover it, and to declare that certain constitutional provisions are no longer operative, because of the changed situation of affairs. It would appear that such a declaration on the part of Congress would be as fully within the sphere of its duty as the withholding of an appropriation to satisfy an annuity demand which an Indian treaty declared perpetual, for the reason that the Indian organization had become extinct. In the latter case Congress merely refuses to carry out the stipulations of a lawfully executed treaty, or we might say, to be governed by the supreme law of the land, because of the fact, that one of the parties to the contract is no longer in being. In the other case it declines to recognize the native communities within United States territory as nations, with whom treaties can be made, although the constitution declared them to be such, because they have actually lost the ability to contract by treaty. Unless Congress can thus determine facts, and authoritatively decide whether or not they continue to be of such a nature, as to still make operative or applicable the law as expressed in the constitution, the provision of the act of eighteen hundred and seventy-one, forbidding further treaties with Indian tribes, is without force or effect, and the President may negotiate with the Indians by treaty, until deprived of the power to do so by a constitutional amendment.

Whether the tribal organizations have undergone such radical change since the formation of the present Government that they no longer retain the national characteristics which they possessed when the constitution was framed and adopted, and whether they have lost all power to make and execute national decisions, can only be ascertained by a comparison of their past and present relations to the United States, a consideration of the causes which have produced modified conditions, and a review of Government action. That action has been so extended, that it is only possible to give it a hasty glance ; but, an attempt will be made to sufficiently exhibit it through a discussion of its more prominent features, to convey a definite idea of its nature, and the method of its application.

Enough has been said for the present, of the powers conferred upon the different branches of the Government by the constitution. It is important to examine the policy inaugurated during the first administration, and afterwards it will be necessary to trace the modifications made in succeeding years. It will be seen, that the essential elements of that policy still remain in force, and only such changes have been introduced as varying circumstances seemed to demand.

The declared objects which the Government desired to accomplish, have always been the same, viz : to remove the native population from the land required for occupancy by the whites, to restrain in the most economical manner its onslaughts upon border settlements, and finally to prepare it for citizenship. The first object has uniformly been attained by purchase under contract or treaty ; the second has been sought through various expedients, generally and when possible of a peaceful character, but all attended with considerable expenditure ; and the last by the introduction of civilized example. These three objects have been steadily kept in view, and any policy which did not ostensibly assist in the accomplishment of all, could not have received popular support. For one class of citizens demanded of it, practical beneficial results to government, financially considered. Another class, impressed with the sacredness of the so-called right of the Indians to territory, and with a duty to make earnest endeavors to fix upon them the customs of civilized and Christian life, demanded of it liberal and benevolent achievements ; while a third class, looking to the future, demanded individual and social improvement. It is plain, therefore, that any policy which assisted in the accomplishment of all these avowed objects, would be generally sustained, and it is not to be wondered at that the friends of every administration, proclaimed that its action toward the native population was both economical and humane, and was at the same time rapidly promoting civilization.

At different periods, however, public attention has been partially diverted from one or the other of these desired results, and the great proportion of the labor expended has been given to that which appeared to be of the greatest temporary importance.

If land was required, endeavors were made to induce the Indians to relinquish it. The commissioners who negotiated on the part of the United States must, under the appearance of fair dealing, keep in mind the pecuniary consideration, and effect the purchase upon the most moderate terms possible. If Indian outbreaks were threatened, attempts were put forth to remove apparent causes of disturbance, and to restore friendly feeling. This might be brought about by placing restraints upon whites, and restrictions upon trade, or by the expenditure of money for the benefit of the Indians, and giving to them some of the needs of civilized domestic life.

All of these experiments were tested. Did the position of Indian nations, in respect to neighboring civil governments, make the future incorporation of the native element with the great body of our population seem necessary, more earnest efforts were proposed in the interest of education and Christianity. Still attempts to produce any of these results might aid in securing the others. The sale of land removed the Indians further from the white population and furnished them with means to improve their social condition. The establishment of trade relations, or the bestowal of implements of husbandry, might induce them to abandon the chase, make them more willing to abridge the limits of their territory, and advance them in the path of civilization. Should educational privileges be extended, they might be prevailed upon to embrace the opportunity of fitting themselves for citizenship, would cease to intimidate by hostile attitude the border settlements, and would dispose of all the land which they did not actually require for cultivation. Every administration then, might with some show of reason, defend the wisdom of its action, whether engaged in the purchase of land and Indian removal to the westward, or in the expenditure of revenue for the benefit of Indians, in order to secure tranquillity upon the border, and to bring about their mental and moral elevation. In any event, contemporary opinion could not decide justly upon its merits, except in so far as immediate practical benefits were obtained. The effect of civilizing influences would not be at once discovered.

A faint sunlight might soon give place to the old shadow of darkness. The good seed cast upon such a waste of waters, might lose its power to germinate before it found congenial soil.

Soon after the formation of the new Government, Congress took into consideration the condition of the native population. Early in August, seventeen hundred and eighty-nine, an act was passed, requiring the Secretary of War to perform and execute such duties as should be "entrusted to him by the President, agreeably to the constitution," relative to Indian affairs. Upon the twentieth of the same month, an appropriation of twenty thousand dollars was voted, to defray the expenses of negotiating and treating with the Indian tribes ; and an intimation of the opinion of Congress, as to the power of the President in the execution of those duties, may be gathered from the provision which fixed the compensation of the commissioners whom he should appoint to make the negotiations.

At this time most of the Indians north-west of the Ohio had violated the treaties which they had made with the Confederacy. The Delawares and Pottawatomies, the Ottawa, Chippewa and Sac nations, had, upon the previous January, agreed to live in peace with the United States, and had, in consideration of goods promised them to the value of six thousand dollars, granted all lands outside of defined boundaries. The contract had never been observed by them, and they continued in hostile attitude. The Southern Indians, with the exception of the Chickasaws, showed an unfriendly disposition. The Government found it necessary to send military expeditions to the North, and to make preparations for the chastisement of the Indians South. On the northern frontier, war continued until seventeen hundred and ninety-four; and at the South, a vacillating course of action was pursued, and treaties establishing "perpetual peace," were quickly followed by warlike demonstrations. At length the British treaty of seventeen hundred and ninety-four, and that made with Spain in the following year, deprived the Indian nations of foreign aid and counsel, and they soon gave up the conflict, and placed themselves under United States protection.

During these five years of confusion and excitement, it was not possible to apply a definite Indian policy. President Washington recommended the enactment of laws to govern the alienation of land by Indians, to provide for their punishment when violating treaties, to remove from their midst evil disposed white people, and to justify the appointment of agents to dwell among them. He advocated throughout the war conciliatory action, "a system, corresponding with the mild principles of religion and philanthropy towards an unenlightened race of men, whose happiness materially depends upon the conduct of the United States."

When the contest had nearly terminated, he informed Congress of the course he intended to adopt. He said in his message of November, seventeen hundred and ninety-four, " The intelligence from our army under the command of General Wayne, is a happy presage to our military operations against the hostile Indians north of the Ohio. * * * And yet, even at this late hour, when our power to punish them cannot be questioned, we shall not be unwilling to cement a lasting peace, upon terms of candor, equity and good neighborhood. Towards none of the Indian tribes have overtures of friendship been spared."

Congress endeavored to propitiate the Indian nations by salutary and liberal legislation. Little public effort had hitherto been made to improve their condition. Now it was proposed to protect them from the impositions practiced by white individuals, and to introduce among them the habits of civilized society. The Government proffered them its protection, and promised non-interference on the part of its citizens. The law of seventeen hundred and ninety prevented the white population from obtaining possession of the lands of Indians, and forbade any trade with them, except under license obtained through the public departments.

The law of seventeen hundred and ninety-three re-enacted similar provisions, and prescribed more severe penalties in case of disobedience. It also forbade white inhabitants to settle on Indian land under penalty of fine and imprisonment, and made crimes committed against Indians by whites, punishable in like manner as those committed against citizens. It also provided, "That, in order to promote civilization among the friendly Indian tribes, and to secure the continuance of their friendship, it shall and may be lawful for the President to cause them to be furnished with useful domestic animals and implements of husbandry, and also to furnish them with goods and money in such proportions as he shall judge proper, and appoint such persons from time to time as temporary agents to reside among the Indians, as he shall think proper," but expenditures for such purposes shall not exceed twenty thousand dollars per annum.

By legislation, and through the treaty-making power, Government also established control over the New York Indians and over the Cherokee and Creek nations. All other Indians, living within State boundaries, remained subject to State authority. This control however was but partial. Government directed the disposition of land, regulated trade and intercourse, and appointed its agents to supervise Indian affairs. It gave to its courts and those of the States concurrent criminal jurisdiction in cases where United States statutory offences were committed against Indians in their country, and within State limits. It admitted the exclusive jurisdiction of the State courts to try crimes committed by whites against whites upon Indian reservations, and even decided that the power had never been conferred upon its own courts, to punish Indians for offences committed against whites, when perpetrated within a State, and outside of a reservation. The Government also re-enacted the ordinance of seventeen hundred and eighty-seven, and provided for the appointment, by the President, of the officers of the North-west Territory: North Carolina ceded the Western lands which it had claimed, and the above mentioned ordinance was extended over all the territory south of the Ohio. This territory composed a single district, and the powers and duties of governor were united with those of superintendent of Indian affairs. Soon after, Kentucky was formed within the jurisdiction of the commonwealth of Virginia, and admitted as a State.

At the conclusion of the war, the Indians were in destitute circumstances, especially those on the Northern frontier. Government commenced a vigorous peace policy, and adopted such measures as seemed best calculated to obtain and make lasting their friendship, and at the same time render them more dependent. Congress appropriated fifty thousand dollars for the purchase of goods, and passed an act for the purpose of carrying on with them a just and liberal trade." Treaties were entered into, by which the United States covenanted to maintain them in the peaceable possession and quiet enjoyment of their territory, and promised permanent annuities. To enable and induce them to adopt civilized customs, and establish fixed abodes, they were furnished with agricultural implements, also with instructors to teach the habits practiced in civilized communities. Some of the nations were even more abundantly supplied. They received the necessary machinery to prepare material for the construction of comfortable dwellings, and to make ready for household use the grain which might reward their labors in cultivating the soil. Educational and religious experiments were also undertaken. Government aid was granted to assist in erecting school houses, and church edifices, and the missionaries, maintained by different Christian denominations, were encouraged in the performance of the good work in which they had engaged.

But the guardianship so carefully entered upon, was calculated to retard the progress of civilization, although it might secure temporary peace. The attempted exclusion of the white population from the Indian country, by the passage of the stringent intercourse act of seventeen hundred and ninety-six, deprived the Indians of the example of law-abiding citizens, and left to them as types of white morality and intelligence, those representatives of debased humanity whom the most severe legal measures yet devised have not prevented from affiliating with the native race. By the provisions of that act the boundary line of the Indian country was to be determined, and no white individual could cross the same and enter that country without a license or passport; and should any one enter for the purpose of trade, or even of hunting, he rendered himself liable to fine and imprisonment.

This law expired by limitation in March, seventeen hundred and ninety-nine, but it was then reënacted and made to apply to any variation of boundary which might in future be declared. It is hardly possible that those by whom it was framed, supposed that it could be rigidly enforced; but they rather intended that it should furnish the requisite authority for the removal of troublesome and evil-intentioned persons, and supply the Indians with the power to rid themselves of those who might give them annoyance. It had the effect, however, to shut out from Indian intercourse that class of individuals who obey simple prohibitions because of conscientious regard for law, and scarcely restrained that other class who are alone deterred from the commission of crime by the fear of incurring penalties.

The "Trading House Act" which was passed in seven-

teen hundred and ninety-six also opposed the social improvement of the Indian, and exercised a demoralizing
tendency upon the officers of the Government. It empowered the President "to establish trading houses at such
posts and places on the Western and Southern frontier, or
in the Indian country, as he should judge most convenient
for the purpose of carrying on a liberal trade with the
several Indian nations within the United States." He was
required to license all traders and to prescribe rules and
regulations to govern their action. The latter should
trade for furs and skins only, and solely on public account.
They were forbidden to receive any emoluments or gain
from trade, but should be compensated for services by
fixed salaries.

The friends of this act, however, did not advocate it in
the interest of civilization.

They wished to accomplish two objects : one of which
was the securing of the friendship of the Indians by supplying their wants, and the other the supplanting of the
British traders in their influence over the Indians. It was
said that France, Britain, and Spain had wisely adopted
such a policy ; that the United States had hitherto pursued war at an enormous expense, and that it was time
to try commerce ; that the Indians had sufficient sense
not to abandon allies who furnished them with necessary
goods.

The Indians had, in fact, more sense than they received
credit for. They could understand the meaning of the
constant encroachments made in the progress of settlement. They saw clearly that their lands were gradually
passing from their possession, and that unless white advances could be checked, they would be obliged to retire
in order to obtain subsistence, or else submit to the dictation of their rivals. That fear influenced their actions
more than the desire for commerce, and rendered them

always willing to assist any foreign force engaged in hostilities against this immediate disturber of their peace and apprehended cause of future grievances.

The act appropriated one hundred and fifty thousand dollars, as the capital stock to be used in the trade, and eight thousand dollars as the yearly compensation of the factors and clerks who should be appointed to conduct the business; but as all barter was strictly confined to the purchase of skins and furs, no Indians could participate in the benefits of the traffic, unless they had those articles for sale. It therefore encouraged a continuance and a more zealous following of their natural pursuits, and had in no respect the slightest tendency to wean them from their nomadic habits.

The act was limited to a single year, but it was revived in eighteen hundred and two. and substantially continued by periodical legislation for twenty years. It furnishes an illustration of the difficulty of destroying any Government system of action, which may possibly bring remote beneficial results, in the creation and duration of which a class of individuals are pecuniarily interested, and of the utter impossibility of confining it within originally intended bounds, while practiced. The law as revived in eighteen hundred and three contained no new provisions; but in eighteen hundred and five, an additional one hundred thousand dollars was appropriated, for the purpose of establishing new trading houses. In the following year, the appointment of a Superintendent of Indian trade was authorized, who should be charged with the duty of purchasing all goods, sending the same to posts, and receiving and disposing of, at public auction, the furs obtained therefor. The capital stock was increased to two hundred and sixty thousand dollars, and ten thousand dollars was fixed as the united salaries of factors and clerks.

In eighteen hundred and nine, the capital stock was

made three hundred thousand dollars; and in eighteen hundred and eleven, the superintendent was directed to purchase and ship to the proper destination, all annuity goods purchased under treaties. Thus was the system continued by legislation until eighteen hundred and twenty-two, when the President was required to cause the houses to be closed, the accounts to be settled, and the proceeds remaining to be used in arranging treaties with, and paying annuities to Indians. It was continued and extended, although it utterly failed to accomplish the objects expected of it, and resulted in a loss to Government from the time it was first organized—the average yearly loss being about three per cent of the money invested, if the salaries paid to officers is taken into computation. The conduct of the Indians, during the disturbances of eighteen hundred and twelve and thirteen, conclusively demonstrated the fact, that foreign governments had not lost their influence over them, and the experiment also proved that the United States cannot compete with private parties in Indian trade enterprises. And yet, notwithstanding the evidences of failure were so clearly apparent that resulting future good could not be reasonably anticipated, the system had become so firmly established, and was so persistently defended and supported by its friends, that it required the most determined efforts to effect its destruction.

The active peace policy inaugurated by Government, after the forced submission by the Indian nations during the latter part of the century, seemingly promised satisfactory results.

President Jefferson, in his first message, informed Congress, that their condition was improving; that they had begun to see the necessity of assistance; that they had not only ceased to decrease, but were actually increasing in numbers. In subsequent messages they were represented as living peaceably, and engaging quite extensively in agriculture, and as disposing of portions of their lands to obtain means to make further advancement. Endowed, he says, with the faculties and rights of men, and occupying a country which left them no desire but to be undisturbed, the stream of population has overwhelmed them, and now, " reduced within limits too narrow for the hunter's state, humanity enjoins us to teach them agriculture, and the domestic arts, and to encourage them to that industry, which alone can enable them to maintain their place in existence. * * We have therefore furnished them liberally with the implements of husbandry and household use. We placed among them instructors in the arts of first necessity. They are covered with the ægis of the law against aggressors from among ourselves ;" and were it not, he intimates, for the evil counsel and example of crafty individuals who had gone among them, their improvement would be decided and lasting.

It is well to note in this connection, that those tribes or nations which were evidently making progress, occupied, or had occupied for a long time, the border of civilization. The southern Indians, says Jefferson, are much more advanced than those north ; and Calhoun, as late as eighteen hundred and twenty, reported as follows : " While many of the Indian tribes have acquired only the vices with which a savage people usually become tainted by their intercourse with those who are civilized, others appear to be making gradual advances in industry and civilization. Among the latter description may be placed the Cherokees, Choctaws, Chickasaws, and perhaps the Creeks ; most of the remnants of the Six Nations in New York, the Wyandottes, Senecas and Shawnees at Upper Sandusky."

The Cherokees stand first, and have two flourishing schools. It is pertinent here to note the fact that progress was really confined to those Indian nations more immedi-

ately in contact with the whites ; because about the date
when Mr. Jefferson gave utterance to the remarks which
have been quoted, a new feature of the Indian policy appeared, destined to become in later years, the one most
important and prominent. It was the plan at this time
suggested and afterwards adopted, of removing the eastern
Indian population beyond the Mississippi River, where it
might be as far away as possible from interference on the
part of citizens or white individuals, and where it would
cease to give annoyance to the white communities, which
were rapidly increasing in the West. Mr. Jefferson entertained the supposition, that such a plan successfully carried
out, would result in benefit to both races. The acquisition
of the Louisiana territory presented the opportunity of
putting it in operation.

Little however at this time was attempted, for popular
opinion was not prepared to favor so radical an experiment.
It had not fully endorsed the proposition of the first Secretary of War. General Knox, who advocated the gradual
removal of the Indians to the West, and the purchase of
such portions of their territory as advancing white population should demand. To extinguish the Indian title to a
vast amount of territory before it was actually required for
settlement, and to remove its occupants by Government aid
involved too great an expenditure, was of doubtful expediency and was possibly inflicting a wrong upon the native
race. No active measures were therefore engaged in,
further than attempts to induce emigration by advice and
slight pecuniary considerations ; and the war of eighteen
hundred and twelve, which destroyed to a great extent the
friendly relations between the Indians and the United
States, rendered the operation of any definite policy impossible. But after the settlement of the difficulties incident
to the war, the question of removal again came up for consideration.

Its friends now advocated the colonization of all the
eastern Indians within two large reservations, or declared
territories—one of which should be created west of the
Mississippi, and the other near the northern frontier.
The plan had many favorable recommendations, whether
examined in a utilitarian point of view, or benevolently
considered.   The Indians retarded the expansion of population, and the development of large tracts of country.
Their presence within State limits caused conflicts between
State and United States authorities, and gave rise to questions of jurisdiction, which were beginning to assume a
serious aspect.   Their scattered condition made it well
nigh impossible to establish over them sufficient control to
prevent serious outbreak, and the inhabitants upon the
border were without the security which they had a right
to demand.   The philanthropist might add, that the Indians could not be improved as long as they remained in
the neighborhood of the whites ; for as situated, they were
brought in contact with the lower classes of society, and
were influenced to imitate vices, rather than to be guided
by examples of virtue.   They should therefore be placed
in localities beyond the reach of crafty and mischief-mak-
ing individuals, where they could be more efficiently protected by the strong arm of the law, and where they might
be under the direction of faithful and competent instructors, who could induce them to assume other habits, and
bring them gradually to a knowledge of the customs of
civilized life.

The opponents of the plan stoutly contested these arguments, and were apparently able to produce as convincing
proofs in support of their own theories.   Much of the reasoning was based upon doubtful and imaginary premises,
because of different opinions entertained respecting the
nature and capacity of the native race.   It was denied that
the condition of the Indians would be improved by thrust-

ing them further back into the wilderness, where they would again take up former practices, and unlearn all that had been taught them.   It was claimed that the territory which they had already relinquished furnished ample room for any increase of population which could be reasonably anticipated during a series of years, and they should be allowed to remain stationary, where they could be better encouraged to make permanent improvements, and thereby acquire local attachments, and the usages suited to a new mode of living.   The objection that it was hazardous to create an Indian territory, and build up a separate sovereignty within the United States limits, was met by the assertion, that the Indians would become civilized before there could be any danger of conflict.   The objection that the execution of the plan would be attended with too great an expense, was answered by the statement, that removal must at some time take place, and that the longer it was postponed, the greater would be the cost attending it.   "It cannot be doubted," said Calhoun, "that much of the difficulty of acquiring additional cessions from the Cherokees, and other southern tribes, results from their growing civilization and knowledge."   A wise economy therefore, directed that the removal be made as quickly as possible.

The measure was strongly favored by Mr. Monroe, and he began to act upon it soon after he had assumed the duties of the presidential office.   In July, eighteen hundred and seventeen, a portion of the Cherokee nation agreed to accept land in Arkansas.   During the following year the Delawares ceded to the United States their possession in Indiana, and the Government agreed to provide for them a country west of the Mississippi, to pay them the value of the improvements which they had made, also a perpetual annuity, and to furnish them with provisions and the necessary assistance for their journey.   Shortly thereafter, President Monroe urged his views upon Congress. He said in a special message relating to the Georgia affairs : " My impression is equally strong that it would promote essentially the security and happiness of the tribes within our limits, if they could be prevailed on to retire west and north of our States and territories, on lands to be procured for them by the United States. Surrounded as they are, and pressed as they will be on every side by the white population, it will be difficult, if not impossible for them, with their kind of government, to sustain order, etc." He then remarks that the United States could adopt a general system for their improvement in their new homes, in which the whole country would take an interest. Again, in his message of eighteen hundred and twenty-five, he says in speaking of the Indians : " Experience has demonstrated, that in their present state it is impossible to incorporate them in such masses in any form whatever into our system. It has also demonstrated with equal certainty, that without a timely anticipation of and provision against, the danger to which they are exposed under causes which it would be difficult, if not impossible, to control, their degradation and extermination will be inevitable."

The work of removal was now energetically pursued, and was made the more important on account of the position taken by the State of Georgia. Her western territory had been relinquished on condition that the United States would extinguish the Indian title to the lands within her agreed boundaries, and she demanded performance of the condition. The Cherokees within that State had, under treaty authority, formed a government of their own, and denied that State jurisdiction extended over them. The case was considered by Congress, and although the weight of opinion upheld the Cherokees in their asserted right of self-government, and also conceded their right to remain within the State until they might be willing to depart therefrom, the best remedy out of the difficulty was thought to consist in the withdrawal of the cause of discontent. A home in the West, "which should never in all future time be embarrassed by having extended around it the lines, or placed over it the jurisdiction of a territory or State," was promised them in the treaty of eighteen hundred and twenty-eight.

The whole subject of Indian removal was debated at length in Congress. In the meantime, the administration zealously labored to execute treaties, by which the Indians should consent to emigrate. President Adams remarked, that the United States had endeavored to advance them and when attempts had been partially rewarded, they were found to exist "as independent communities in our midst." He recommended therefore, that they be sent West. President Jackson advised, that Congress set apart an ample district west of the Mississippi, and without the limits of any State or territory, to be guaranteed to the Indian tribes as long as they shall occupy it ; each tribe having the management of its own portion of the district, and being "subject to no other control from the United States, than such as may be necessary to preserve peace on the frontier, and between the several tribes. There the benevolent may teach, and an interesting commonwealth may be raised up, destined to perpetuate the race, and attest the humanity and justice of this Government."

Congress passed an act authorizing the President to cause the necessary territory lying west of the Mississippi River, and not included within any State or territorial government, to be divided into a suitable number of districts, and to exchange land with those Indians with whom the United States had treaty relations. The President was also authorized to guarantee title, and to promise the Indians aid to remove to, and protection in, their new residence.

Assurances that the tribes who agreed to the exchange should be undisturbed in the control of their own affairs, were omitted in the act, but were fully set forth in treaties, which generally contained the stipulations, that they might enjoy their own form of government, and make their own laws—subject however, to the regulations of Congress in the matter of intercourse—and that their lands should never be included in any State or territory of the Union.

The plan of removal had now received governmental sanction. The views of several administrations respecting its importance, the zeal with which it was prosecuted, and the benefits expected to result therefrom, can be briefly presented by the introduction of a few extracts from presidential messages and official reports. The annual message for eighteen hundred and thirty informs Congress that the speedy removal of the Indians to the West is important to the General Government, the State governments, and to the Indians themselves. It will prevent danger of collision between general and state governments, will free the Indians from the power of the States, and enable them to pursue happiness in their own way. It will retard decay among them, and they may possibly become interesting and civilized communities. Treaties had been made with the Choctaws and Chickasaws, "*probably the last that will ever be made with them,*" which are "characterized by great liberality on the part of Government."

The annual message for the succeeding year contains the following : " It is confidently believed that perseverance for a few years in the present policy of the Government, will extinguish the Indian title to all lands lying within the States, and remove beyond their limits every Indian who is not willing to submit to their laws."

In the message of eighteen hundred and thirty-two, the following is found : " I am happy to inform you that the wise and humane policy, of transferring from the eastern to the western side of the Mississippi, the remnants of our aboriginal tribes, with their own consent and upon just terms, has been steadily pursued and is approaching I trust its consummation."

The message of eighteen hundred and thirty-three announces the fact, that if the several treaties entered into for the relinquishment of territory and migration of the Indians are ratified, provision will have been made for the removal of almost all the tribes, remaining east of the Mississippi. The Indians, "have neither the intelligence, the industry, the moral habits, nor the desire of improvement, which are essential to any favorable change in their condition." If the fate of disappearing before a superior civilization is to be averted, it must be brought about by removal. Those who have emigrated are reported to be doing well.

The message of eighteen hundred and thirty-four states : "No important change has during the season taken place in the condition of the Indians. Arrangements are in progress for the removal of the Creeks and Seminoles. The Cherokees east of the Mississippi have not yet determined to remove. The experience of every year adds to the conviction, that emigration and that alone can preserve from destruction the remnants of the tribes yet living among us." In his report of eighteen hundred and thirty-three, the Secretary of War commends the policy of Government in removing the Indians to the West, where they might physically and morally improve, and alludes to the advancement which those who have emigrated were making. They were rapidly improving, were "erecting dwellings, and laying the foundation of a social system, which it is to be hoped will afford them security and prosperity." He says, that the whole country north of the Ohio and east of the Mississippi, as far as the Fox and Wisconsin Rivers, has been cleared of the embarrassments of

Indian relations ; for the Indians have either migrated or
have stipulated to do so within short periods. They will
be comfortable in their new homes, " unless indeed the aid
and efforts of the Government are rendered useless by their
habitual indolence and improvidence." The Cherokees,
occupying portions of land in Georgia, Alabama, North
Carolina, and Tennessee, numbering about eleven thousand,
are the only Indians south of the Ohio and east of the Mississippi, with whom an arrangement has not been made,
either for emigration or for a change of political relations.
President Van Buren, in his message of eighteen hundred
and thirty-eight, said that the measures lately pursued
" have rendered the speedy and successful result of the long
established policy of the Government upon the subject of
Indian affairs, entirely certain. The occasion is therefore
deemed a proper one, to place this policy in such a point
of view as will exonerate the Government of the United
States from the undeserved reproach which has been cast
upon it through several successive administrations. That
a mixed occupancy of the same territory by the white and
red man is incompatible with the safety and happiness
of either, is a proposition in respect to which there has
long ceased to be sufficient room for a difference of opinion.
* * * The remedial policy, the principles of which were
settled more than thirty years ago under the administration of Mr. Jefferson, consists in an extinction, for a fair
consideration, of the title to all lands still occupied by the
Indians within the States and territories of the United
States, their removal to a country west of the Mississippi,
much more extensive and better adapted to their condition
than that on which they then resided ; the guarantee to
them by the United States of their exclusive possession of
that country forever, exempt from all intrusions by white
men, with ample provisions for their security against external violence, and internal dissensions, and the extension to

them of suitable facilities for their advancement in civilization. This has not been the policy of particular administrations only, but of each in succession since the first attempt
to carry it out under that of Mr. Monroe." The manner
of its execution has given rise to conflicts of opinion ; "but
in respect to the wisdom and necessity of the policy itself,
there has not, from the beginning, existed a doubt in the
mind of any calm, judicious, disinterested friend of the
Indian race, accustomed to reflection and enlightened by
experience." Mr. Van Buren then indulges in prophetic
fancies, and romantically exclaims : "and if in future
time a powerful, civilized and happy nation of Indians shall
be found to exist within this Northern continent, it will be
owing to the consummation of that policy which has been so
unjustly assailed." He then speaks of the Cherokees lately
removed, to whom Government granted in fee thirteen
millions of acres, in exchange for nine millions, and stipulated to pay a large sum of money, "thereby putting it in
their power to become one of the most wealthy and independent communities of the same extent in the world."
He further remarks that "the case of the Seminoles con-
stitutes the only exception to the successful efforts of the
Government to remove the Indians to the homes assigned
them west of the Mississippi."

Mr. Tyler, in his message of eighteen hundred and forty-
two, thus speaks of improvement among the Indians :
"With several of the tribes, great progress in civilizing
them has already been made. The schoolmaster and the
missionary are found side by side, and the remnant of what
were once numerous and powerful nations may yet be preserved as the builders up of a new name for themselves and
their posterity." And again, in eighteen hundred and
forty-four, he says : "The Executive has abated no effort
in carrying into effect the well established policy of the
Government, which contemplates a removal of all the tribes

residing within the limits of the several States, beyond those limits, and it is now enabled to congratulate the country at the prospect of an early consummation of this object. * * * We may fondly hope that the remains of the formidable tribes which were once masters of this country will, in their transition from a savage state to a condition of refinement and cultivation, add another bright trophy to adorn the labors of a well directed philanthropy."

Mr. Polk maintained and pursued the same Indian policy, and in eighteen hundred and forty-seven, Secretary Marcy reported as follows : " Our relations with the tribes is yearly extending, and in many respects assuming a more interesting character. The wise policy of separating the Indians residing in States and organized territories, from contiguity to, and intermingling with, the white population, and of settling them in a quiet home, removed as far as practicable from the reach of influences so pernicious to their well being, has been steadily pursued, and generally with favorable results."

From the first report of our first Secretary of the Interior, made in eighteen hundred and forty-nine, we are led to believe, that the wisdom of the policy had not been over-estimated, and that it was about to yield the abundant harvest of good which had been so confidently promised. He says : " Most of the tribes located permanently on our western border, and particularly the more southern, continue steadily to advance in civilization, and in all the elements of substantial prosperity. The establishment of manual labor schools in charge of missionary societies of various religious denominations, is working a great moral and social revolution among several of the tribes, and if the department had the means of extending the benefits of these institutions to those now destitute, it would no doubt be productive of like happy results."

But a decided change in the tone of state papers and

official reports is about to take place. It is suddenly perceived that the Government, if it has not committed a palpable error, has at least failed to accomplish the objects desired. Much of the labor and expense attending the execution of the sweeping plan of removal, and subsequent education of the native population, have been barren of beneficial results. Says the Secretary of the Interior in his report of eighteen hundred and fifty three : " It is folly to attempt to conceal the fact, that under the present system, the Indians have not for many years past advanced in morality, integrity, or intelligence. * * * Much of the philanthropy and charity manifested for them, has been wrongfully directed."

The Commissioner of Indian Affairs, who had that year returned from a visit to the Indian territory, reported that what had been said about the advancement of the Indians was in a great measure false. They had houses, but they did not live like white people. They refused to work, and showed a decided inclination to consume all the ardent spirits they could by any possibility obtain. Later, and in eighteen hundred and fifty-five, the Secretary of the Interior thus addressed President Pierce upon the subject of the removal of the Indians, and the guarantees which the Government had given them : " The country was congratulated by one of your predecessors, upon the removal to their new homes, and the dawning to them of a new and happy era was publicly proclaimed. But this guarantee has not been fulfilled, and that propitious time has not yet arrived. A quarter of a century has not elapsed before the same state of things, so much deplored, is found to exist, and the evil that was intended to be remedied appears in a far more appalling form. The strong arm of the Government is constantly invoked to stay its progress, and the guarantee is continually held up to us for faithful performance. Our only reply to all the appeals made, is, that "the force of circumstances has rendered it impracticable."

From such and many similar expressed opinions of that period, it is safe to conclude, that the policy which successive administrations had acted upon, had not been advantageous to the Indian, or had not at least, advanced him in the moral or social scale,—whatever may have been the substantial benefits which it secured to the General Government. It would appear in fact, that the Indian had retrograded since the completion of his westward pilgrimage. The Secretary of the Interior, in eighteen hundred and fifty-one, spoke in commendatory terms of the New York Indians, who upon the petition of the citizens of that State had been permitted to remain in their eastern home. They were then making gradual advances in agriculture and civil pursuits, and although they had been constantly subjected to all the destructive influences of contiguous white neighborhood, were living under their own government, and bid fair to surpass their formerly more favored southern brethren in acquiring the habits necessary in a progressive social development. They were undoubtedly in much better circumstances than they would have been, had they removed to the Indian territory as they stipulated to do in the treaty of eighteen hundred and thirty-eight, and received the one million acres of land, together with the pecuniary consideration, which had been promised them. Their condition at the present time is probably more advanced than it would have been had they migrated and recommenced the labor of improvement. The progress which they have made during the last half century, exposes the fallacy of the doctrine, that Indians cannot exist in the presence of, and in contact with, a superior cultivated race, and also shows that they are no more subject to decay, or disorganization, when thus situated, than when dwelling apart by themselves.

It also shows, when compared with the progress of the southern nations since their settlement in the Indian country, that the red man is more rapidly improved when in constant communication with the whites, than when debarred from intercourse with them—even if supplied liberally with instructors from whom he can derive a knowledge of the habits and practices of a people occupying a higher plane of existence.

Expediency may have dictated the removal of the more populous Indian nations to a country beyond State limits, in order to check conflicts of State and Federal authorities. It may have warranted such removal on the ground, that the powerful, independent, and irresponsible communities endangered the scattered white inhabitants, retarded the growth of newly-planted settlements, prevented the cultivation of large tracts of productive land, and finally arrested general development. But the less important tribes, and especially the insignificant bands with which the Government treated, should have remained in the east, in the possession of convenient and much abridged reservations, where circumstances would have induced them to copy, by degrees, the customs of those by whom they were surrounded.

The plan of removal was too thoroughly executed. As viewed in the light which the experience of years has thrown upon it, it did not benefit the Indian, and only brought relief to the country by the temporary elimination of a troublesome element in society. As far as it brought relief, it might be rationally defended ; but when the necessity of removal did not actually exist, in order that disturbing causes might be displaced, it cannot be supported. Government committed an error, in forcing into the wilderness those straggling bands which had already become partially civilized. The money expended in fitting them out with guns, blankets, kettles and tobacco, for their journey, and in furnishing them with a year's provisions, could have been better employed in administering to their wants in their former habitations.

De Tocqueville's remarks upon the uncharitableness of the country, called forth by witnessing the poverty and wretched appearance of Indians who were awaiting transportation across the Mississippi, and the criticisms of American citizens who opposed the administration, contained much deserved censure, and now appear more significant than the declarations of Presidents Van Buren and Tyler, who so confidently proclaimed the wisdom and liberality of their action.

More particular attention will be given to the effect of the policy, when hereafter its cost and the measure of advancement attained by those who have been longest under its influences are considered. It has not within the last quarter of a century been pursued to any great extent. An occasional removal to the Indian territory has been accomplished, but the scattered tribes have for the most part been allowed to remain upon portions of their own lands, having relinquished, under treaty, possession of such portions as Government could persuade them to dispose of when it wished to concentrate them, so that they could be more readily supplied, or to open up tracts of country for settlement, or to disencumber routes of travel. Still, the idea of gathering the native population within two or three large territorial reservations, to be devoted exclusively to its use and occupation where it could not be contaminated by contact with overreaching and demoralized whites, and where it could be easily controlled and possibly taught the essential requirements of a higher and better life, has never been abandoned.

The tribes which inhabited the country adjacent to the present Indian territory have been placed within its boundaries, and inducements have been held out to those more remote to remove within the same, but they have generally proved unavailing. The Commissioners appointed under the act of eighteen hundred and sixty-seven, to meet and negotiate with certain hostile tribes, were empowered to select a district or districts, which should become and remain the permanent home of those Indians who should consent to live therein. The Commissioners advocated the establishment of an additional Indian territory, situated above the Nebraska line, and recommended that nearly all the northern tribes roaming east of the Rocky Mountains be there concentrated, while those at the south be gathered within the territory already existing. The plan was adopted and the new reservation declared ; but owing to the bitter hereditary feuds actively maintained by members of the different tribes, or an inclination on their part to continue nomadic habits, the undertaking met with little success. Now the Indian Bureau is again attempting to draw the northern bands to the old Indian territory— especially those which have made progress in civilization.

We will glance, for a moment, at the general Indian legislation of the country, during the period which has thus been hastily traversed, to ascertain more fully the methods adopted by the Government, to restrain the native population, and by what especial branches of the executive authority, control has been exercised.

From the organization of the Government until eighteen hundred and forty-nine, when the Interior Department was created, the management of Indian affairs devolved upon the Secretary of War. For many years the expenditures, except when active hostilities existed, were light. But few agents were appointed, but few expensive treaties were made, and but little money was disbursed for the general welfare and improvement of the native race. As communication with the interior was opened, and population spread itself over the western territory, our

Indian relations were correspondingly extended and the duties of control necessarily increased. In eighteen hundred and eleven, the Superintendent of Indian Trade, appointed under the trading-house acts, was directed to attend to the distribution of annuities ; but when that office was abolished in eighteen hundred and twenty-two, the direct supervision of all Indian matters again fell upon the War Department, and so continued until eighteen hundred and thirty-two, when the Indian Bureau was created, a Commissioner of Indian Affairs appointed, and a separate office established at an annual cost of ten thousand dollars.

This Commissioner, though placed under the authority of the Secretary of War, and subject to such regulations as the President might prescribe, had " the direction and management of all Indian affairs, and of all matters arising out of Indian relations." and passed upon all accounts connected therewith, which were by him referred to the proper accounting officers of the treasury.

The act transferring the Bureau to the Home Department, authorized the Secretary of the Interior to exercise all the supervisory and appellate powers formerly exercised by the Secretary of War, in relation to all the acts of the Commissioner.

The War Department had executed the labor of Indian removal, had established relations with nearly all the tribes roaming over the United States territory, and had developed a system of conducting business, as similar in form as that which characterized army transactions, as legislation and circumstances permitted. Army officers and Indian agents had been answerable to the same authority. Their spheres of duty were distinct, but they were often called upon to act in unison, when Indians became refractory, or threatened to break out into rebellion. As they derived their separate powers from the same source, and as those powers were well defined, there was little probability that conflicts would arise, when united action became necessary. Responsibility to the same head, also created a common interest, and the different branches not only became mutually reliant, but were sharp observers of each other's derelictions of duty. They occupied the same field and were in constant communication. The agent was present to discharge Government obligations, the soldier to restrain and to inflict punishment when merited. The War Department held within its own grasp these distinct forces, and applied them to suit the variable conditions of different tribes.

The Interior Department assumed the management of Indian affairs, without the power to coerce disobedient bands, and expected to accomplish its work through persuasion. In fact an argument in favor of the transfer of the Bureau, was, that too much force had hitherto been used, and too little attention paid to milder methods; and for that reason Indian advancement had been unsatisfactory. Said Commissioner Brown : "Among the more important duties of this office, are those which relate to the civilization of our Indian tribes," and the Secretary of the Interior, in eighteen hundred and fifty-one, said that civilization "must be commenced by substituting kindness for coercion, by feeding and clothing, rather than by warring upon and driving them from their territory." It is possible that the Interior Department did not intend to manage rebellious tribes. The first Secretary refused to accept the Florida Indians until they had been properly punished, and manifested a willingness to be improved. In the possible event that any of the tribes could not be controlled through kindness, it was easy to turn them over to the army for chastisement.

Another consequence of the transfer was the creation of apparently separate interests, on the part of the officers of the two departments. Each class felt independent of the other.   The feeling of mutual reliance was destroyed, and there sprung up in its stead a spirit, if not of jealousy, at least of distrust, lest either party might make unwarranted assumptions, or declarations of authority.   The checks formerly existing upon illegal or fraudulent transactions, by reason of the watchfulness which a conscious common responsibility produced, were removed. and the scattered agents, if not strongly armed with intelligence and integrity, became the willing or unwilling prey of tricky contractors and designing knaves.

The Interior Department has retained the management of Indian affairs to the present time.   Since eighteen hundred and forty-nine, the labor and responsibility incident thereto have greatly increased.   Remote tribes have been brought within treaty relations, and have been placed under special guardianship.   The provisions of the trade and intercourse laws have been extended, by legislation, over the Indian nations transferred to us by Mexico, and indeed over all of those within United States jurisdiction who occupy the Pacific slope, including the inhabitants of the territory of Alaska.

This management has, from year to year, become more independent and exclusive.   Congress, in eighteen hundred and fifty-one, strangely abridged the constitutional right of the President to select commissioners or ministers for the purpose of framing Indian treaties.   It enacted, that all such negotiations should be conducted by the officers and agents of the Indian Department, who should not receive any additional compensation for the extra services. The President was still allowed, and even compelled, to designate the party by whom a treaty should be negotiated, but was confined in his selection to the particular class of persons amenable to the authority of the Commissioner of Indian Affairs.

Congress might as lawfully have stripped the Executive

of all discretion in appointment, as to have thus fettered
its action. It can as well take away as limit a power conferred by the constitution. The Interior Department
could as well have objected to this act upon legal grounds,
as to that of eighteen hundred and seventy-three, which
deprived the Indians of formerly recognized treaty privileges. It did not, however, but quietly submitted to the
new provisions. The law placed the entire native population more completely under its control, and its agents
could frame and negotiate treaties according to its dictation. It not only did this, but it also augmented the responsibility of the Indian Department in the expenditure
of money, since that department created the treaty obligations under which a considerable portion of the money
was disbursed.

The system of management does not materially differ
from that which was adopted when the Government was
inaugurated. Agents to exercise general supervision, instructors in husbandry, and the mechanical arts, dwell
with the various tribes. Mental and spiritual improvement is sought through the labors of secular and clerical
teachers. The practice of feeding those Indians unable to
subsist themselves, has frequently been resorted to for the
last fifty years. The "Peace Policy" of the late administration differs from past Indian policies, chiefly because it
furnishes a greater amount of subsistence, and attempts
more thorough instruction.

The general Indian legislation of the country is mostly
embodied in the Indian Trade and Intercourse laws, and
the yearly appropriation acts. The particular relations
which different tribes hold to the government have almost
universally been brought about through treaties. There
are a few instances in which the status of certain tribes
has been modified, and even radically changed by special
laws, unconnected or unsupported by treaty agreements.

As for instance the act of eighteen hundred and sixty-three, which cancelled all United States obligations in favor of specified bands of the Sioux nation, and declared their rights in lands forfeited. But special acts affecting such relations, unless passed to make operative treaty conditions, have been of such rare occurrence, that the above statement might be made without qualification.

In a preceding portion of this chapter, the idea is advanced that the Indian nations have lost all the national characteristics which they possessed at the time when the constitution was framed and adopted. No effort has been made to support the theory announced by a recent chairman of the Senate Committee on Indian Affairs, that it was "a solecism from the very start," to recognize that they held any of the elements of sovereignty ; but their former ability to contract by treaty has been admitted. If they have lost that power, they have either been deprived of it or they have surrendered it. If it has been taken from them without their assent, it has been effected through the medium of general legislation, since special acts referring to particular tribes have, as a rule, been passed to carry out the provisions of treaties, by which those tribes surrendered or forfeited their national attributes.

But the majority of the Indian nations consented by treaty, even before the intercourse laws were extended over them, to live under such regulations as the United States might deem necessary for their welfare, and nearly all of them have since willingly acquiesced in the regulations under which they have been placed. Like the Navajos, and neighboring nations, they have acknowledged in council that they are under the protection and jurisdiction of the United States, and that all laws in force for regulating trade, and preserving peace with the Indian tribes are binding upon them. Therefore but few of the native national organizations, embracing but a very limited proportion of the native population, have been unwillingly deprived of any of the attributes of sovereignty. The great majority of those organizations have yielded them up, and have solemnly and irrevocably consummated the act of surrender. At least they have accepted for the most part those modifications of former political condition which have been effected by the provisions of the trade and intercourse laws.

Congress however derived its power to enact those laws from the constitutional provision which permits it " To regulate commerce with foreign nations, and among the several States, and with the Indian tribes." It has frequently availed itself of the power thus conferred, and if we allow the decisions of the courts to govern our conclusions, we must admit that its action in this respect has been lawfully exercised. In " the United States vs. Rogers ;" Chief Justice Taney held, that the United States could extend its criminal jurisdiction over all persons, whether whites or Indians, who resided within its territorial limits, and without the limits of organized States. Certainly if such a power was carried to its utmost legitimate extent, not one of the native tribes would retain a single national qualification.

From the organization of the present Government to the beginning of the century, five trade and intercourse acts were passed, nearly all limited in duration to a short period of time. They were evidently intended to secure the good will of the tribes, while they increased their dependence. They aimed to protect the Indians from the frauds of private and irresponsible parties, to elevate their condition by imparting instruction, to cut them off from communication with citizens of foreign powers, and to allow of no business transaction on their part, with people other than of their own race, except they were conducted under the supervision of regularly appointed Government officials. These acts authorized the appointment of agents, forbade the carrying on of trade outside of State limits, by any person except a trader legally licensed ; declared invalid all sales of land by Indians, unless executed "at some public treaty, held under the authority of the United States ;" defined the boundaries of the Indian country, prohibited whites from settling therein, and proclaimed public routes of travel within it ; made the penalties for crimes committed against Indians, within their territory, the same as if committed against citizens ; allowed State courts to arrest and punish Indians, if detected in the commission of depredations at any place over which the jurisdiction of the courts extended ; and finally authorized the annual expenditure of a small amount of money, "to promote civilization among the friendly Indian tribes, and to secure the continuance of their friendship."

There seems to be nothing in these laws which deprived the Indian nations of any of the acknowledged rights which they enjoyed when the country was under the supremacy of Great Britain, or during the existence of the Confederation, unless the more stringent restrictions placed upon intercourse, and the more effective guardianship sought to be established over them, may be supposed to effect it. These are moderate in comparison to later statutes. The law of eighteen hundred and two, without expressed limit as to the time of its operations, contained the essential provisions of all the laws above mentioned, and but little of importance that was new. The law of eighteen hundred and sixteen forbade any foreigner to enter the Indian country, without first securing a passport. The law of eighteen hundred and seventeen extended the criminal jurisdiction of the United States Courts over the Indian country, and gave to them power to punish Indians who should commit offences against whites, even in their own territory. The act of eighteen hundred and twenty-two enabled the courts to take cognizance of civil causes arising in the Indian country, in which Indians should be opposed to whites as claimants.

The statutes of eighteen hundred and thirty-four substantially re-enacted all the important provisions of former trade and intercourse laws, and readjusted the boundaries of the Indian country. It abridged the liberties of the Indians, as it restricted their trade with the outside world to the disposition of their robes and furs, which they procured in the chase, and made the appointment and retention of those with whom they were alone permitted to transact business, dependent upon the will or caprice of the agents who presided over them. It obliged them to deliver up for trial any of their number accused of crime, and declared, "that so much of the laws of the United States as provide for the punishment of crimes committed in any place within the sole and exclusive jurisdiction of the United States, shall be in force in the Indian country, provided the same shall not extend to crimes committed by one Indian against the person or property of another Indian." The law of eighteen hundred and forty seven, amendatory of certain sections of that of eighteen hundred and thirty-four, allowed the agents to pay over annuities due under treaty stipulations to families, instead of to chiefs, as formerly, and forbade the agents to make payment to Indians while the latter were intoxicated, and only upon condition that the chiefs and head men of tribes would pledge themselves to use all their influence to prevent the introduction and sale of liquor in their country. It also deprived the Indians of the power of entering into agreements which could be enforced, as it made null and void all executory contracts for the payment of money or goods, to which they should become parties. The act of June, eighteen hundred and sixty-two, provides that when Indians of treaty tribes wish to adopt the habits of civilized life, and have lands allotted to them, they shall be protected by their agents against trespassers, and if a chief molests them he shall be temporarily deposed. This, under a plausible construction, might enable an agent to overthrow the entire political organization of a tribe, should tribal authority interfere with an Indian who was attempting to cultivate a patch of ground assigned him by the agent. Agents have so frequently dethroned chiefs for slight causes, and disregarded the desires of majorities in making new appointments, that it requires no effort of the imagination to believe, that such an interpretation might be given to the law upon an attempt at practical application.

What liberties have these trade and intercourse laws left to the Indian nations? What national prerogatives do they enjoy, and what essential privileges of a free people do they retain? In what does that sovereignty consist, which enables the Executive and Senate under the treaty-making power of the constitution, to make to them solemn pledges, and to bind our national faith for the performance of the same? The Indian nations have not the independence of the counties in the States of the Union. They have not now a single right except to live within their territory and control their own domestic relations. They can, it is true, freely rob, murder, and trade with each other, without incurring responsibility to the United States Government. Yet that freedom, or license, has been taken away from the treaty Indians. For them the fountain of all authority is to be found in the Interior Department. The agents are their immediate rulers, and are vested with arbitrary, almost despotic power. Their civil and political condition is so well expressed in a section of an act passed in eighteen hundred and sixty-three, and intended to apply to a portion of the Sioux nation, that it might not be amiss to quote. It reads as follows : " Said Indians shall be subject to the laws of the United States and to the criminal laws of the State or Territory in which they may happen to reside.   They shall also be subject to such rules and regulations for their government, as the Secretary of the Interior may prescribe ; but they shall be incapable of making any valid civil contract with any person other than a native member of their tribe, without the consent of the President."

CHAPTER IV.

INDIAN TREATY SYSTEM.

THE Indian treaty system, continued by Government until the year eighteen hundred and seventy-one, admits of extended criticism. Unless presented, our Indian policy would be but feebly portrayed. The limits of a single chapter are barely sufficient to allow a mention of the action taken under the treaty-making power, and the responsibilities which have been thereby incurred ; but an endeavor will be made to show within those limits, how that action has been applied, and to point out some of the most notable results.

A discussion of the subject, though meagre, involves questions both of law and of expediency. The legality, or at least the legal consistency of Government action, in entering into many of the treaty obligations, is occasionally suggested, as an examination into the changes of political relations wrought through the treaty system is pursued.

Inquiries as to the amount of disbursements made on account of our Indian population become necessary, since nearly all of the expenditures have been covered by treaty promises, and the further inquiry is also pertinent, have such disbursements been judicious and economical?

More than three hundred and sixty treaties are recorded within the statute books, which have been made by and between the United States and the Indian nations, since the adoption of the constitution. In many of them, a number of distinct tribes or nations entered conjointly, and thus the same tribe has assumed sacred national obligations under the most solemn sanctions upon very numerous occasions. In seventeen hundred and ninety-four, twelve nations north of the Ohio executed the same instrument. Should such joint action be considered in every instance as made up of independent acts, equal in number to the separate national organizations which thereby mutually pledged their faith, our Indian treaties would be numerically increased threefold.

This surprising exercise of the treaty-making power has not been distributed equally through successive periods of time. Often for a term of years but very few of these international agreements were entered into, and then there might follow a season remarkably fruitful in treaty covenants. Nor has every Indian nation, of the sixty or seventy within our boundaries, had the same opportunities to frequently renew promises for friendly or reciprocal relations. The Missouri River, above the State bearing its name, was not reached by our commissioners until eighteen hundred and fifteen, and afterwards for the succeeding twenty years, the North-western tribes were seldom invited to enter into negotiations. Many treaties were made during the early years of the Government, stipulating peace, alliance, or cession of territory. Again, after the war of eighteen hundred and twelve, peace was established with the Indian tribes through the formalities of treaties; and then, from eighteen hundred and twenty-five to eighteen hundred and thirty-eight, emigration from the east to the territory west of the Mississippi was conducted under treaty agreements. Since that period, the tribes which have permanently roamed over the country west of the Mississippi and Missouri Rivers, have occupied the greater share of the attention of Government. These treaties have been made for the accomplishment of definite objects, and when the attainment of those objects was specially desired. As our white population was constantly extending itself, land for settlement was needed, and as Congress had early announced, that all purchases of land from Indians must "be by treaty entered into pursuant to the constitution," treaties became necessary in order to extinguish Indian right of occupancy. During the first twenty-five years of our existence, thirty-eight treaties were ratified, by which it was claimed, that this right of occupancy to two hundred millions of acres was extinguished. Possession of land was the chief object to be accomplished, and in fact about the only thing wished for in the absence of hostilities, or during undisturbed peaceful relations. The tribes then retarding the advance of white population, because of occupation of country, or because of threatening attitude, are those which have been most frequently met in council. Of these, those formerly north of the Ohio, and two or three of the southern nations were prominent. The Pottawatomies alone have entered into thirty-eight treaties with the United States—thirty-five of which were executed before they made final disposition of all their eastern lands.

Commissioners, freely chosen by the Executive, conducted these diplomatic transactions on the part of the United States until eighteen hundred and fifty-one, and for the remainder of the treaty period, they were for the most part under the control of the Indian Bureau. About two-thirds of the treaties are prior in time to the above mentioned date. The succeeding twenty-five years yielded nearly seven of these international compacts annually. But, during this term, the tribes roaming over the territory received from Mexico, and those inhabiting the country to the north of the same, as well as those along our northern boundary, west of the Mississippi, were brought in contact with our spreading settlements, and were necessarily called upon to make concessions, by relinquishing portions of their hunting grounds.

We shall now attempt a brief consideration of a few of the treaties, confining ourselves to recent dates, and commenting only upon those provisions which appear impossible of execution, or which might be justly avoided, and those which, from the condition of parties, might be considered unconstitutional by the courts of the United States.

Among the first mentioned, we would include those which promise the performance of acts which in the nature of things cannot be accomplished ; those which cannot by any reasonable supposition be peaceably fulfilled, if carried to their fullest extent, and those which might be resisted by the Indian nations on account of illegality.   In the second class, we would place those in which the Government, in entering into them, carried the treaty-making power beyond its legitimate sphere.

In a certain class of treaties the position in which the Indian tribes are placed is simply absurd.   United States Commissioners, knowing full well the willingness of Indians to assent to any course of future conduct in order to obtain a present advantage, and wishing as it would seem to make their work complete, have induced the representatives of the Indian nations to promise on behalf of their people an immediate change from the habits of barbarism to those customs of another race which are the result of the struggle of centuries after individual and social improvement.

These tribes are not only pledged to correct public action, but also to virtuous private conduct.   Their representatives have not only dealt with subjects which were general and national, but have attempted to surrender the personal liberty of their constituents.

The treaty of eighteen hundred and fifty-five with the Mississippi and other bands of the Chippewas, furnishes an illustration of the obligations resting upon some of these freedom-loving and but recently independent communities. In this instrument, the bands, after jointly and severally agreeing "to conduct themselves at all times in a peaceable and orderly manner, and to submit all difficulties between them and other Indians to the President" of the United States for arbitrament and decision, stipulate, " that they will settle down in the peaceful pursuits of life, commence the cultivation of the soil, and appropriate their means to the erection of houses, opening of farms, the education of their children, and such other objects of improvement and convenience as are incident to well regulated society, and that they will abstain from the use of intoxicating drinks and other vices to which they have been addicted."

Equally ridiculous and as impossible of fulfilment are certain provisions in treaties made during the same year with the Oregon and Washington tribes. Every Indian in that region is the victim of a strict temperance pledge. All are under international covenants to live in peace, to surrender all offenders against United States laws, and not to trade or transact business outside of United States limits ; and by a supplemental treaty of eighteen hundred and sixty-five, these Indians relinquished the right to fish and hunt outside of their reservations, and agreed to live under the laws of the United States and the regulations of the Indian Department, and not to go beyond the boundaries of their reservations for any purpose whatsoever, without the written permission of the agents whom our Government might place over them.

Many treaties having like and similar provisions are still in force. Do these covenants of absolute sobriety and upright conduct continue to run with the nation while remaining under contract, and are they binding upon rising generations ? Is the individual liberty of the child circumscribed by the act of the parent ? Large money considerations support these treaties, and it is certainly for the interest of the United States Government that the opposite parties to the bargain remain at peace and at rest, and cease to practice the vices to which in the past they have been addicted. Perhaps Congress might find sufficient facts to justify a declaration, that the Indian tribes have not scrupulously kept their faith.

A great latitude of action has been exercised by our Government in its ratification of treaties. In some instances material amendments have been made by the Senate, without the knowledge of the Indian tribes who entered into the original contract, and the amended instrument has been deemed valid, although never submitted to the tribes for concurrence. The labor and expense of collecting the scattered bands of an Indian nation, especially when roaming over a great extent of western country, is so considerable that the reassemblage of a council for the purpose of considering and agreeing to amendments, unless the same are vital to a proposed treaty, might be pardonable. The Senate amended the Cheyenne treaty of eighteen hundred and sixty-one by striking out its eleventh article, and in the opinion of the Executive, the treaty became at once legally operative without further negotiations. In that article the Arapahoes and Cheyennes displayed a more thorough knowledge of the laws adopted by our Government for the disposition of its public lands, and a higher appreciation of hospitalities received from their white brethren than is common among the border Indians. They respectfully requested that, "in consideration of the kind treatment received from the citizens of Denver city and the adjacent towns, the proprietors of said cities and adjacent towns be permitted by the United States Government to enter a sufficient quantity of land to include said city and towns, at the minimum price of one and one-quarter dollars per acre." This constituted the article which was unsatisfactory to the Senate, and the

Arapahoes and Cheyennes were held to their contract, notwithstanding the denial of their request. But how could the treaty of eighteen hundred and fifty-one, entered into by Government with the same Cheyennes and other Indian tribes, be regarded as finally ratified and operative upon the action of the Senate, when that body disallowed a large portion of the money consideration which the Indians demanded in payment for the property and privileges by them transferred ?

Many important provisions of the Wyandotte treaty of eighteen hundred and fifty were stricken out by the Senate without the consent of that tribe ; and other cases might be cited, where a similar course has been pursued. An acceptance of the consideration given by the terms of the treaty as modified by the Senate, might estop the Indians from pleading its illegality, as in law they must be supposed to know the conditions of the contract under which they receive benefits. This mode of procedure was not however general, and in a few years became entirely unnecessary, because of a discovery made by the commissioners of the Government selected by the Indian Bureau.

It consisted in the insertion of a proposition in the treaty itself, to the effect that, if modifications were deemed desirable, the same might be made at the pleasure of the Executive and Senate, and therefore become valid without the formality of reference for acquiescence. The seventh article of the treaty of eighteen hundred and fifty-nine, with the Kansas tribe of Indians, is as follows : " In order to render unnecessary any further treaty hereafter with the United States, the President, with consent of Congress, shall have full power to modify or change provisions of former treaties, to such extent as he may deem necessary for their welfare and best interests."

A similar article was incorporated in the Cheyenne treaty of eighteen hundred and sixty-one. A number of treaties made in eighteen hundred and sixty-five contain this article : "Any amendment or modification of this treaty by the Senate of the United States, shall be considered final and binding upon the said band represented in council, as a part of this treaty, in the same manner as if it had been subsequently presented and agreed to by the chiefs and headmen of said nation."

In commenting upon the constitutionality of Government action under the treaty-making power, it is only intended to present a few suggestions.   During a hasty review of the more important Indian treaties, the question of the legitimate scope of the treaty-making power is constantly recurring.   The puzzling problem as to whether the power could be carried to its fullest extent, when employed in conducting negotiations with our Indian communities, is also continually presented to the mind.

The power is of course general, and extends to all subjects of national concern.   Says Story : "It embraces treaties for peace or war, for commerce or cession of territory, for alliance or succor, for indemnity, for injuries or payment of debts, for the recognition or establishment of principles of law, and for any other purpose which the policy necessitates or interests of independent nations may dictate."   Its limits are not fixed by the constitution, nor can they be defined, since they may be varied by circumstances.

Each of the departments of Government must however have its appropriate sphere of action.   The Executive, in the exercise of powers which the constitution confers, cannot intrench upon the constitutional rights and privileges of the Legislative Department.   The President and Senate acting unitedly, cannot take from Congress its expressed or implied authority.   To such statements there can be no possibility of dissent, and they might be announced as fundamental rules of government.   But when an application of these rules is attempted upon questions of Indian control, great difficulty arises, from the fact that the Indians have been placed in irreconcilable, or at least anomalous positions.   Viewed as independent nations, they were vested with treaty rights, and considered at the same time as a portion of our population, they were subject to legislative dictation.   Were their treaty rights abridged because of their occupancy of United States territory ?   Was the control of Congress limited because of their conceded national independence ?

These questions have received the study of our courts for three-quarters of a century, but no satisfactory or at least conclusive answers are obtained from a review of the decisions.   The earlier and more important cases arose upon the interpretation of treaties.   The President and Senate, proceeding under that constitutional provision which bestowed the treaty power, had acted with great latitude, and the courts were called upon to define the true scope of the provision.   The conclusion reached seems to have been this : That the power to make Indian treaties, enumerated in the constitution, was general, and carried with it authority to treat upon all subjects of an international character, excepting those prohibited by express legislation.

The second question, whether legislative control over the Indians was limited because of conceded national independence, has also been partially answered by the courts.

They affirmed that our Indian territory composed a part of the United States ; that all Indians residing therein were a portion of our population, and were subject to congressional authority.   It was of late decided in the celebrated Boudinot case, that a general law of Congress annulled specific stipulations of an existing treaty ; that certain privileges conferred upon members of the Cherokee nation who were engaged in trade, were taken away by

the revenue laws of eighteen hundred and sixty-eight,
because Congress had declared that the provisions of the
latter should be operative in all parts of the United States.
and they were in conflict with the terms of the treaty.
The courts also maintain that the ability of Congress to
extend over the Indian nation a criminal code of laws is
unlimited. Chief Justice Taney speaking for the court in
the case of " The Government against Rogers," which was
cited in a former chapter. said. that when the country occupied by the Indian tribes " is not within the limits of
one of the States. Congress may by law punish any offence
committed there. no matter whether the offender be a
white man or an Indian."

To either question. considered separately. the answer
appears to be explicit : but how can such opposed theories
be reconciled ? Our Indian communities were quasi independent nations. capable of maintaining with the Government the relations of war and peace. and rightfully controlling their own internal affairs. As such. they were
distinct from United States subjects. and could only be
reached under the forms of international law. In the
language of Justice McLean. of the Supreme Bench :
" The President and Senate, except under the treaty-
making power. cannot enter into compacts with the Indians or with foreign nations." Again they were part and
parcel of our population. holding tribal relations only by
sufferance. every member of which was individually
amenable to such laws as Congress might choose to enact.

As independent nations, the treaty-making power of
the Government could establish, maintain, or modify political relations with them : as residents within the territorial
limits of the United States. they could be placed by Congress in entirely different political conditions.

Here, then. were two separate powers of the Government, exercising Indian control by virtue of the authority

conferred in the constitution,—a control which the courts failed to limit in either case—and the action of the separate powers became therefore confused and antagonistic. Had those separate powers confined action within agreed and harmonizing rules, results legally considered would not have been so perplexing. Had Congress respected that sanctity which it is claimed attaches to assumed international obligations, and refused to legislate upon matters which had practically been adjusted by treaty, legal conflicts might have been partially avoided. But the rule of law, that a treaty may be abrogated by a legislative act, furnished to the House of Representatives a check upon the proceedings of the Executive and Senate. Under the threat of withholding appropriations, it was enabled to secure the passage of statutes which modified treaty stipulations, and made them more in consonance with its own views and wishes.

The same rule of law compelled the courts to declare null and void articles of existing treaties, when interpreting general enactments. As in the Boudinot case, cited above, the revenue laws applied "anywhere within the exterior boundaries of the United States," and the court, gathering the meaning of Congress from the language employed, decided that conflicting Indian treaty stipulations were thereby overthrown.

Had, on the other hand, the President and Senate confined Indian action to subjects which arise between independent powers, and left undisturbed the internal and individual affairs of the tribes, Indian matters might have been less complicated. But unfortunately, having obtained jurisdiction from the fact, or fiction, whichever it was, that those tribes were independent nations, they immediately proceeded to manage them as a portion of our dependent population, and assumed to confer those privileges, and exercise that restraint, which was clearly within the province of Congress. They severed and dissolved Indian political organizations, and bestowed upon the members thereof American citizenship. They bartered away the public domain, conveying lands in permanency to individuals. In the absence of statutory provisions, they regulated trade and intercourse, and negotiated upon every subject which could possibly arise or grow out of our Indian relationship. The Wyandotte treaty of eighteen hundred and fifty-five declared the Indians of that band to be citizens of the United States. The treaty of eighteen hundred and sixty-two with the Pottawatomies, placed it in the power of the President to confer citizenship upon the members of that tribe. A treaty of the same year stipulates that the Ottawas "having become sufficiently advanced in civilization, and being desirous of becoming citizens of the United States," shall be permitted to terminate their relations to the Government as an Indian tribe, after the period of five years, when they shall be declared citizens, and shall be entitled to the rights, and subject to the laws of the United States, and of the State in which they reside.

It is plain, that the President and Senate could not bestow citizenship upon aliens, unless under some enabling congressional act. Admission to the privileges of a citizen, can only be gained by following certain rules prescribed by the legislative branch of the Government; for the constitution leaves the matter of naturalization solely with Congress. A treaty stipulation that inhabitants of territory about to be acquired shall receive citizenship in case they comply with the naturalization laws of the country, would undoubtedly be good, but a stipulation declaring citizenship without making necessary such procedure on the part of those seeking the same, would have no validity.

But the Indians are not aliens, and the courts have de-

cided that the naturalization laws do not apply to them ;
still, it would appear, that it was competent for Congress,
and for no other power, to confer political rights upon our
inhabitants.

The Executive and Senate however, abandoned the process of making citizens by simple declaration.   In the
Delaware treaty of eighteen hundred and sixty-six, they
compelled the members of that tribe who sought citizenship, to appear before the United States District Court,
and be naturalized in the same manner as aliens.   They
first converted them, in theory at least, into foreigners, and
then made applicable the laws of naturalization, notwithstanding the decision of the courts that the same had no
relevancy to such cases.   Yet the Indians were also made
to furnish proof, that they were sufficiently intelligent and
prudent to control their own affairs, that they had adopted
the habits of civilized life, and that they had been able to
support for five years themselves and families ; so that, if
naturalization turned out to be a useless operation, there
might still remain a judicial transaction upon which to
base the doubtful proceedings.

But the most surprising portion of the treaty is that
clause which proposed to consider the children of these declared citizens as aliens, for they upon arriving at the age
of twenty-one years, were to elect whether they would
enter the tribal organization, or seek citizenship through
the forms and ceremonies followed by their fathers.

The status of the parent did not descend to them, but
they were Indians, by birth and inheritance, and not only
bereft of political rights, but were without membership in
the Delaware nation.

Again Indian treaties which stipulate for the acquisition,
cession, or exchange of territory, are considered legitimate,
while it is extremely doubtful if a treaty with a strictly foreign State, could convey any portion of our public domain.

The power "to dispose of and make all needful rules and regulations, respecting the territory, or other property belonging to the United States," rests in Congress. The Ordinance of eighty-seven, ordained that all the territory east of the Mississippi River should forever remain a part of this country. Disposition of lands to foreign governments was probably never contemplated by the framers of the constitution, and the early enactment of the above mentioned ordinance gives weight to the presumption. Aside from the argument, that absolute cession carries with it political control, which is incident to the legislative power; or sovereignty, which belongs to the people and cannot be lawfully surrendered, it might be affirmed, that the nature of the Government forbids the dismemberment, and the unconditional transfer of any portion of its territory. Should, for instance, the treaty-making power undertake to dispose of Oregon, or New Mexico, to a foreign State, Congress would at once consider that it was its constitutional duty to interfere, and stop the negotiations, and for reasons purely political. Still, grants of large tracts of unoccupied country to Indian tribes by treaty have been adjudged valid, because since Government retained the ultimate fee, control of Congress in all things, except in the temporary disposition of the land, remained unimpaired.

Here likewise the Executive and Senate obtained the right of action on the ground that the Indian bands were sufficiently independent to be possessed of treaty privileges, and having thus acquired it, they were enabled to enter into negotiations which would have been illegal had those bands been strictly sovereign in every particular. They obtained jurisdiction because of the existence of a fact, and exercised it freely because that fact was simply a legal fiction.

The truth of this statement will more fully appear as this subject is pursued. Congress early proclaimed that Indian country should only be acquired through treaty, but once unincumbered it could not be reconverted without its own coöperation. It set apart the Indian territory for Indian use and occupancy, and the Executive and Senate delayed the work of removal until the necessary statute was passed. But during recent years, the latter has not only considered the treaty power competent to purchase title but also to dispose of the ultimate fee to the Indians themselves. Treaties of eighteen hundred and fifty-five, and some prior to that time, allotted to individuals small tracts in reservations ; but as the right of alienation was expressly withheld, these tracts continued to retain their character as Indian lands, and the grants were therefore harmless. Subsequent to that period, in a few instances, the treaty-making power entered into stipulation to confer citizenship upon the individual members of tribes, and to convey to them in fee simple, by absolute patent with all needful covenants, parcels of land of which they held possession— thereby severing Indian national organizations, investing the members of the same with complete political privileges and converting them into landed proprietors. Such a scope of action can only be sustained upon the plea, that the treaty-making power, or Congress, could alone legally exercise unlimited control over our Indian population, when once either obtained the right of direction or administration in any particular whatever, or for any expressed purpose ; that although the former obtained authority to act, because of the legally recognized independence of the communities into which this population was divided, it might carry its authority to an extent which could not be upheld, except on the ground that they were not independent.

But what elements of sovereignty was it necessary that these communities should possess, in order to allow the treaty-making power to negotiate with them ? The determination of that question rested, it would seem, in the discretion of the authority exercising the power, and was not therefore subject to control.

It has never been answered, and we must look for a solution to the practice pursued. Numerical strength was of no importance. A tribal political organization was immaterial. It did not make the slightest difference whether a so called Indian nation numbered ten thousand or five hundred, nor whether the entire or only a portion of a tribe could be reached.

The treaty power met either the Sioux or the Ponca in council; and if it could not gather an entire tribe, was content to enter into stipulations with its irresponsible fragments. It never failed to discover sufficient nationality in any band of Indians to warrant the exercise of its functions—no matter what previous political modifications had been effected through treaties. nor what changes legislation had produced. As long as the semblance of a tribal organization remained, so long did the agents of the Indian Bureau, acting as Commissioners on the part of the United States, invite its members to enter into international compacts. The necessity of obtaining land in a constitutional manner might be proffered as the excuse, but the occasions were deemed suitable for the settlement of all vexed problems.

We find, therefore. that the treaty-making power, and Congress, were engaged in the same vocation, dealing with the same persons, and effecting identical results—the one by contract, (and it supposed with a party fully capable of entering into the agreement,) the other by enactment over a subject people, in every way answerable to its laws. We find Congress, equally with the Executive and Senate, severing tribal relations, conferring citizenship, and directing the ultimate fee of Indian lands to be given to individual Indians, where they might be able to furnish the proof, and take the oath of allegiance required of aliens, and could show to the United States courts that they were sufficiently intelligent to take care of themselves, and had done so for the five previous years.

The correctness of the proceeding on the part of Congress, in so far as the change of political status, (if voluntary on the part of the tribes,) and the final disposition of land were concerned, cannot be questioned. But its ability to divide territory before the Indian right of possession had been otherwise extinguished, is extremely doubtful. If that had been consummated by treaty, congressional control would have been complete and supreme ; for nothing remained to which the treaty power could attach action. Granting then, that a tribal association of any character, holding occupancy of soil, stood in treaty relationship with the Government, it would seem that no single department of the latter could dissolve that organization, dispose of its lands, and admit its members to the full privileges of American citizenship.

The President assisted by the Senate, and Congress, must each apply their offices before so radical a change could be effected ; for land title could not be extinguished except by treaty, and political rights could only be bestowed by congressional enactments. Each, too, must operate independently within its own constitutional sphere. Congress cannot give validity or direction to the action of the treaty-making power. Should it claim the liberty to review, and overrule treaty proceedings, it must first obtain jurisdiction upon facts already existing and established. Even then, it cannot give interpretation or pass upon the legality of those proceedings, (since such dictation is judicial in its nature, and belongs to the United States courts,) but can only destroy them. If therefore authority to declare citizenship, and to direct the conveyance of the public domain, is vested in the President and Senate, it is there by virtue of the constitution, and Con-

gress can no more define, control, or limit it, than confer it.

These suggestions are here advanced, because of the
existence of an impression, that the illegalities, or at least
inconsistencies, of treaties, might be cured by explanatory
or declaratory statutes. As early as eighteen hundred and
twenty-seven, we find a bill introduced into the House, to
settle the nature of the estates conferred by treaty of
eighteen hundred and twenty-four, upon certain chiefs of
the Quawpaw nation, and to determine whether they held
" in fee as citizens from the United States, or of their
tribe as Indians." We find an act passed in eighteen
hundred and forty-eight, affirming that certain persons holding land under the treaty of eighteen hundred and thirty-
two, with the Pottawatomies, shall be considered to hold
estates in fee simple, provided that deeds of conveyance
made before or after the passage of the act, should not be
valid unless approved by the President. Notwithstanding
the well established rule that " Congress has the sole
power to declare the dignity and effect of titles emanating
from the United States," and that it may place such limitations upon its grants as it chooses, the courts must determine the quality of an estate passed by treaty, and
define the same in accordance with maxims settled by legal
precedent. If they determine that territory can be conveyed by treaty, they must then be governed by the language employed in the contract, and apply the rules of
construction pertinent to such cases. Should such course
be followed, it might be discovered, that tribes and individual Indians were holding estates of every name and
nature known to the law—the tenure oftentimes being far
different from that intended by the commissioners who
executed the treaties on the part of the Government under
which those estates were conveyed.

An impression has also prevailed that Congress was

competent to direct the treaty-making power in its action ; that under its instructions the latter might negotiate in regard to subjects which otherwise would not come within its province. An act of eighteen hundred and sixty-three confers upon the President the privilege to treat with the Kansas Indians for exchange of territory.

An act of eighteen hundred and sixty-seven authorized the President to appoint a Commission to meet hostile Indians, and to make treaty with them for their permanent settlement in a district of country to be made by selection, subject to the approval of Congress.

A more perfect manifestation of this impression is contained in the act of eighteen hundred and sixty-seven, which was subsequently set aside. It repealed "all laws allowing the President, the Secretary of the Interior, or the Commissioners of Indian Affairs to enter into treaties with any Indian tribes"—thereby showing conclusively that in the opinion of those who framed and passed the laws, Congress possessed not only authority to instruct the President in the exercise of the treaty power, but could effectually limit his action in that direction.

Yet under such and similar legislation the President has often called the Indian tribes to council, and has based upon it many stipulations which have subsequently received the sanction of the Senate. They stand upon our statute books as solemn international obligations, for the performance of which the nation's faith is plighted. But they are not treaties in fact.

The President, in making such negotiations, was engaged in the execution of a law of Congress, and was not exercising a power conferred upon him by the constitution and which the Legislative Department is helpless to define or control.

They are simply Government contracts, made with a people subject to congressional dictation. The ratification of the Senate does not give them any greater binding force nor a more sacred character. As contracts they are valid and should be fulfilled.

In so far, however, as the President and Senate have carried proceedings beyond the legitimate province of the treaty-making power, and have not been supported by any so called enabling congressional act, their negotiations with the Indian tribes can neither be called treaties nor contracts, since they are without warrant of law. That many of the treaties entered into contain doubtful provisions in this respect is apparent.

Attention has been more particularly confined to naturalization, and traffic in public lands, simply because of the difficulty to understand how such subjects having been specially placed under the management of Congress by the constitution itself, could be regulated or interfered with in any way by any other governmental power.

But a casual glance at many of our Indian treaties of recent date, will show to what extent this treaty system has in its development laid hold of other matters, which are equally the concern of Congress, and with which the representatives of our foreign policy, however considered, have nothing whatever to do. The course pursued might be viewed as ridiculous, were it not for the danger to be apprehended in allowing proceedings under it to fall into contempt, and for the vexed questions which the courts must meet in endeavors to place upon them proper construction. For we find the treaty-making power, which is clothed with the majesty of the Government, and can only be properly brought into exercise to consider and adjust those subjects which arise between sovereign and independent States, delegated as it were, by act of Congress to the Indian Commissioners, and made use of, to arrange the social and domestic affairs of a band of dependent barbarians. We find that power, which is supreme in its sphere,

making promises to a few ignorant Indian chiefs, whom
the United States Indian Agent under existing acts of
Congress, might to-morrow depose, and which can only
be fulfilled under the instructions and management of
that agent, acting under the regulations prescribed by
Congress.

We find that power which has been created only to
deal with independent sovereignties, contracting with individual Indians, who occupy small reservations in our
States and territories, for the erection of cabins, the conveyance of farms, and the delivery of oxen ; or with their
headmen, for the support of schools, churches, and work-
shops. Surely any fair-minded person must admit, that
such proceedings are inconsistent, if not manifestly illegal;
that they are calculated to bring our treaty system into
disrepute and contempt, and tend to diminish the regard
due to sacred international compacts, which serve to unite
the civilized world into a common bond of friendship, and
which depend for their existence, upon the courtesy, enlightenment and morality of nations.

But there were not wanting many accomplished individuals, who strenuously defended the Indian treaty system down to its final overthrow in eighteen hundred and
seventy-one. In the belief of some, it was iniquitous to
deny in our strength, a right which was conceded to the
Indian tribes while the Government was weak. They
seemed to forget that the legal relations of the parties had
become entirely changed ; that those tribes had parted with
every vestige of freedom they might be supposed to have
once possessed, and were in fact dependent upon the bounty
of Government for the necessaries of life. Others thought
the system practicable, and should be continued, until the
tribes could be brought more thoroughly under restraint.
That by it, the Indian Bureau exercised an immediate
authority which was necessary to a successful prosecution

of our Indian policy. They would accomplish objects through questionable methods. They ignore correct political status, and are intent upon methods of control, else they would acknowledge the duty of Congress to exercise entire supervision of Indian matters; nor would they fail to recognize the peril into which the late system has brought constitutional law, and the troublesome problems to which it has given rise to perplex the courts. Those problems are already sufficiently numerous. A very large number of the Indian treaties are still in force. The act which forbade a continuance of the system, provided that nothing therein contained should be construed to invalidate, or impair the obligations of any treaty, which had been lawfully made and ratified with any Indian nation or tribe. All treaties ratified to the date of the passage of the act, were considered legal, and all remained operative, excepting those which had expired by limitation, or those which had been annulled by new agreements. Appropriations are still made under some of them, which were entered into before the commencement of the present century, and are to be eternally continued, unless means can be devised to extinguish these permanent claims upon Government. Therefore, many intricate questions yet require decision, before a definite settlement of the rights of Indians under existing circumstances can be reached. The true scope of the treaty-making power in its application to fragmentary bands of dependent Indians; the meaning of a patent of lands, which the courts have held to be the superior and conclusive evidence of perfect legal title, and which under treaty passes to an individual a qualified fee; the nature of a treaty provision, which exempts land patented to a citizen Indian from taxation for a long term of years, although the same may be situated within State limits; the true status of an individual, though an Indian, made a citizen by simple treaty declaration, are all delicate and practical questions, any one of which may at any time be presented for judicial determination.

The proceedings, based upon the treaties of eighteen hundred and sixty-six with tribes in the Indian territory, will further illustrate the abnormal condition of affairs which the system has produced. A civil government exists there, and is in a measure confessedly subject to congressional legislation. It was not organized, nor put in operation, pursuant to any organic act. There has never been a statute passed to control it or define its powers. It was devised by treaty commissioners, and has been constructed upon treaty stipulations.

It is the legitimate product of the system, and as such becomes of interest. Under agreements that they should never become subject to State or territorial authority, and that they might "enjoy a government of their choice, and perpetuate such a state of society" as might to them seem best, these tribes were led to this El Dorado of promise. There they existed for a long time as independent communities, with antagonistic interests. When it became desirable to abridge the tracts of land which had been granted them, and consequently to draw them into closer neighborhood, and place over them a code of laws, the treaty provisions already made and remaining in force placed difficulties in the path of simple and direct procedure. The ordinary course of legislation in the erection of territorial governments was blocked in this instance, and it became necessary for the treaty-making power to invent a government. He who wishes to ascertain what its duties and privileges are, must consult the treaties upon which it is founded.

It might be briefly defined as a confederacy of nations, dependent upon the United States for protection, support, continuance, or dissolution. Its legislative assembly takes cognizance of "all rightful subjects, and matters pertaining to the intercourse and relations of the Indian tribes and nations resident in said territory" and represented, but is restrained from passing any act inconsistent with the constitution of the United States, the laws of Congress, or existing treaty stipulations; or any act affecting the tribal organizations, laws, or usages. Its courts, required for the administration of justice and the interpretation of its regulations, are organized and vested with jurisdiction by Congress. Its Executive is the Superintendent of Indian Affairs, and thereby becomes *ex-officio* Governor.

The commissioners who negotiated on the part of the United States, builded thus far very ingeniously. Legislation must necessarily be harmless, since the power to overthrow or enforce it, rests with United States officers. Congress, if unfettered, could not have invented a more innocent expedient to harmonize the conflicting interests of the separate organizations thus associated, and allow them opportunity to work out undisturbed their own civilization.

But glance further at the treaties and mark the peculiar political complexion of the government promised the tribes which compose this confederacy. Each is independent of the Grand National Council in matters of home concern. Each has its constitution and laws, its legislature, executive, and judiciary. The treaties accord them the power of self-control, and deny to Congress the right "to interfere with, or annul their present tribal organizations, rights, laws, privileges, and customs." Their courts have exclusive jurisdiction in cases both civil and criminal, and are of last resort. They are in semblance small principalities. Citizens of the United States are not permitted to remain therein unless bidden, and then they become members of the nations, and are subject to all the laws of their new domiciles. In some instances, the Indian land held in common by authority of the act of Congress of eighteen hundred and thirty, may be finally disposed of by the legislative assemblies.

Such are some of the chief political features of the tribal organizations of which the territorial government is made up. Their proceedings, although confined within the limits prescribed in the treaties, might give rise to many puzzling questions ; and indeed they are given a breadth of action which the law does not justify. Should a white man become a member of a tribe by adoption, and commit a crime forbidden by the Indian trade and intercourse laws, could the courts of that tribe exercise exclusive jurisdiction in the case ? Should he commit a murder, taking the life of an Indian, would he not be amenable to trial by a United States court under existing statutes ? A treaty cannot set aside an act of Congress. The latter remains in force in defiance of a treaty agreement. And yet, a few years ago, the conduct of a United States marshal was condemned, because he attempted to take forcible possession of a United States citizen, who was also a citizen of the Cherokee nation, and who was accused of the murder of a Cherokee squaw. The Cherokee court claimed that its jurisdiction of the case was exclusive, when in fact it was not concurrent. The process of the United States court could have been executed, even if a trial of the accused by the tribal courts had been in progress. Again, the treaties not only ostensibly set aside United States statutes, but they limit the transactions of Congress in the matter of control. That body, out of scrupulous regard for the national faith, might avoid special legislation having application to these particular tribes ; but a general Indian statute without any saving clause would at once dissolve those stipulations of a treaty with which it was at variance.

A careful reading of the instruments suggests many inconsistencies of similar import. The commissioners in preparing them, evidently took under advisement all the solemn guarantees and written covenants which had not become nugatory, and determined that all should be sacredly observed. The construction of the tribal governments therefore became very difficult, and the labor was probably as well performed as circumstances and material permitted. They attempted impossibilities under the law. The object sought, too, was new. Formerly, the treaty-making power had been engaged in placing the tribes more thoroughly under United States authority. Here, the experiment of confining that authority, and making them less dependent, was to be tried ; plainly a much more arduous task.

If now, after this casual review of these promised political regulations of the tribes, we again glance at the construction of the territorial government, we should find that while comparatively harmless in its operation, it might be difficult to administer.

The organizations of which it is composed must retain sole direction of their own affairs, for the treaties make it imperative. Only such matters as are of general concern, or such as may arise between parties of separate tribes, are placed under the management of the territorial council. The field of legislation would, in the language of the treaties, include such subjects as the "arrest and extradition of criminals escaping from one tribe to another ; the administration of justice between members of the several tribes of said territory, and persons other than Indians, and members of said tribes ; the construction of works of internal improvement, and the common defence and safety of the nations of said territory." The field appears very narrow and the governor as such has few duties to perform. Still, being at the same time Superintendent of Indian Affairs, he has direction of the Indian agents of every tribe. As Governor, he executes the mandates of a council established by virtue of treaties, which might unitedly be considered the organic act, or constitution, of the territory. As Superintendent, he executes the laws of Congress, and can by a skillful manipulation of his agents, hold every tribe represented in that council in complete subjection. He therefore virtually conducts the tribal assemblies, and also the territorial legislature; and it might oftentimes become difficult for him to place proper bounds to his official action.

The United States Court, which has exclusive original jurisdiction in all matters arising between parties of separate tribes, must recognize all tribal rules, customs and laws not inconsistent with the constitution and laws of the United States. How far this recognition must extend depends in a great measure upon the agreements of Indians contained in treaties. If they have promised to adopt our usages, to live and govern themselves as do our civilized communities, a barbarous custom might be considered inconsistent with the supreme law of the land, because the treaties interdict it; otherwise, a virtuous and enlightened judge might be sorely troubled concerning the duty of recognition, for the constitution and acts of Congress allow the Indian bands to abuse and destroy each other at their pleasure. When this Indian territory of promise, progression, and of intended expansion, receives within its elastic folds the as yet uncivilized Indian nations, those nations should (as promise by treaty is no longer possible) be forced to declare, and in a manner which the law will hold binding, that they discard the practices of their fathers, or Congress should take away the license which they have hitherto enjoyed. Whatever may be their social condition, it is evident that a court which attempts to administer the laws of the United States, the laws enacted by the council of the Indian territory, and at the same time gives full faith and credit to "the public acts, records, and judicial proceedings" of every tribe, as well as legal recognition of all their customs which are not inconsistent with the constitution and the acts of Congress, might have before it a fertile province for the production of fine spun theories and masterly decisions.

Thus, the legislative department is restrained within narrow boundaries, while the executive and judicial branches presided over by United States officers, are really the vital moving forces of the confederacy. The different powers are either not properly adjusted, or are out of proportion. They have not their true spheres and balances, and the machinery of such a government will not work without the constant assistance of some external agency. The aid must come from Congress, and the territorial government in its movements must conform to the demands of the United States, and must submit to such amendments and modifications as the force of circumstances may require, or its long continued existence is impossible. Those modifications will in the end change its entire structure. Whether the tribes become civilized, and the members thereof are incorporated with the great body of our own citizens, or whether they remain in a semi-barbarous condition, a government so completely opposed to all other forms of State and territorial governments, cannot be maintained and administered in the heart of a future thickly populated country.

This confederacy may be viewed as the crowning achievement of the Indian treaty system. Notwithstanding the extremity to which the treaty power was carried, and the silent acquiescence of all interested parties in the action taken, the result, practically considered, is but a temporary arrangement. Had not the usage of contracting by treaty been destroyed, the power might again have been called into exercise for the correction of manifest imperfections. But in such an event our commissioners might have become perplexed in attempting to decide upon the particu lar authority which should be invited to negotiate with them. They might be at a loss to know whether the confederacy possessed the sovereignty, or whether it still belonged entirely to the tribes which were confederated. The absurdity of entering into international compacts with the territorial governor—a United States citizen holding the office of Superintendent of Indian Affairs—might solve the mystery in the commissioners' minds, and quickly lead them to the discovery that the tribes had never surrendered any portion of their nationality. A readjustment of the territorial machinery would then require a number of new and distinct agreements, equal to the separate organizations for which it was intended, before the drama of Indian self-control under a united government could be reënacted.

Fortunately, it is no longer possible for the circumstances to arise, which would necessitate such a proceeding. Congress has finally asserted its right to conduct Indian matters, and the simple contract, made under the explicit directions of that body, has been substituted for the agreement by treaty. The change should have been made a quarter of a century ago ; but our courts, and all people who respect constitutional provisions, and who desire simplicity of construction and homogeneity in our political institutions, should be rejoiced that it has been no longer delayed. If our continuing promises—such as are to remain in force until certain doubtful events transpire, are avoided—if conditions which are to endure " for all future time," or " as long as grass grows and water runs," are no longer entered into ; if, in fine, contracts are only made to meet exigencies as they arise, our Indian tribes will begin to assume their true relationship to Government and the confusion of the past upon Indian matters will gradually give place to correct understanding.

7

Thus far in this chapter, attention has been invited to the frequency with which the treaty power has been called into service for the settlement of Indian difficulties, the astonishing range of subjects which it has undertaken to deal with, the absurdity and apparent illegality of many of the provisions, and the effect of its sweeping action in restraining judicious congressional legislation, in establishing incongruous political organizations, and in creating legal perplexities. The practical, financial results of the treaty system, or the substantial benefits which the United States have obtained by means of that system, have only been occasionally referred to. Its advocates claimed that it furnished the best mode of conducting Indian affairs. That under it, the Indians received humane and Christian treatment; that it was best calculated to allay hostilities and to promote moral and mental improvement, while it cheaply secured the Indian estate in territory, and that it was therefore most economical in its workings. We do not propose to discuss at this time, the mental, moral, or Christian influences which it exerted, either upon those engaged in its administration, or upon the Indians. We know that it threw all power into the hands of the Indian Bureau, which made all treaties, attended to their execution and fulfillment, and was therefore, in a great degree, responsible for the honest performance of contracts arising under them. If they have been faithfully carried out, the Indians must have received a sufficient amount of teaching to permanently impress the dullest of natures, and enough substantial aid to win their continued gratitude. Education and the spirit of thankfulness have not, however, been so largely developed as to repress their savage passions, nor to cement a lasting friendship. As a rule, they have been ready to break off amicable relations with the Government, whenever their strength promised them a successful issue to hostilities. A distinguished bishop of the

Episcopal church, who has labored zealously in the field of Indian missions, and who has given considerable study to the causes of border disturbances, publicly asserted a few years since, that Indian wars had cost us five hundred millions of dollars. The statement, at first view, appears exaggerated; but a little reflection drives one to the bishop's opinion. I could believe, that fully two-thirds of that amount of money had been expended during the last century. in conquering by force of arms, the tribes which were rebellious, and in the permanent retention of troops for the express purpose of intimidating those which were turbulent. During the first ten years of that period, more than ten millions of dollars were disbursed on account of expeditions on the northern frontier. The numerous wars since waged, have been attended with disbursements in like ratio. The Seminole war cost some twenty-five millions, and the Cheyenne war, according to good authority, thirty millions of dollars. The treasury is yearly called upon to liquidate the claims of the territories for expenses incurred in battling with the race which is being supplanted. The present Sioux war, far from being terminated, will exhaust large money appropriations; so that an estimate of one hundred and fifty millions of dollars, as the actual sum paid out in conquering peace with the various bands and tribes of the malicious aborigines, might be supposed reasonable.

The expenses incident to the support of the additional troops required, because of the presence and attitude of interior tribes, may be roughly approximated. The erection and maintenance of costly military posts in territory roamed over by the natives, has been deemed expedient, in order to render secure routes of communication, and to protect the white inhabitants of the borders. Such labors might have been for the most part dispensed with, if the country had not been occupied by Indians from whom attack was anticipated.

If now from the total expenditures of the War Department, there be deducted the cost of our foreign wars, that of the late rebellion, and that of our probable peace establishment, the remainder,—had there not been in our midst an uncivilized population of doubtful intentions,—would be mostly made up of the particular expenditures sought after. The disbursements of the War Department since the foundation of the Government, aggregate four thousand millions of dollars ; of which amount about one hundred millions were paid out on account of the war of eighteen hundred and twelve and that with Mexico, and about three thousand millions during the rebellion. Without these foreign and domestic difficulties here mentioned, and with no Indian population, the necessary annual expenses of the War Department, for the first sixteen years of that period, would not have been more than eight hundred thousand dollars, not more than three millions of dollars for the succeeding forty years, and for the following thirty years, not to exceed eight millions of dollars. The remainder which we seek is therefore upwards of five hundred millions of dollars.

Such calculations are however vague and unsatisfactory. But the object of here introducing them is accomplished, if the fact is recognized, that notwithstanding the politic system of civil control which has been pursued, the war expenditures involved in holding the Indian population in check has been very burdensome to the country ; that the money saving resulting from the humane and Christian treatment which the Indians have received under the treaty system, with all its elevating influences, and consequent moral restraints, is too indefinite to be appreciated. No other system has been tried, and it could not therefore be shown, that some other plan of operation would not have been more economical in its financial bearings, but it is doubtful if the enforcement of law, applicable to the true legal status of the tribes, carried out in letter and spirit, and by force if necessary, would have been more exhaustive to the United States treasury.

The civil disbursements of the Government, on account of our Indian population, can be ascertained. They were almost entirely made under treaty stipulations until the practice of subsisting that population was inaugurated.

An occasional donation by Congress, or an official appointment under the trade and intercourse laws, have cost small sums of money, but the amounts are so insignificant when compared with the total expenditures, that they are hardly deserving of mention. Those disbursements may be stated in round numbers, at one hundred and sixty-five millions of dollars. During the sixty years in which the Indians were managed by the War Department, the disbursements on their account were not more than fifty millions, and during the last twenty-eight years, they have therefore been one hundred and fifteen millions of dollars. The annual average of appropriations for the first twenty years of the Government's existence, was about ninety-five thousand dollars ; and for the last twenty years about four and one-half millions of dollars. The cost of the entire service of the Indian Department has increased one hundred fold, and it now amounts to about eight hundred thousand dollars annually.

The United States are still largely in debt to the Indians under existing treaties. It yet requires four and one-half millions of dollars to meet those stipulations which call for definite payments at expressed dates, while the annual liabilities of the Government, on account of contracts with the tribes, and which are not limited as regards duration, exceed one and one-quarter millions of dollars. Of the last stated amount more than one-third must be annually continued for all time, but the yearly payment of much of the remaining portion is discretionary, and may be discontinued. A fraction of this liability is covered by interest upon investments in public stock, made and held in trust by the United States for certain tribes, but nearly a third of the stock thus held does not pay interest, and Congress is obliged to make the same good by repeated appropriations. How long an admitted expediency may insist upon carrying out the stipulations of treaties indefinite as to time, and what limit may be fixed to the duration of permanent annuities, are problems of too uncertain a character for arithmetical calculation. The sum of money then which must be yet applied to fully execute these contracts, cannot be exactly ascertained ; still it is safe to place it among the tens of millions. This added to the one hundred and sixty-five millions already disbursed, would force the civil expenditure of our Government, on account of our Indian population, in the neighborhood of two hundred millions of dollars. What benefits have been received for this outlay ? We wish to consider the question from a strictly business standpoint, and not in its philanthropic and Christian aspects.

It might be suggested, that the expenditure has resulted in the civilization, to a certain degree, of a portion of our population ; has partly prepared it for labor and citizenship, and thereby secured an aid in the development of the nation. But most men would confess that the total loss of this element at the present time would prove favorable to the financial interests of the country. Yet this element is destined to remain, for it cannot be removed by any action which the law of nature would sanction, and therefore, in so far as Indian advancement has been achieved, the Government has been benefited.

Another, and the only other, recompense or consideration received, is the possession of territory of which the Indians held the conceded right of occupancy ; or rather, to be more explicit in statement, the immediate and peaceable possession of territory actually occupied by Indians, title to which had been previously acquired by conquest and purchase from foreign nations.

The money value of this acquisition has not been as important as generally supposed.

We cannot ascertain the extent of actual Indian occupancy at the various dates of foreign conquest and purchase. We cannot even tell the extent thereof at the time of Indian relinquishment, nor compute the term of probable Indian possession, had the Indian estate been allowed to continue free from outer molestation until it expired from tribal causes. We will proceed, therefore, upon the supposition that the Indians held a perfect title in the lands with which they parted by treaty, and also that they legally possessed the entire territorial area of the nation, outside of the boundaries of the thirteen original States, and those States which retained their public land upon admission to the Union. Even upon this erroneous supposition, the treaty purchases cannot be shown to have been very successful financial speculations.

It is true, that the Government holds an unencumbered public domain of magnificent proportions. If the statements of theorists, and indeed of our public men, are to be regarded as facts, cheapness and fertility of soil, and salubrity of climate, invite the oppressed of the world to there seek asylums, and establish for themselves happy and prosperous homes. Says a distinguished law-maker : "No nation ever held so rich and vast an estate in lands as has been, and now is, held by the United States, and nowhere have been found lands of equal fertility, with such a diversity of soil and climate, to be disposed of so cheaply." Granted for the present that the lands are attended with all these favorable conditions, while a brief examination is made into the action of the Government, thus far, in regard to acquisition and disposition.

The area of the United States, outside of the States above referred to, the territory of Alaska also excepted, is nearly fifteen hundred millions of acres.

The tribes still own one hundred and sixty millions of acres, which is contained within described reservations. On the supposition then, that the Indians formerly held complete and rightful possession, the United States have purchased about thirteen hundred millions of acres. Of this amount some six hundred millions of acres have been surveyed, and a little more than five hundred millions of acres have been disposed of ; so that the unencumbered public domain embraces, at the present time, nearly nine hundred millions of acres. Proceeding on the supposition that the Indians originally held perfect title, the cost of the land might be presented as follows : Paid to Indians, one hundred and sixty-five millions of money ; expense of surveying, of selling and of managing the land which has been passed to private parties, thirty millions ; amount yet due on executory Indian contracts, twenty-five millions of dollars ; total cost, two hundred and twenty millions of dollars. The total receipts thus far obtained from the sale of land is about two hundred millions of dollars, or twenty millions less than entire expenditures. But the Government has still nearly nine hundred millions of acres to dispose of. Most assuredly it has, yet the present pecuniary value is insignificant. Time is required to convert it into currency. Conceding that ten millions of acres will be taken up annually, and that the treasury will yearly receive therefrom four millions of dollars, (certainly a supposed rapid disposition with most liberal returns if the experience of the past is to be a guide in determining the results of future speculation) what profits would be realized ? The expense of survey, and of completing sale, might be fixed at twenty cents per acre ; and the transfer of ten millions of acres would cost two millions of dollars.

The annual interest of the twenty millions of money already paid out, would at six per cent, be one million two hundred thousand dollars. The yearly profits would therefore amount to eight hundred thousand dollars. At such a rate, twenty-five years would pass, or the sale of two hundred and fifty millions of acres would be consummated before present deficiencies could be made good.

Viewing the entire proceedings which have been taken in the acquisition of territory from the Indian tribes, as a single contract, one might admit that Government had secured favorable terms could the parties withdraw from all future relationship. Unfortunately the tribes by fulfillment on their part, have been placed in conditions which enable them to demand large additional compensation. They relinquished the means of support, in giving up tracts of country and accepting small reservations. They were reduced from a self-sustaining to a dependent condition, and thus they will remain until their intentions, ideas, and even natures, undergo a radical change. Until that far distant day, they will pray for extra awards of money, basing their claim upon the demands of natural justice. They will represent that they bartered their territory for money and government protection ; that they have endeavored to fulfill the stipulations of the contract, but in their earnest trials to adopt the habits, and secure the necessaries of life, by following the pursuits of their white brethren, they have met with failure. Might not a broad interpretation of the contract entitle them to relief ?

The officers of the Indian Bureau, in those portions of their reports wherein they call attention to economy in administration, and to the small consideration promised for land purchased, forget to mention the implied covenants which are assumed. The report of former Commissioner Harris, rendered in eighteen hundred and thirty-six, occurs to me in this connection. He reports, that the United

7*

States had, within eight years, acquired title to more than
ninety-three millions of acres of land, and had stipulated
to give therefor twenty-seven millions of dollars, and
thirty-two million acres of land. He looks upon those
transactions as financial successes, while they were at the
same time characterized by great liberality on the part of
the Government; for, as he says, during the early days,
only from ten to thirty cents per acre was allowed, whereas the price had risen to seventy-two cents per acre. He
did not attempt an estimate, nor even mention in any way
the liabilities which the Government had incurred, by
stripping the Indians of their hunting grounds, and impliedly promising them food and raiment until they became civilized, or at least able to maintain themselves by
growing the products of the soil. The actual purchase
money for the four hundred and twenty millions of acres
of land, transferred by the tribes during the first fifty
years of the Government existence, is not yet paid, and it
may still require fifty years to exhaust the Indian claim.

This view may be erroneous, but it is obtained from the
consideration of those official reports, in which we are
taught that the public domain is being cleared of encum-
brances at a trifling expense, taken in connection with
those yearly public statements, made when large appropriations are sought, from which we learn that almost the
entire amounts asked for are due to the Indians, and cannot in any sense be deemed charity. That they are due to
the Indians, in "consideration of their relinquishment to
the Government of the United States, of large tracts of
country which they formerly occupied."

But we may be reminded that the ideas advanced in
regard to the value of the public domain are exceedingly
narrow; that its worth cannot be measured by its market
price; that cash receipts are of slight importance, compared with the benefits derived from the various uses to

which it has, and is being applied, the inducements for national growth which it offers, and the promise of future national greatness which it insures. Limited only by great acres of the earth's surface, it is of sufficient dimensions, notwithstanding its waste and desert places, to sustain the increase of population for centuries. There beneficent laws grant free homes to the poor and industrious, thereby inviting large immigration. It enables Government to foster magnificent enterprises, and to assist the cause of general education. The land now sold for cash, is but one-tenth of the amount actually transferred. The cash sales are to the homestead entries as one to four, and to the gifts in aid of schools and colleges, as one to three.

This comprehensive opinion of value is willingly accepted. In confining attention to actual cost and market rates, the subject was brought within the argument of those who proceed upon the hypothesis, that the Indian tribes held legal possession of this vast area of country, and who thereupon attempt to show that by judicious purchase under treaty, they were cheaply obtaining the land required for settlement, and that the nation was constantly reaping pecuniary successes from their sagacity and labors.

Admitting the priceless value of the public domain, the supposition that any considerable interest therein was ever secured from the Indians is pronounced untenable. Whatever speculations as to abstract rights moralists may indulge in, it cannot be denied that the whole country was bought by the blood and treasure of our ancestors from foreign governments. Indian treaties gave us nothing except the right of immediate possession to those sections of territory which the tribes legally occupied. The extent of such occupancy has never been determined. If the tribes sold more than they held by virtue of the occupants' claim, the treaty commissioners purchased that which already belonged to the United States. That they did so is very probable, even if they purchased the possession of one-half of our former public domain ; for the idea that three hundred thousand Indians could legally possess eight hundred millions of acres would hardly be indulged in by the most benevolent of minds. As before intimated, the pecuniary value of this actual interest in possession cannot be measured, but it was insignificant in comparison with the great reversionary interest which a short period of time would have brought into being, whatever might have been the nature of the policy pursued towards the Indian race. The treaty power paid well for the Indian right and at the same time built up a political relation between the Government and the tribes which has proved expensive and unfortunate. We believe therefore, that in the interest of economy the treaty system has not proved a success. The assertion will appear more convincing when its effects upon the tribes are considered.

CHAPTER V.

INDIAN TREATY SYSTEM.

In the preceding chapter, the result of action under the treaty system, as it affected the government, was chiefly considered. Little was said of its effect upon the tribes.

An attempt to discuss this aspect of the subject necessarily opens a broad speculative field; for since no other system of control has been resorted to, we cannot furnish proof to show that a different method of treatment would have been more satisfactory. The difficulty which presented itself when seeking the errors of Government under the system, still attends us. The assertion that the tribes might have been more rapidly advanced in civilized life, and controlled at less expense, had their proper political status as a portion of our dependent population been imposed upon them, is again met by the answer, that the treaty system was wise and humane, and has proved successful.

Even the best of our public men, who confess disappointment that our Indian policy has not produced more happy results, are apt to attribute failure to the improper manner in which it has been carried out, and not to its radical defects. Criticism might therefore in many instances be acknowledged as just, while suggestions as to an entirely different mode of procedure would be rejected. Hence, it is much easier to point out the errors of the treaty system, as applicable to the tribes, than to advocate a course of action towards the Indians which is directly antagonistic to former practices.

In the preceding chapter, we endeavored to expose some of the serious evils which have been entailed upon Government, because of the recognition of the tribes as nations vested with treaty rights. We tried to show that those evils would have been avoided, had the tribes been placed under congressional dictation. We shall now attempt to make it appear, that the greatest good of the tribes demanded from the first, their entire subjection to legislative control, and consequently has not been promoted by their treaty privileges.

The proposition conducts us to ground as yet untrodden. Thus far in the discussion, we have remarked upon the rise and growth of the treaty system, have spoken of its adoption by the present Government, and referred in brief to the law by which it has been upheld. Now we shall endeavor to maintain, that error was committed in considering the tribes as independent communities in any particular whatever, and that they have not been benefited by the course of action which has been pursued.

The new domain which we are obliged to enter teems with speculations upon abstract rights. The wisdom of our fathers, who placed upon record the opinion that the Indians were entitled to self political control, and legally held possession of all that vast territory over which they roamed, will be questioned. This is an unfilial, and according to the old Roman teachings would be almost a sacrilegious, undertaking. It is also a presumptuous task, since their recorded verdict, embodied in the constitution of the United States, as the earlier decisions of the supreme court give us to understand, was presumedly based upon their interpretation of natural, or positive law, as well as upon their judgment in regard to expediency. If the law of nature awarded to the tribes the powers of independent nations, that verdict rested in justice, and was therefore correct; for a constitutional provision or enactment of any kind which is not in harmony with that law, is clearly wrong. If that law conferred upon the tribes national attributes and gave them title to American territory, such recognition by our Government was right, notwithstanding the claims of expediency.

Unless then, it can be made apparent, that positive law did not compel the establishment of the political relation which has so long continued between the Government and the Indian tribes, there is no foundation for an assertion, that our ancestors did wrong in acknowledging the national independence of the latter, whatever may be the teachings of a century's experience.

We propose here to take but a single step in advance of the position assumed in the third chapter, wherein we remarked upon the legality of the congressional act which took from the treaty-making power control of the native population. There we affirmed that the special circumstances which decided action at the time the Government was organized, had become so changed as to render constitutional provisions inoperative; that the Indians had given up, or bartered away, all the national prerogatives which they ever possessed, and should be recognized as communities subject to the dictation of Congress. Now we contend, that even at the time when those provisions were adopted, the tribes were in no sense independent sovereignties, as judged by the law of nature or nations, and that all opinion to the contrary is founded upon an erroneous appreciation of the special circumstances which then existed.

The proposition does not therefore imply that the framers of the constitution were wanting in theoretical knowledge of positive political rights. They studied more deeply the subject of civil liberty, and the science of government, than the statesmen of the present day. They sought more earnestly the ultimate sources of political power, than any class of men of any other age. The practical training which they received in that severe contest, wherein they struggled for the success of principles, founded, as they claimed, upon the law of nature, fitted them to ably expound that law, and to render righteous judgments. But they might have been deceived in regard to the particular circumstances upon which they were called to administer, and have therefore made mistaken decisions, although they did not entertain any misconceptions of the law intended to be realized. This is all that our proposition contains. They were wrong in their opinions of the strength, importance, and organization of the tribes, and of the condition, ability, and characteristics of the Indians.

Besides, theirs was a time when right was contending against established power, and when many advocates of the former, strengthening their opinions by every plausible argument, were liable to embrace extreme political views. It was a time when the interests of the Indians would be most sure to receive recognition, and to be most strictly guarded. It was a time when the cause of the red man was eloquently supported at home and abroad, and especially so by Frenchmen, although their own nation was shortly to engage in the sale, purchase, and exchange of populous civilized provinces, regarding them merely as commodities of trade. The reply of Jefferson contains an expression of the better sentiment of the American people : " It may be regarded as certain, that not a foot of land will be taken from the Indians without their own consent. The sacredness of their rights is felt by all thinking persons in America, as much as in Europe."

Stripped of sentiment, the facts which are now known to have then existed, may be plainly stated as follows : The European claims of property to, and within, a large territory, had been acquired by the United States. All title and interest therein vested in the people of those States, and by the rules governing the actions of nations of the civilized world, they could manage or dispose of it as they pleased. Over that extended country roamed a few barbarians, numbering less than two hundred thousand, who were unconditionally transferred with the soil. They were separated into many clans, which were determined by consanguineous relationship, and maintained for personal security. Confederations of bands were sometimes found—the bond still consisting in relationship, as indicated by identical stock language, and the object being war or defence against savage enemies. Their rude societies were governed by no law, except that of retaliation, which was interpreted and executed only by the individual who considered himself aggrieved. They did not have the remotest idea of the law of real property. With no permanent abodes, their wanderings were limited by the range of the wild game on which they, for the most part, subsisted, by choice of climate, by inclination for particular features of country, and by fear of encounters with hostile tribes. They had no political organizations, in the modern acceptation of that term. In peace, they were not subject to any legalized authority, for none was placed over them. In war, they united under a leader from desire and not from compulsion. Their rude councils never considered questions of tribal management, but fixed upon and declared purposes for the ruin and distress of surrounding bands. The only object of inter-tribal assemblies was the purchase of peace, or the formation of combinations for war. Their occupation was destruction, and such seemed to be their mission —destruction of man and beast and indeed of everything in nature.

This brief description is true of the majority of the Indian population, when transferred by Europe. There were tribes which had long lived in proximity to the white man, had learned from him the benefits of settlement, and had adopted many of his habits. This individual advancement improved the tribal structures, but they were still of too primitive a mould to display the rudiments of simple government.

As opposed to the above estimate of Indian characteristics and condition, let us set out the opinions of an earlier period : " When wild in woods the noble savage ran," when his mental ability, his superstitious beliefs, his domestic and social life, and, if we may so speak, his national peculiarities, furnished perplexing riddles which were generally solved to his advantage ; when his ancestors were sought among the lost tribes of Israel, or with those Carthagenians supposed to have been separated from Hanno's fleet during his periplus. We will not however, quote the extravagant conceits of that day, but further present the mature conclusions of Jefferson. He says : " It is in North America that we are to seek the original character of the Indian; and I am safe in affirming, that the proofs of genius given by the Indians of North America place them on a level with whites in the same uncultivated state. * * * I believe the Indian then to be, in body and mind, equal to the white man. I have supposed the black man, in his present state, might not be so, but it would be hazardous to affirm that, equally cultivated for a few generations, he would not become so."

To say the least, this comparison between the red and black man, is unfair. The former Seminole negro slaves are far in advance of their old masters. Experience proves that the African excels the Indian in aptitude to conform to our customs, and in ability to receive our instructions. The supposition that the Indians and the whites would be equal, if in the same uncultivated state, is doubtless true, but place the white man in that supposed condition, and he becomes an Indian, with all the latter's superstitions and wicked propensities, and would be equally averse to the teachings of the civilization of the whites. The two are radically different by nature, and would, if left to themselves, pursue divergent paths.

Yet, the above cited convictions of Mr. Jefferson are moderate, as compared with the opinions of many of his contemporaries. The Indian, the untutored child of the forest, the subject of absurdly imaginative contemplation, was the psychological enigma of the New World. Educated by nature, he must naturally have been governed by noble impulses. His cunning cruelties might be attributed to natural revenge for wrongs inflicted upon him, but treated with kindness and moderation, and allowed full freedom of action, he would cheerfully welcome his white brother, and gaining from him new ideas of life and duty, would soon develop into an intelligent and conscientious member of society.

No less erroneous were impressions regarding the number and strength of the tribes, as has already been shown, of the quantity of territory which they actually occupied, and the constitution of the tribal authority under which they had gathered. Such impressions gave rise to what would now appear unreasonable assumptions. It is not fifty years since the United States Senate was addressed as follows: "I insist, that by immemorial possession as the original tenants of the soil, they hold a title beyond and superior to the British crown and her colonies, and to all adverse pretensions of our confederation and subsequent union. God, in his providence, planted these tribes on this Western continent, so far as we know, before Great Britain herself had a political existence. However mere human policy, or the law of power, or the tyrant's plea of expediency, may have found it convenient, at any or in all times, to recede from the unchangeable principles of eternal justice, no argument can shake the political maxim,

that where the Indian always has been, he enjoys an absolute right still to be, in the free exercise of his own modes
of thought, government and conduct."

Such sentiments, stand in direct opposition to those
which are now announced in the Senate : "There is no
law of nations, no law of morality, no law of religion, that
gives the Indian title to one-half of this country," exclaims
one of our leading jurists, and he is assisted by a member
who thus interprets divine economy : "God gave the earth
to nourish man, and He never intended that a few barbarous wretches should·possess a great extent of territory."

The application of law to circumstances as formerly
understood might consistently result in decisions impossible to be reached upon actual facts.   Distinguished scholars, however, who made the science of positive law a life
study, and who construed the law of nature as applicable
to the Indian tribes in their relation to civilized nations,
did not maintain as extreme views as many of our former
statesmen.   Vattel says : "The whole earth is appointed
for the nourishment of its inhabitants ; but it would be
incapable of doing so was it uncultivated.   Those people
like the ancient Germans and modern Tartars, who having
fertile countries disdain to cultivate the earth, and choose
rather to live by rapine, are wanting to themselves,
and deserve to be exterminated as savage and pernicious
beasts.   *   *   *   Though the conquest of the uncivilized empires of Peru and Mexico was a notorious usurpa-
tion, the establishment of many colonies on the Continent
of North America, may, on their confining themselves
within just bounds, be extremely lawful."

This doctrine is concurred in by our own lawyers, and
Justice McLean of the Supreme Bench enlarged upon it,
while insisting upon the legality and binding force of
Indian treaties.   We quote from his decision : "The
abstract right of every section of the human race to a

reasonable portion of the soil by which to acquire the means of subsistence, cannot be controverted ; and it is equally clear that the range of nations or tribes which exist in the hunter's state may be restricted within reasonable limits.

" The law of nature which is paramount to all other laws gives the right to every nation to the enjoyment of a reasonable extent of country, so as to derive the means of subsistence from the soil. Our ancestors might have taken possession of a limited extent of the domain, had they been sufficiently powerful, without negotiation or purchase from the native Indians."

The meaning to be derived from these expressions, is, that the Europeans had a perfect right under the law of nature, to appropriate to their own use all the land needed for actual settlement. The inference might also be drawn, that as land was subsequently required on account of increased population, the same might be forcibly seized, and without attempt at negotiation, provided sufficient was left remaining to the native race, from which to obtain subsistence by cultivation.

These opinions have not, it is true, any weight except as they influence other minds. They are not spoken *ex-cathedra*, and in so far as they appear in decisions, are *obiter dicta*. Unfortunately, the designs of Providence are only known to us as the wishes of the highest excellence of which we are able to conceive. They are subject to as many different interpretations as there are diversified types in the wide range of human convictions. But the legal profession should base its conclusions upon its knowledge of facts. The enthusiast is apt to first ascertain convictions upon an imagined existence of circumstances, and then force the facts to support those convictions. He finds upon a matter of belief a conclusion of law. He finds as matter of belief, that " God, in his providence, planted the tribes on the Western Continent," and gave them liberty to follow their inclinations, as regards habits of life, and then announces as a political maxim, that, where God placed them, they " have an absolute right still to be, in the free exercise of their own modes of thought, government and conduct." The legal profession would first determine, as far as possible, the facts actually existing. It would perceive a people, seeking territory from which to derive support by tillage ; a people desiring to expend labor in the production of articles for consumption necessary for the maintenance of mankind, and demanding land for that purpose. It would perceive on this Western Continent, a great extent of waste and fertile country which might be made available, roamed over and claimed by insignificant bands of barbarians, and serving no purpose except to nourish the game which fed the idle, destructive and depraved representatives of humanity who constituted its sole inhabitants. Upon these facts it would seek to apply the law of natural right. That God, in his providence, had placed the Indians here with the intention that they should be unmolested to follow their heathen practices, notwithstanding the needs of civilized communities, would be considered unsound doctrine. It would not be amiss to presume that most persons, having a fair appreciation of morals, would upon such a presentation of facts, be convinced that the claim of the Indian should in justice give way to the demands of the crowded population of the old world.

Again, the Christian philanthropist is liable to fix unchangeable rules, by which to measure virtuous personal action, and does not properly weigh extraneous circumstances. His code is simple and severe when applied to himself, but of great latitude when it concerns others. Whereas, a more practical and less conscientious mind, giving little reflection to the correctness of motive, finds in outward circumstances an excuse for proceedings. The former might determine at once, that he would not be justified in taking possession of property not clearly his own by express law, whatever might be his wants, while the latter would, before coming to any decision, pass upon the merits of all adverse claims. These different modes of determining consistent conduct, employed to ascertain the equities presented in this question of American territory, would produce opposite conclusions. The one would support the native race in all the ridiculous pretensions which have ever been raised in its behalf, while the other, viewing the Indian "as a savage and pernicious beast," would award the country over which he wanders to those who require it for use and occupation, and condemn him to extermination in case of resistance. Representatives of either theory may be found to-day in large numbers. The Indian's advocates and staunchest friends dwell generally in the eastern States; his would-be executioners are his neighbors. If the accusation of bias because of self-interest is brought against the latter class, it should be admitted that its estimate of Indian character, however erroneous it may be, is formed from practical experience.

But neither of the above mentioned conclusions would be just. A rule of individual action, though unobjectionable in its proper sphere, is not always to the purpose if called into use to guide the movements and transactions of great communities. The continued practice on the part of a nation, of those virtues of private life, such as mildness, charity, denial, and uncomplaining suffering under insult and wrong, would prove disastrous. The law of protection and preservation, the exigencies of moral and physical development, the maxim that the greatest good for the greatest number is to be sought, must all be taken into consideration and allowed weight, in the settlement of questions of abstract national right. Nor can any people ignore the claims of those holding interests antagonistic to its own. All classes of men have rights and immunities. Because they do not make the best use of property in possession, is not, of itself, a reason why it should be taken from them. Although the law of nature both commands and condemns, a nation is only bound by its directions, and is not called upon to inflict its penalties. It is a law which executes itself. If it condemns the Indian, as undoubtedly it does,—a truth which is seldom remembered by the admirers of this simple child of nature —it still compels the white man to extend to him kind and humane treatment. The sentence which it pronounces against him, and which is and has been for a long time in process of fulfillment, cannot be mistaken. No pardon will be granted until his uplifted hand raised against all mankind is stayed, nor until he ceases his wanderings and betakes himself to those peaceful pursuits which Providence directs him to follow. We may be the instruments employed to enforce this sentence, but we cannot assume that he has forfeited by his conduct all claims to consideration, and thereupon ignore or forcibly wrest from him his inheritance, although we wish to devote it to laudable purposes.

Conceding that certain abstract rights belonged to the Indians, which the United States were bound by the law of nature to respect, it is well to ask concerning the quality of the same, whether individual or national, and to ascertain the extent to which the presumption that they were of a national character has been carried in legislation. The answers to these inquiries, could they be obtained, would make it appear whether the legal recognition granted by Government, has been in accordance with justice and consistency as determined by the dictates of conscience or an approved code of morals.

Excluding all arguments of expediency, we maintain

that if the tribes were entitled to be recognized as nations
or independent sovereignties in any degree, they should
have been so recognized in all particulars, and were entitled to all the rights and privileges which are incident to
those conditions ; since, as far as the Government was
concerned, they had never been abridged by the voluntary
act or permission of the tribes ; that those rights and
privileges were, in violation of the law of nations and of
nature, greatly curtailed by the Government when the
political status of the Indians was fixed. We also contend
that if the tribes only possessed those rights which pertain
to individuals or dependent communities, they should not
have been recognized in any sense as national powers, and
that by such recognition on the part of the Government,
they became vested with property to which they could not
otherwise have set up a valid claim.

The propositions briefly stated are these :—If the tribes
were nations, their rights were wrongfully withheld ; and
if not, they have been treated with a liberality beyond all
reasonable expectation. As nations, each had a basis
upon which to rest a legal title to all territory contained
within such boundaries as the tacit consent or sufferance
of surrounding tribes had permitted to be established as
the rightful limits of tribal occupancy, or such as has
been maintained by long continued force. As nations,
they owned this territory absolutely, and had the authority,
unless they had voluntarily parted therewith, to convey
the unconditional, unqualified fee to whomsoever they
wished. As nations, they had the right, in case they had
not given it up by stipulation, to hold intercourse and
negotiations with all foreign powers, and could also determine by what provisions they would continue relations with
the United States.

The latter thus recognized them : As nations, holding
national domains, with power to dispose of them carefully

8

restricted by its own unauthorized act ; as nations, capable of contracting international obligations, but with ability to treat, trade, and hold intercourse only with other Indian tribes, and with the United States.

If nations, how, by any known law of nations, could they be thus fettered, without their coöperation or consent ? The argument that such were the conditions imposed by Great Britain, and could be continued, is not valid. If that power placed them in an unnatural condition, we had no right to prolong it. The law of nature does not legalize a wrong, by any statute of limitations. The United States could not substitute itself for Great Britain, and thereby become a party to the treaties which the latter had entered into with the tribes. And even if that act could be accomplished at the will of the former, the non-treaty tribes were not bound by any obligations to accept the position assigned them, which was that of dependent nations.

If the Indians did not possess rights of a national character, they had only those which belong to the individual. The fact that they dwelt in assemblages, that they had gathered themselves into bands or communities, did not enhance or increase their rights, except with the societies in which they had cast their lot. With those, to be sure, membership created a relationship, from which sprang mutual duties and privileges ; but it could not confer a status cognizable by any known system of international law. Their rights then, if not national, were, in so far as this Government is concerned, those pertaining to the person ; and there is no authority in the code of nature, which human ingenuity or research has yet discovered, that bestowed upon them title to any more land than the quantity which they could occupy and utilize. That doctrine of a former century, which affirmed that title to new country vested in the government of the subject who made the discovery, was very fragile, and was accepted in order to avoid distressing wars. It would however appear substantial, compared with the vague theory, that individuals, or societies of individuals, could absolutely hold a legal interest, unconnected with any superior sovereignty, in vast tracts of country, which they had neither the power nor inclination to make productive.

But consider this matter for a moment from an Indian stand-point, and see if the case is made better. The members of tribes did not own land in severalty, but held it in common. In their minds, it was not property. Their interest in territory was this : the exclusive privilege to roam over it, and appropriate to their own especial use the natural products which it contained. Comparatively insignificant in numbers, they claimed to be the legally constituted, sole recipients of all that share of those blessings and benefits which Providence has freely bestowed for the good of the human race, which were to be found within a large portion of the earth's surface. Surely such an assumption is not in accordance with divine will, and would not be defended even by the Christian philanthropist who a short time since was introduced in these pages. Yet, this claim to extended territory admits of no other interpretation, unless immemorial enjoyment of an advantage permitted under favorable conditions, necessarily developed into a vested right ; or unless long continued modes of obtaining subsistence could be perpetuated, to the detriment and exclusion of fellow men, simply because they had been long practiced.

Whether, therefore, the natural right of the Indians to land was judged from their own or from the European position, the validity of their claim to large tracts of country could not have been upheld, except on the ground that it was acquired while the organizations into which they were collected possessed the powers of independent nations. And if a large portion of the American continent belonged to the Indians when the United States Government was created, they owned it as nations, and in no other capacity.

Let us pursue further this question of character of rights, and endeavor to shut out from consideration the subject of territory, which constantly obtrudes itself in all discussions upon Indian matters. Why it does so, is probably for the reason that the relation established between the Government and tribes is so apparently fictitious, or intangible, when placed upon any other foundation than that of territorial ownership, that it becomes exceedingly difficult to understand. The response to the inquiry were the tribes nations, is to the effect that they must have been, since they held extensive domains. Should I ask if the Indians were the rightful proprietors of American soil, I should be answered, yes, in their character of nations they originally possessed the continent. This reasoning is unsatisfactory. It is admitted that if they held extensive domains they were nations, and were consequently the rightful proprietors of the soil of this continent ; for extended dominion necessarily supposes sovereignty. But we assert, that if they had not been sovereign powers they could not have supported any title to large tracts of country, because it is only in sovereignty that such a claim could rest. We now deny that they were nations, and consequently their claim to territory is denied. The facts as they existed must be judged by the law of nations, which is, in this respect, the conceded law of nature, and judged by that law, what evidences can be discovered to prove that the tribal organization possessed the requisites of national powers ?

A body of people, the members of which act at times in concert, but from individual will, and not in obedience to an expressed or understood rule ; a body of people dwelling in the same locality, but not subordinate to any general authority; a body of nomadic people, congregated in self-defence. or attracted by the ties of relationship, love of superstitious observances, and opportunities for social intercourse, numbering when united a few hundreds, or possibly thousands, but without a code of laws or government of any kind, does not constitute a nation in a single particular.

But the tribes were organized and had their chiefs and grand councils ! To be sure they had ; and any party of men who should determine to cut themselves loose from civil restraint, and enter a wilderness. would organize themselves under a leader, and the ablest of the party would become its advisers. The tribal organization was of the weakest pattern. The chief was a leader in war, but an equal in peace. The members of the council did not become such by appointment or election, but assumed and maintained their positions from acknowledged ability in speech and deeds. There was nothing in the organizations which could be denominated government. Not even the bands which formed the Iroquois league, nor those embraced within the southern confederacies, could unitedly show the essential elements of nations, as now defined, unless it might be in strength to maintain themselves under adverse circumstances, in the possession of privileges which they had usurped. View the tribes as we please, we fail to discover nations, kingdoms, principalities, or powers—nothing in the majority of cases, but bands of uncivilized people, who did not hold themselves responsible to any law, but acted in accordance with will, as caprice or passion moved them. We fail to find that the decrees of nature invested them with the dignities and immunities of national existences, or upheld their claim to the extended country over which they roamed. We are led to believe, in conclusion, after weighing many probabilities, that the

position assigned them by our Government, as lawful occupants of the soil, subject to a qualified dependence, was
not, in truth, given because supposed to be in consonance
with positive law, but only because expediency and charity
combined seemed to dictate a continuance of the policy
which Great Britain had followed. It was thought that
the status which was declared and fixed, which accorded
them internal sovereignty, free tribal intercourse, and possession of territory, until extinguished under governmental
authority, would prove satisfactory to all parties, and would
result in concord. For this reason the course pursued
was adopted, and not that it was made imperative by any
imagined higher law, or natural commands.

If conclusions thus drawn are correct, the effects of the
treaty system upon the tribes may be viewed as the results
of voluntary measures of public policy, and not as the at-
tendants, or consequences of a line of action which was
necessarily followed. We intend to consider them as the
results of measures deemed expedient, and put in operation
to meet the requirements of existing circumstances, and
shall endeavor to show in what respects the system was unwise or erroneous.

The questions which naturally suggest themselves in
the outset of the inquiry, are these : What changes in the
condition of the Indian population were sought ? What
ends did Government wish to accomplish ? They may be
briefly answered. The mental and moral improvement of
the Indians, indeed their complete transformation in habits
of life and modes of thought, was desired. " The ultimate
design was to incorporate into our own institutions that
portion which could be converted to the state of civilization."

Whether proceedings under the treaty system were calculated to bring about these results in the speediest and
most natural manner, even if faithfully conducted, is made

doubtful, for the reason that the improvement demanded was personal, and not national or tribal, and that the subsequent intended incorporation must be effected by the acceptance of individuals, and not of entire communities, into the great body of citizens. The needed reformation consisted in individual progress, and the Government system delayed it, since it assisted to perpetuate the tribal relation, which was the outgrowth of barbarism, and the product of savage customs. It attempted to reach the person through an institution both social and political in part, which was built up on idleness, superstition, and crime, and which encouraged the Indians, even if it did not compel them, to persist in those practices which it fostered and preserved. It vainly thought it possible to remodel the social structure under which they lived, and make it conform to those of civilized society ; when on the contrary, efforts should have been made for its gradual destruction, since it was one of the chief difficulties in the path of true progression.

We will not here say that violent measures should have been resorted to in order to effect this destruction. Never try to reform by law or force that which ought to be changed by custom, is a sound political maxim. The Indians should have been allowed to retain their tribal institutions until they could have been prevailed upon to make modifications therein themselves or really to abolish them ; but Government should not have adopted a course of conduct tending to influence them to hold fast to their organizations, which it did by its recognition, and its transactions under the treaty system. It should have ignored their claims as independent communities, and have placed them individually as much as circumstances allowed, under its subjection.

This is no modern idea. It has been advocated by eminent men of various times, and now, after a prolonged experience of determined effort followed by constant disappointment, appears to have an important meaning. It is clearly expressed in Mr. Monroe's presidential message of eighteen hundred and eighteen. He says, speaking of the Indians : " To civilize them and even to prevent their extinction, it seems to be indispensable that their independence as communities should cease, and that the control of the United States over them should be complete and undisputed. The hunter's state will then be more easily abandoned and recourse will be had to the acquisition and culture of land, and to other pursuits tending to dissolve the ties which cement them together as a savage community, and to give a new character to every individual."

The requisites of Indian civilization were and still are, localization, mental and moral regeneration, and personal responsibility to law.

Not until the first condition is established can substantial success be attained. This is attended by radical innovations in those pursuits by which the necessities of life are acquired. It begets in time the desire for acquisition from which springs the incentive to labor and which is repugnant to community of interest. It develops the individual and weakens the tribal influence. As soon as permanent settlement is made the opportunity to impart instruction by teaching and example arises. A change of habits creates new modes of thought. In so far as the customs of the white man are copied, just so far does his instruction become practical. It will therefore be understood and will assist to shape conduct. Agriculture accompanies and succeeds to pastoral pursuits. With commodities for disposal, attention is turned to trade, and the subject of barter and exchange, as practiced in the civilized world, is studied.

Anything that influences the Indian to fix his abode, serves to wean him from his nomadic career, and opens to him a new channel for ideas ; and although an evil in itself, it proves to him at least a temporary benefit. There was truth in the old saying of the southern congressman : "Give an Indian a slave and you make a man of him." Not that the relation created had any elevating effect, but because the negro bondsman cultivated the fields of his master, compelled him to supervise his labor, and to dispose of the products of the soil. Slavery, as it existed in Oregon, degraded both bond and free, as would have been the case among the Indian tribes of the Southern States, had it not insured localization, increased agriculture, and given rise to new processes of thought and reflection.

With settlement comes also the opportunity to enforce law. In a country as extended as our own, in which the tribes are permitted to wander at will over the untenanted territory, it has been found impossible to execute the few statutes which affect the person of the Indian. He is practically removed from responsibility by the protection which the tribal organization furnishes. To it he can flee for refuge, and although it has not any constituted authority, either to shield or to surrender him, he can there find sufficient unorganized force to enable him to elude justice. This is as unfortunate for his race as it is for the Government; for, while such a condition of affairs exists, the night of barbarism is prolonged. The first glimmerings of the dawn of perfect and lasting civilization appear in obedience and self-imposed restraint. The savage, if left to himself, rarely learns to practice these cardinal virtues. Aid is required, and it must come from without his own social sphere. It manifests itself in the forms of definite and concise law, attended by the power to inflict sure and speedy punishment. If obedience is demanded and exacted the subject soon educates himself to curb his violent passions and to check his vicious tendencies. The rigid enforcement of a simple criminal code, which prohibited Indians from committing crimes against each other, as well

8*

as against the whites, would more quickly place the red man in the path of substantial improvement, than all the instructors in arts, morals, and religion who have ever visited him. The Romans fully comprehended the accuracy of this doctrine. They may have carried it too far in practice. They may have resorted to tyranny, when milder methods would have answered. Yet they laid the foundation upon which has been built modern European civilization.

The doctrine is accepted and acted upon by Great Britain at the present day. It is frequently asked why have not the eighty thousand Indians who inhabited her territory in the North-west given trouble. Explanations are as often ventured, to show why the peaceful policy of the Canadian Government has proved so successful. We are told that it results from honest administration. It is a mistaken idea. Honest contractors, and conscientious agents, with money and goods without limit, could not correct the roving disposition of the native, nor elevate his standard of morality. The full performance on the part of the Government of every treaty stipulation ever entered into, would not insure Indian advancement. To be sure, integrity of conduct, practiced by the supervising race, would have a certain influence, and would remove the present causes of complaint, but it would not of itself work substantial benefit.

The Indian will not easily receive permanent impressions of a virtuous character. He is not in the plastic state of childhood. His whole moral and mental system is diseased. The tablet of his mind is covered all over with heathen prejudices and cruel superstitions, and no space remains upon which to inscribe the golden rule of duty. The tablet must be cleansed before new impressions can be made. Quiet example, or gentle persuasion, will not do the work, while the temptations and allurements of unchecked tribal life continue. The latter prove stronger than the temporary convictions produced by exemplary conduct and argument.

Honest administration, by which is here meant the faithful execution of all promises which the Government has made, would not ameliorate the condition of the native, if unrestrained by physical force, and permitted to practice that license in which he is encouraged by propensity, superstition, and long-existing customs. The commendable behavior of the native population of Great Britain is not due, to any great extent, to upright dealing, fidelity, or capacity, on the part of agents, but it may be reasonably attributed to the fact, that every individual of that population is a subject of the Empire, and is personally responsible for the violation of its laws. Should he engage in murder or robbery, no sentimental plea of deep cherished wrongs would be advanced in his defence, to shield him from legal punishment. The sword of justice would surely fall upon him, and he is fully conscious of it. Dread apprehension of merited retribution deters from crime. It is more effective than gifts or speech, and more appreciated than the greatest forbearance. To this feature of Great Britain's Indian policy is success with the undomesticated tribes mainly due. It is, with that Government, the initiatory step, and is followed by localization and incorporation. She does not force back the native race into the wilderness, but settles, disciplines, and educates it, (although for education through hired instructors little is done,) as speedily as the territory over which it roams is needed for use or white occupancy.

The late Indian treaty system of the United States seems to have been admirably suited to delay the establishment of the condition we have named, as requisite to the attainment of civilization. It opposed definite settlement within reasonable boundaries. By its recognition of the tribes as independent communities, it ignored individual accountability for criminal action, in so far as the safety of its citizens would permit, and gave immunity from legal restraint. The remaining condition, mental and moral advancement, would consequently be of slow and tedious acquirement.

Look now a little farther into this subject. One might possibly be convinced by a careful examination, that the treaty system has not only delayed Indian improvement, but that, in many respects, it has actually exerted a direct injurious influence. We have said that it perpetuated the tribal relation. It did more. It gave to that relation a fictitious and pernicious importance, which strengthened a feeling of independence from government control, and nourished a spirit of vanity. The Indians could not appreciate the benevolent, or rather munificent, measures which invested them with the continual possession of the territory over which they were accustomed to roam in pursuit of food. They could not properly value the moderation which accorded them the management of their internal affairs. Such action they looked upon as concessions which belonged to them of right, and which were granted because of their consequence, and through fear of incurring their displeasure. The treaty councils, wherein United States commissioners sued for peace, and the representatives of the tribes arrogantly declared terms, aptly exhibited to view the false impressions the latter were under regarding their correct status, and the power of the Government to punish them for their conduct. Arrayed in barbaric splendor, assuming to be rulers of vast domains, they even demanded compensation for the water which the white man drank from their lakes and rivers, insolently denied the right of the Great Father to enter their country, and exacted large sums of money upon their naked promises to cease from murdering American citizens.

Is this great nation degrading itself in negotiating by treaty with a few savages in the hope of controlling them and promoting their welfare at the least expense, exclaim the friends of the treaty system. We shall not attempt a reply, but content ourselves by pronouncing the proceedings a hollow mockery. We will say that it deceived and injured the Indian, and that by creating within him an erroneous sense of his importance increased crime on our frontier.

It is impossible to purchase lasting peace of the barbarian, unless he is placed in a situation where he is restrained by a fear of righteous judgment. That appropriation of half a million of dollars which was expended on the Fort Peck Indians a few years ago, wonderfully developed a consciousness of strength. The whole peace policy has proved a failure, simply because it lacked the one great essential element to make it successful. The hostile tribes, flattered and subsisted, received the abundant stores of goods which were sent to their reservations, and which were intended to appeal to gratitude, as tribute or the price of peace. No coercion was attempted. Indeed the larger reservations were without system, regulation, or government of any kind, with which to control the uneducated, inharmonious and passionate population there collected. A few instructors in written language and the catechism, a few experts in the use of agricultural implements, were expected to employ the attention of this people of leisure, maintained in indolence and insolence, and by persuasion, encouragement and example, to thoroughly revolutionize them in thought and pursuits.

The treaty system also produced an injurious effect upon the tribes, because they were permitted and induced to enter into stipulations which they had no intention of regarding, —which they knew from the nature of circumstances, could not be complied with on their part. They promised, in order to obtain the consideration which generally preceded performance. Allusion has already been made to the absurdity of certain provisions which many of the treaty instruments contain, and it is not intended that another reference shall now be made to them. We have in mind those stipulations, which involve disagreeable duties, or unpleasant action from the members of the tribes and which we consider impossible of execution, on account of the weakness of tribal authority, and the utter absence of any species of coercion over individuals.

What honesty of purpose could inspire a chief of a wild tribe to enter into a contract, binding all heads of families of his people to fix permanent residences, to cultivate land in future, and to keep children of certain ages at schools ? He knows that his constituents will not plough ground, nor plant extended fields in corn, as long as there is any thing to hunt. He is fully aware that obedience is no part of a child's instruction ; that parental restraint ceases, or at least will not be exercised, after the boy is able to draw the bow, and that those heads of families not only do not wish their sons to attend school, but could not force the unwilling ones to do so. He may however entertain confused ideas concerning the manual labor schools, which are said to be intended, "for the education and training of the youth, in letters, agriculture the mechanical arts, and housewifery," and imagine that they may present some irresistible attraction to the young, else he would be in honor bound to reply to those asking for promises as did the Iroquois chief to the Pennsylvania Commissioners in seventeen hundred and fifty-four : "The Indians are not inclined to give their children learning. Our customs differ from yours."

Such and kindred stipulations which cannot be enforced ought not to be entered into. The chiefs comprehended and the commissioners should not be ignorant of the fact, that the tribes will not and cannot fulfill them. They must tend to destroy the moral force and binding effect of treaties, bring the Government into disrepute, and encourage the Indians in the commission of deeds of lawlessness.

But how, it might be asked, if tribal restraint and influence is so feeble, and the moral tone of the native is such as has been represented, can reliance be placed upon the fulfillment of treaty conditions of any nature ? Probably very little credit or importance is attached to the majority of them. The action of the Government has generally been experimental, and has not been attended with a confidence that the opposite party would put forth strenuous efforts to perform its part of the agreement. Still, that confidence has in almost all cases been too strong. Very few treaties have ever been regarded, except as to those provisions which relinquished title to territory (and which of course could not be evaded) unless the tribes which entered into them occupied positions which rendered continual government aid necessary to their existence or preservation.

The cause of this repeated violation of faith is excused by a large class of our citizens, on the ground that either our own authorities do not observe the contract, and are the first transgressors, or that our white inhabitants make unwarranted encroachments upon the rights and commit injuries upon the persons of the Indians. The extent to which opinions are sometimes carried in this direction, is sufficient to excite surprise. They are not of late origin, but the extravagant expressions to which they have given rise may be found in the written history of every generation of our people since settlements on the American coast were permanently established. I turn back nearly one hundred and seventy years and find the Governor of Virginia saying : " The Indians never break with the English without gross provocation from persons trading with them." The public press of the present day scatters from time to time the proclaimed opinions of those who advocate certain pretended rights of the native, and seek to cover his crimes with the mantle of charity. We have, say they, never known the Indians to first break faith with the white man. Disturbances are always caused by the aggressions and dishonesty of the whites.

Why do not these gentlemen rather show us instances in which the Indians have kept their faith when overwhelming physical causes did not oblige them to do so ; or to present more convincing examples in proof of their theory of Indian honor and fidelity to plighted word, why do they not bring forward illustrations which would not involve the policy and action of the white man ? Let them instance treaties to which the tribes are sole parties— treaty agreements made by and between the tribes, and with which the white man had nothing whatever to do. They are of frequent occurrence, and we venture the remark, that they never healed a long existing difficulty. We have heard of great inter-tribal councils called for the purpose of removing hereditary feuds, at which the calumet was smoked, eternal friendship pledged, and magnificent presents in ponies and goods exchanged ; and we have been informed that the old strife was almost immediately resumed, and that the ponies presented in token of sincerity of the sentiments expressed in the council were soon stolen and captured, and placed in the possession of the original owners. In fact, we have witnessed the apparent honesty of intention amounting to earnestness which characterizes such assemblages, and have believed for the time but mistakenly that peace solemnized with so great ceremony would be preserved.

Tribes which have been at enmity for a considerable period of time, and which are not obliged for actual preservation to unite their fortunes against a common foe, cannot of themselves effect a permanent reconciliation, although one is sometimes merged in the other, after severe chastisement. The reason is plain. Even if the chiefs and principal soldiers who make the treaties are serious and peaceably disposed, the members of the tribes cannot be controlled. With them future welfare is of slight consequence, compared with the gratification of the passions ; and by individual action they bring back the condition of hostility. It is next to an impossibility to cure an internal tribal feud. The parties to the quarrel are likely to separate, and thenceforth live apart, and at war with each other.

Yet notwithstanding these proofs of inconstancy, a numerous class of citizens discover in the conduct of the whites, the only cause for Indian violation of treaty obligations. Such explanations furnish too sad a commentary upon the boasted civilization which that same class is endeavoring to induce the natives to accept, and they should not be taken without qualification, unless it can be made to appear that the Indians are as Columbus is reported to have found them : "A race of men whose minds, far from being wedded to any system of idolatry, were prepared, by their extreme simplicity, for the reception of pure and uncorrupted doctrine."

Every fair minded person will confess that there have been occasions when wanton, ill treatment by the whites has suddenly put an end to a languishing peace ; that the frequent applications made by our authorities to change provisions of treaties which the Indians had been instructed should be forever undisturbed, have quickened and given direction to a natural unrest. But the assertion that the savage butcheries and fiendish atrocities which have been committed on the border citizens, are due to any considerable extent to the crimes of the white man or his Government, is based upon an assumption which history and experience will not sustain, viz : that the native is by disposition mild and tractable, and by nature sincere and faithful.

Perhaps a clearer idea of the effect of the treaty system upon our Indian population might be conveyed, should a practical exposition of its workings be attempted. Some tribe from among those which have been from the first under its influence, might be selected as an example, to make more intelligible the views which have been advanced. Let us go to the Indian territory, where, according to an official report made in eighteen hundred and seventy-two, "the partially civilized tribes, numbering about fifty thousand souls, have, in proportion to population, more schools and with a larger average attendance, more churches, church members, and ministers, and spend far more of their money for education, than the people of any territory of the United States," and where, as the same report informs us, "life and property are more safe, and there are fewer violations of the law," than in the regularly organized territories. Let us make selection of the Cherokee nation, which is acknowledged to be the most influential and most enlightened tribe of that section, and to which the believers in the ability of the Indian to speedily acquire our civilization, and the supporters of the treaty system, are accustomed to turn for encouragement and consolation.

For evidence as to its condition in culture and wealth, we will confine our search for the present to official statistics, which undoubtedly present facts in their most favorable colors. The tabular statements, prepared by the late Commissioner of Indian Affairs, show that the Cherokee nation numbers eighteen thousand six hundred and seventy-two souls ; that they owned, until recently, eleven millions of acres of land, and that they now hold a reservation of five millions ; that they have seven thousand

acres under cultivation, and possess four hundred and sixteen thousand head of stock; that the eighteen thousand
six hundred and seventy-two inhabitants have, strange to
say, that exact number of dwelling-houses, also have
seventy-four school buildings, and thirty church edifices;
that the average attendance of scholars for the year eighteen hundred and seventy-six, was fifteen hundred and
twenty-five; that there are seven thousand church members, and twelve thousand persons who are able to read;
that the stocks, bonds, and funds, which are held in trust
by the United States, amount to two millions six hundred
thousand dollars, and that the annual interest on the same,
which is paid regularly, is more than one hundred and
forty thousand dollars.

It appears from the report of the agent, that this
nation inhabits a very fertile section of country; that its
people live in stone, brick, and log houses (in which can
be seen the sewing-machine and piano) with surrounding
grounds "adorned by ornamental trees, shrubbery, flowers,
and nearly every improvement, including orchards and
choice fruits;" that they sustain a newspaper ably edited
by native Cherokees; that they have a constitutional government, with legislative, judicial, and executive departments; that they own public buildings worth two hundred
and sixty-one thousand dollars; that "among their citizens are men noted for their talents and learning;" that
their government "is conducted with marked ability and
dignity," and that although "it has been but a few years
since the Cherokees assembled in council under trees, or in
a hewed log house, with hewed logs for seats, now the
legislature assembles in a spacious brick council house,
provided with suitable committee rooms, senate chamber,
representative hall, library and executive offices, which
cost in erecting the sum of twenty-two thousand dollars."

Surely this people seem to be superior, in many respects,

to the whites living within the organized territories, and may be favorably compared with the inhabitants of any county, in our most wealthy and populous States. A hasty computation would show the value of their real and personal property to be from sixteen to twenty millions of dollars,—one thousand dollars to each man, woman, and child. It is doubtful if many communities can boast of greater riches. They exceed those of the people of New York, and are greater by one-half than those of the people of the United States.

The Cherokees also manifest a greater regard for religion than white communities, if the reported number of church-members are properly impressed with Christian doctrine. They expend larger sums upon education, in proportion to their population, than any State in the Union. The current expenses of the common school system in some of the Eastern States, is less than four dollars per scholar. In the South, they average from five to ten dollars, and in California they are sixteen dollars, while among the Cherokees they have been thirty-five dollars per scholar.

The attendance among the latter is small, however, for the ratio of scholars to the population is as one to twelve ; whereas in the entire country, it is as one to six. Yet the reports show, that the number of their people able to read is greater in proportion to their strength than the number of those of the same ability in the entire United States, where there are four and one-half millions of inhabitants more than ten years of age, who can neither read nor write.

The figures and extracts which have been produced from official statistics indicate that the Cherokee nation is rapidly progressing in cultivation, and that it has already secured a high degree of civilization. But let us examine more carefully into its actual condition, and ascertain if possible by what means, through what processes, and in what period of time it has been reached. That population of eighteen thousand is made up of eight thousand full and ten thousand mixed bloods. Some of the native Cherokees have the blue eyes and light hair of the Saxon, and in many the lineaments of the European predominate. In two centuries the nation has lost one-quarter of its Indian stock, which has been absorbed by the white and negro races, and if past relations continue, another two hundred years will nearly efface the distinguishing features of its progenitors.

The effect of this infusion of white blood is mental as well as physical. It has been said, that "the union of the Englishman and the Hindoo produces something not only between races but between moralities." Whatever may be thought of the union of races on this continent, it is true, that the offspring inherits, to a certain extent, the mental, moral and religious peculiarities of either parent. With him, consistent action is rather due to legal restraint than conscientious motive, and he seldom becomes a good citizen making his conduct subservient to a regard for social order. He is often strongly imbued with the traditional superstitions, the sentiments and passions of the pure Indian, and with the same quality of restlessness and a dislike for labor.

The leaven of blood therefore which has been introduced into the Cherokee nation, has only measurably conditioned individual habits and social life. It has modified national character, but its influence in the past has not been sufficient to bring about any very marked transformations. The advancement then may be considered that of the Indian race, assisted and stayed we might say by its partially white representatives.

The extent of the Cherokee civilization, as compared with our own, cannot be determined by computing the number of persons who are able to read, and who attend churches, nor by an estimate of the wealth of the inhabitants, which has been given to and preserved for them. Nor is it shown by the faithfulness with which our laws and institutions have been copied. It should be judged from the uses the people make of the advantages placed in their possession, and from the manner in which the laws are obeyed and executed.

The reservation occupied by this tribe, consisting of five millions of acres of land, cannot be surpassed. Delightful climate, remarkable fertility of soil, and central location, render it the most desirable section of country within the United States for the pioneer and immigrant. Yet the tribe only cultivates seven thousand acres, and the crops raised might be grown on a less quantity. Even as light as agricultural labors are, the work is largely performed by white individuals. Fifteen hundred whites lawfully reside upon the reservation, whom the Cherokee farmers are obliged to employ in order to secure a crop.

What the United States Indian Agent remarks of the Choctaws and Chickasaws, is partly true of the Cherokees, although the latter employ far less white labor, and cultivate much less soil than the former. He says : "A great many white people are scattered among these two nations, either hired by the Indians as laborers, or renters of Indian farms ; and where the right kind of white men, of temperate and industrious habits are, there will be seen the prosperous Indian farm." The remark needs no comment. It plainly conveys the truth of Indian inferiority or indolence.

Many of the native inhabitants are educated. College bred men are found among them, but they make little practical use of their acquirements. They are content oftentimes to pursue their studies in filthy cabins. The schools are maintained at the expense of the United States Government ; or as this assertion might be disputed, we will say, by the interest on moneys promised the tribe under treaty stipulations, which it receives each year, and which cannot be expended for any other purpose. Notwithstanding the large amount paid out, there results a yearly surplus which is consumed in the erection of costly buildings. In fine, the native Cherokee is provided with land in abundance, with educational and religious advantages, with a government, and all the needed institutions of society, from the returns of the money held in trust by the United States. He receives all the public benefits of well organized communities, in so far as the same can be conferred, without taxation or expenditure of any kind, and can devote his entire property and the earnings of his labors, to his personal comfort.

Well may the Board of Indian Commissioners of eighteen hundred and seventy-two exclaim, that the tribe has more schools, more churches, and spends far more of its own money for education, than the people of any territory, provided it shows the source from which this money comes, and the impossibility of using it for other objects. But from another portion of that report which asserts that life and property are more safe, and violations of the law less frequent, than in the territories, we must dissent. We could only credit that statement on the supposition, that the Board had in mind, when making its comparison, all the inhabitants of the territories, both white and Indian. It must have reached this conclusion either by guess, or after the judicial records had been consulted. Had it pursued the latter course to its fullest extent, it might have discovered, that crimes among the most virtuous communities of the States were enormous, as compared with the offences of the Cherokee nation ; for with the former, law is executed in letter and spirit, while among the latter it is neither obeyed nor enforced. At the time this report was submitted, murders and assassinations were of frequent occurrence. Internal feuds, some of which had existed seventy years, kept the passions of the people inflamed. In the words of one of the citizens of that tribe : " The law is no more to be relied on here, than it would be among the Comanches. There is no more perfect despotism, as regards the expression of opinion, on earth, than exists now among the Cherokees."

Matters have not greatly improved. The public press refers at short intervals to the unsettled condition of affairs in that section, and recounts the commission of outrages. The law is too feebly administered to make secure person or property, and desperadoes seldom receive the demands of justice. Take away the strong arm of the General Government, and social disorder would be certain to result. The few enterprising, liberal minded, and industrious citizens who encourage order and progress, could not withstand that larger class which is controlled by passion and prejudice, and blinded by ignorance and superstition. The civilization of the Cherokees, regarded as a body or in mass, is of a low order. It is a foreign tree which has not yet taken deep root, and which will require long protracted attention to make it flourish in the soil in which it has been planted.

The reports which have so glowingly depicted the condition of this tribe, convey an impression that its advancement has been accomplished within a few years, under the Government's fostering care. The Indian Department presents it as a result of the wise and philanthropic policy which it has pursued. A brief review of the history of the Cherokees will enable us to point out at least, the long and sinuous path which has been trodden, from barbarism to semi-civilization. The journey has consumed centuries, and the blood and treasure of the white race has been lavishly expended, to accelerate the tardy movements.

They had been in constant communication with the whites more than one hundred years before the existence of the United States Government, and had copied more generally from the European than any other tribe on the Continent. We find them in war with the colonies long before Carolina became a royal province, and afterwards engaged in the English interest against the French. As early as seventeen hundred and fifty, they dwelt, it is said, in comfortable houses which were surrounded by cultivated fields. During our revolutionary war, when the American troops ravaged their country, one thousand of their houses, and fifty thousand bushels of their grain were destroyed by a single expedition, and as many of their goods were taken as sold for one hundred thousand dollars. The treaty of Hopewell, executed in seventeen hundred and eighty-five, granted them a delegate in Congress, and described by metes and bounds the territory which was assigned to them. Four succeeding treaties of the last century purchased of them land, at a cost of about forty thousand dollars, and at the commencement of the present century, we find them in possession of nineteen millions of acres, or four times as much land as is contained within the boundaries of Massachusetts. Machinery and grist mills were appearing among them. They were quite largely engaged in farming, and were availing themselves of slave labor.' Eight years later, they represented to the President, that they were divided in councils ; part wished to secure western hunting grounds, and part wished to remain in the east and cultivate the soil ; and we find the President engaged in correspondence with them, advising the adoption of a republican form of government, and explaining the necessary steps to be taken. In eighteen hundred and twenty-seven, their population had increased from twelve to thirteen and one-half thousand, they had formed for themselves " a constitution on republican prin-

9

ciples," they lived in good comfortable houses, cultivated large farms, owned twelve hundred and seventy-seven negro slaves, and had five hundred children in school—nearly one-half of the entire number of children of all the Indian tribes then attending school. By periodical sales of land, they had received large sums of money, and before the treaty of eighteen hundred and thirty-five was entered into, they had a school fund of fifty thousand dollars, which the United States preserved for them. At the last mentioned date, the land which they still held amounted to nine and one-half millions of acres, which they sold for six millions seven hundred and sixty thousand dollars, and thirteen and one-half millions of acres of land in the Indian territory, whither they all removed, excepting the remnant which remained in North Carolina.

The civil expenditure of the Government on their account up to the present time, has probably equaled twenty-five millions of money; and the amount paid out to punish them, and to preserve peace through the presence of a military force, if added, would double that sum. So that every representative of that tribe, man, woman, and child, white, black, copper-colored, and mixed, has cost the United States about twenty-five hundred dollars, and they are numerically stronger to-day than ever before.

Should then the advocates of the old treaty system, who cite the Cherokees in illustration of their theory, that our native population will speedily accept civilization under mild and persuasive teachings ; and that proceedings under the past policy were best adapted to accomplish the great end desired, properly present them in their actual condition, and exhibit the expenditure of Government on their account, they might be able to show with a fair degree of plausibility, that all of our Indian tribes could be elevated to the same civilized plane at a cost of five or six hundred millions of dollars. But no, a second thought convinces us that they could not even do that ; for it must be remembered, that the advancement of the Cherokees did not commence within recent years, but long before they began to receive the benefits of the United States treaty system. They were more enlightened a century ago than the wild tribes now are, and therefore an additional sum must be taken into the reckoning, which could not be very well expressed in figures.

The mistaken policy of the Government, in conferring upon the Cherokees, who had been hostile to the United States interest during the revolutionary struggle, national prerogatives, and a large extent of territory, was a direct blow to their progress, as well as an extravagant public measure. Had it terminated hostilities on their part, it might have appeared more reasonable ; but the spirit of opposition was not quieted until they had been made to feel the power of the force which they had attempted to oppose, and had become aware of their inability to cope with it. They then slowly improved in spite of the system which was adopted to control them. Individual progress was made, notwithstanding the tribal relation—which swallowed up personal acquisition in a common appropriation and destroyed individual responsibility—was encouraged, and in fact made necessary, since it was the only medium of intercourse. Deluded into the belief that they constituted an independent nation, falsely conscious that they could not be held responsible for their conduct, advised and persuaded to imitate our own institutions, political and domestic, they have been groping along in the darkness of superstitious ignorance, and have vainly endeavored, with much outside assistance, to assimilate their tribal organization to our own Government, while at the same time, they have continued to live under the customs which it upheld and perpetuated. Would it have cost more money to have given them correct impressions at the

outset ?   Would it not have hastened their advancement ?
My own impression is, that had they been located within a
small and fertile section of country, easily accessible, and
placed under a few simple regulations directly applicable
to the person, merely as a preparatory measure to the final
extension over them of our entire criminal code ; that had
a kind but firm policy been adopted, calculated to ignore
as much as possible community of interest, to encourage
labor, and to protect individual rights, that we should now
have among us as the descendants of the Cherokee tribe,
instead of a troublesome nation, a body of useful and industrious citizens.

Why attempt to improve a tribal structure, which is
but the outward manifestation of a barbarous condition of
a people ?   Why attempt mediate action through an irresponsible agency, in order to reach the person ?   A truth
seems to have been forgotten, viz :—that society is exactly
what the individuals of which it is composed make it, and
that it cannot be elevated until a change is effected in its
elements.   Tribal improvement means nothing more nor
less than progress among the members who constitute the
tribe.   The speediest reform can be attained by bringing
outside influences and forces to bear directly upon the individual.   The practical question is this : What are the
primary wants of the Indian in order to advance him and
fit him for citizenship ? and not, how can tribal organizations be improved.   He requires that which cannot be dispensed with, even in the case of civilized humanity,—active
law with speedy physical punishments, administered with
justice and moderation.   He needs a stable rule of action
to restrain him from committing injuries on the rights and
property of others, and should be punished and coerced
until he submits to be guided by that rule.   The germ of
civilization is obedience to law.   Implant that in the sav-

age breast, and the beginning of a better state is positively secured.

Government has finally learned the necessity of localizing the tribes, in order to advance their condition, but the more necessary measure of enforced repression does not seem to be appreciated. Should a tribe to-day break into rebellion, the ministers of peace would be sent out to purchase submission. There is danger now that the Sioux nation may be paid or hired to settle down under its mere promise to desist from robbery and murder. Far better would it be for its ultimate welfare, should hostilities continue until it is obliged to beg for mercy, and seek pardon through prayerful intercessions, even though it be at the expense of all its possessions and a large fraction of its numbers. A misconceived spirit of utility and philanthropy would stay the hand engaged in teaching it the rudimentary lesson of modern civilization, and which must soon be again uplifted unless indelibly fixed upon this occasion.

CHAPTER VI.

REPORTED CORRUPTION IN THE INDIAN BUREAU.

The period of bitter popular criticism of the action of the Indian Bureau has again returned. As has generally been the case, it follows some hopeful effort at reform, or a pretended determined test of some particular feature of Government policy.

The early trials at enlightenment and trade proved ineffectual. The colonization measure with its attempted seclusion of race was added to the programme and still success was not attained. The transfer of the Indian Bureau to a peace department, and the substitution of the olive branch for the emblems of force, did not bring promised results. The practice of furnishing subsistence was adopted, and yet this ungrateful people would not appreciate the efforts put forth for its preservation. Education, Christianity, and commerce were freely offered to the tribes in all the variable positions which they passed through. So sparingly have they been accepted, that two opinions upon the possibility of Indian advancement have been reached. One, that the Indian is incapable of civilization, and the other, that the responsibility for a failure to civilize him rests upon the Government.

Those administrations which have professed a marked concern for the welfare of the native race, and especially those which have undertaken experiments in management, have been so confident in their assurances of a speedy triumph, that popular belief has been deluded into an expectation of the final realization of a long deferred hope. But after a few years of expensive delusion, anticipations have been blighted and former convictions have been again embraced. Never were people more despondent than during a brief period prior to the inauguration of the so called peace policy. Successive experimental methods had miserably failed. The party which retained faith in the capacity of the Indian to accept our practical civilization, savagely arraigned the past policy of the country and the inefficient operations of the Indian Bureau. The commission, appointed in eighteen hundred and sixty-nine to coöperate with the Administration in the management of Indian affairs, fully expressed the views of the enlightened majority of citizens in a report which was that year submitted. That commission said : " The history of the Government connections with the Indians is a shameful record of broken treaties and unfulfilled promises. The history of the border white man's connections with the Indians is a sickening record of murder, outrage, robbery and wrong committed by the former as the rule, and occasional savage outbreaks and unspeakable barbarous deeds of retaliation by the latter, as the exception." We quote at length from another portion of this report, as the impediments supposed to have retarded the advancement of the tribes are tersely mentioned.

" Paradoxical as it may seem, the white man has been the chief obstacle in the way of Indian civilization. The benevolent measures attempted by the Government for their advancement have been almost uniformly thwarted by the agencies employed to carry them out. The soldiers sent for their protection too often carried demoralization and disease into their midst. The agent appointed to be their friend and counsellor, business manager and the almoner of the Government bounties, frequently went among them only to enrich himself in the shortest possible time at the cost of the Indians, and spend the largest available sums of the Government money with the least ostensible beneficial results. The general interest of the trader was opposed to their enlightenment as tending to lessen his profits. Any increase of intelligence would render them less liable to his impositions, and if occupied in agricultural pursuits their product of furs would be proportionally decreased. The contractors' and transporters' interests were opposed to it, for the reason that the production of agricultural products on the spot would necessarily cut off their profits in furnishing army supplies. The interpreter knew that if they were taught, his occupation would be gone. The more submissive and patient the tribe, the greater the number of outlaws infesting their vicinity ; and all these were the missionaries teaching them the most degrading vices of which humanity is capable. If in spite of these obstacles a tribe made some progress in agriculture, or their lands became valuable from any cause, the process of civilization was summarily ended by driving them away from their homes with fire and sword to undergo similar experiences in some new locality."

This is almost the language of invective. Never had Indian management been more scathingly denounced. The commission had reviewed past operations, and met to fix upon and recommend a new system of control. In its opinion all public measures which had been adopted had tended to demoralize the Indians instead of making them better, simply because they were wickedly executed. It concluded that the custom of meeting the tribes as independent nations was unwise, and proposed that the treaty farce be discontinued, although it substituted the tribal contract with the Government, which in so far as the Indians were concerned was nearly as detrimental to their interests as the treaty proceedings, since it insured a continuance of tribal organizations. The remaining recommendations contained nothing novel, except the proposition to establish a judicial tribunal in the Indian territory, and the taxation of "civilized tribes," which existing treaties forbade, and the transfer of such of those branches of education as are necessarily acquired through the medium of schools and churches, to the religious denominations of the country. Colonization and exclusion were to be carried to the utmost limit. The most determined efforts were to be made to induce the Indians to turn their attention to agriculture, at least in so far as persuasion and material aid could accomplish it. Education and religious instruction were to be pursued with energy, and the Indian service was to be thoroughly purified.

Management under this union of church and State was commenced. Men well grounded in Christian doctrine and of marked piety were selected to superintend and conduct affairs, from the distinguished commissioner to the lowly agency farmer. The country poured out its treasures with a lavish hand, that the auspicious season of reform might be attended with full advantages, and that the disinterested labor might be prosecuted to a glorious consummation. In the words of the report from which we have quoted, the Government seemed determined "to protect the Indians, to educate them in industry, the arts of civilization and the principles of Christianity, elevate them to the rights of citizenship and to sustain and clothe them until they could support themselves." After a trial of eight years, and an expenditure of over fifty millions of dollars, the Indian seems as far removed from the desired condition of improvement as formerly. The people again cry out against the faithless policy of the Government, and the fraudulent transactions of those engaged in the application of its measures.

An arraignment of the Indian Bureau on account of the looseness with which it has conducted business, and the

9*

disregard it has manifested for the integrity of its agents and factors, might strike a responsive sentiment in the popular mind. But whatever sins we might be able to discover, we could not advocate the opinion so widely prevalent, that Indian advancement has been materially checked thereby. Much less could we agree to that still more ultra belief, that our Indians have been rendered more depraved either in actions or intention by the frauds which have been practiced upon them. In their native state they did not have sufficient virtue to allow evil example to injure them. They were not susceptible to demoralization. The society of the whites, even of dishonest and immoral whites, made them better. The crimes of contractors, of reservation agents and employés, have not plunged them any deeper into the mire of besotted ignorance. In fact, all the reservation Indians have gradually improved, notwithstanding all good and law-abiding citizens have been excluded. They have been slowly acquiring an intelligence which manifests itself in a perceptible progress in their modes of life. They might have occupied a still higher plane, had they been constantly under the supervision of saintly men, who had daily pressed them with wholesome instruction and advice, distributed to them all the charities of Government and given to them dollar for dollar in trade. We say that they *might* have improved faster under such conditions, for we are not sure but that a persistent course of argument and persuasion, would have been crowned with partial success, although it is by no means probable, that they would have voluntarily practiced to any extent the teachings received. Still the force of an ever present virtuous example, would undoubtedly produce some degree of good. As for Government bounties and honest exchanges in trade, independent of the commendable influence exerted, it would make little difference whether the Indian received much or little. It mattered not, as far as their future welfare was concerned, whether the provisions and clothing purchased for them were reduced in quantity by the action of the agent and contractor, whether their numbers were greatly over-estimated when requisitions for supplies were made, and amounts in excess of actual needs were subsequently stolen, or whether they received a great or small price for the robes and peltries sold to their traders. Large receipts and returns rather encouraged indolence. They did not tend to increase the agricultural field, and they made the labors of the chase less necessary.

But if the dishonest practices of the contractors and employés of the Indian Department have not demoralized the native race, they have exerted a most corrupting influence upon the public service generally. The expert application of the principles of casuistry, which agents and contractors have been enabled to make, the frauds which have become deep rooted because legalized by sanctioned custom, have continued to debauch those who do business with the Indian Bureau, and has sadly affected public morals throughout a large section of the country. The tendency has been from bad to worse, and the strenuous efforts put forth to purify the service, have not even arrested unlawful transactions.

The would-be reformers attribute their failure to various causes. They seem to lose sight of the fact, that the nature of Indian management and the circumstances which have attended it, have been calculated to produce corrupt action. The Government policy was created in deceit. The recognition of the tribes as nations was an artifice. Negotiations with them have been conducted with a fictitious dignity, and many stipulations indicate that our commissioners resorted to finesse and skillful manipulation. The most stupid white men of the West, who have practical knowledge of the Indians, detect the falsehood which has been practiced and ridicule its absurdity. What wonder then, that those more gifted should be tempted by the spirit of deception, and be inclined, when opportunity offers, to avail themselves of advantages under their control. A policy founded in deceit, although with laudable intentions, would naturally shed an unhappy influence over those engaged to carry it out. There are several other and much more cogent reasons, which might be assigned in attempting to account for fraudulent practices in the Indian service. The business of the Bureau, as indeed business in all the Departments of Government, is carried on through circuitous channels. Transactions begin with the agents and are completed under their supervision. They report the numerical strength, condition and necessities of their tribes, which outside of the treaty stipulations govern appropriations. They receive and distribute the supplies which are purchased in the large markets, and transported under contract to the agencies. They disburse or witness the payment of money annuities to the treaty Indians. An efficient agent would not only look after those matters which come directly under his observation, but would inform himself of the exact amount of the yearly appropriation intended for his own particular tribe, would know the cost of supplies at the places of purchase, and the actual expense attending transportation. He would carefully verify all stores received, estimate their probable value and attend to their distribution or preservation. He would, by following such a course of conduct, allow but slight opportunity for peculation to the middle men, or to those who stand between him and the head of his bureau in business relations. With honest, zealous and capable agents, the Indian service, even as now constituted, might be purified ; but reform is impossible as long as they are roguish or incompetent. They are responsible in a certain sense for nearly all the iniquity which has been perpetrated. even if innocent of the sin of commission, since they might have discovered and reported it, and have been the instruments in bringing the guilty to punishment.

The difficulty in securing an upright and well qualified class of agents would not appear to be very great, but it has proved insurmountable. It requires marked ability of a practical nature, to control efficiently a large Indian agency. The responsible person of a well peopled reservation, should also possess in a high degree the Christian virtues of patience under repeated failures, and hope under bitter disappointments. Character and intelligence combined have a high market value, and the Government endeavors to obtain them at the moderate sum of fifteen hundred dollars per year. This is impossible unless men endowed with those qualifications can be secured, who are willing to sacrifice their personal comforts and private interests for the public good. The churches inspected their flocks to find such men for appointment, but honesty was unaccompanied by capacity, and when competency was acquired, integrity was too often wanting. Many, who had previously sustained excellent reputations, were charged with the grossest frauds and were allowed to retire from the Indian country. Some who were in straightened circumstances when they undertook the management of an agency, now compute their wealth with very expressive figures.

Let no one smile at these exhibitions of weakness and corruption. It is more surprising that a few of the recently appointed agents have resolutely performed their duties than that a large share have betrayed their trust. We do not advocate the rejected doctrine of a former age, that the moral sentiment is begotten and lives in utility. We believe in the continued and wide-spread existence of vicarious suffering, and think that self-imposed restraint is frequently due to the mere love of truth and right. But we also believe that professed morality is as often the consequence of public opinion as of individual conscience.

Faultless conduct on the part of the Indian agent is not incited by a surrounding social impulse. He is not inspired by the healthy moral atmosphere which pervades a civilized Christian community. Far removed from those hitherto attendant influences which have assisted to support and stay him in other pursuits of life, constantly mingling of necessity with the squalid natives who practice every form of vice, he is dependent on conscience only for guidance. If his moral perceptions are not clear and positive, in fine, if he is not a law unto himself, his steps are certain to deviate from the straight and narrow path of rectitude. The evils which beset him give him unceasing battles. He daily passes through temptation in the wilderness. Unless thoroughly governed by philanthropic or missionary motives, he is apt to turn from the pittance allowed him as compensation and which would barely support him at a far off agency, to be reached only over long routes of travel, and endeavor to ascertain the emoluments belonging to his office. Here he generally strikes the rock which wrecks him. His initiatory schemes to improve his pecuniary condition in a way which shall neither defraud Government nor wrong his wards, are worked out with marvelous dexterity, and carefully measured by the rules of a persuaded conscience. Instructors in a very pliant code of ethics attend him in the persons of contractors and assistants—all of whom are interested in his decisions, and soon under the circumstances moral convictions cease to impede the celerity of his mental processes. When an agent embraces the error that emoluments attach to his position, and considers them as a portion of the compensation to which he is entitled, the chances are that he will descend from moral wrong to positively criminal proceedings. As long as he maintains and is governed by the correct opinion that private gain cannot be acquired through official transactions; that the Government is entitled to all the benefits of his business operations ; that he is honorably bound to exert himself for the good of the service in which he has engaged and for the welfare of the tribe placed under his superintendence; that the word emolument as applied to his situation is but an agreeable name for plunder or unlawful exactions, he stands secure against all solicitations and assaults.

There is another class of agents who enter the Indian service without fixed determinations to honestly perform their duties, but really for the purpose of enriching themselves. Given appointments in consideration it may be of labor performed in the interest of political parties, or possibly at the instance of influential friends, they seem to put off and securely pack away at their homes their moral and religious convictions, with the intention of returning and again assuming them when they shall have accumulated fortunes. They seek to commit and conceal crime if by so doing they can acquire money. The avenues of fraud open to them are many, and are so loosely guarded that they can be traveled without much fear of detection. Both the Government and the Indians are at the mercy of these men. The former has no effective system by which their offences can be brought to light, and the latter are too ignorant to understand the meaning of their dubious practices. They can choose either of the two to proceed against, or can operate upon both at one and the same time. As a question depending only for its determination upon the material interests of the two parties, the tribe offers the best point of attack, since its losses would not be of serious importance, while the Government must replace all amounts stolen. If the agents, through a wrongful enumeration, receive for distribution more stores than are allowed the Indians under existing regulations, and appropriate the excess to their own use, or convert it into money for their own benefit ; if they base profitable private bargains upon official agreements, either in the award or fulfillment of public contracts, they draw from the substantial wealth of the United States, because they take from the treasury that which must be replaced by taxation. But the majority of Indian supplies are intended for consumption. They are eaten or worn out and yield no resulting profit. It is a matter of little moment to the tribes whether or not they are cut short upon their promised subsistence in case they dwell in a region abounding in wild meat, nor whether they receive few or many blankets if robes can be easily obtained by them.

The experienced agents take this view of the subject. They perceive that the food and raiment furnished, are not used to sustain labor, nor expended in production ; that they do not assist to fix upon the tribes more civilized habits. Their crimes then in keeping back parts of those classes of annuities or presents, do not present themselves in their real magnitude. They are also conscious that money payments to Indians, especially to those undomiciled, and the teachers, mechanics, farmers and laborers employed for their instruction, in accordance with treaty stipulations, are of slight advantage in promoting permanent improvement. If then they can by a skillful rendition of accounts make forced vouchers support asserted disbursements ; if they can by carefully prepared rolls of mythical employés, or of persons actually serving but at a less rate of monthly compensation than that reported and allowed by the Government ; if they can by such or similar falsifications enrich their pockets, they are not in their judgments guilty of great enormities, as they have not inflicted serious injury upon third parties.

He who attempts to soothe his conscience by reflections of this nature, has made considerable progress down the slippery inclined plane which terminates in moral depravity. He would be willing to confess that by solemn contract with the Government, the Indians were entitled to the money and goods he had appropriated, but his argument runs in this wise : " They would not do the Indians any good, and I might as well have them as to see them thrown away. I have not stolen from Government, but have merely saved that which the Indians would have wasted."

It would seem that the conscience which could be quieted by this fallacious reasoning, too thin even to be termed sophistry, had lost all power of reproof ; but words of like import are sometimes heard in palliation of offences. Could we discover the questions which engage the mind of its possessor they would probably resemble these : " Can I hope to conceal my action ? Can I do this thing and escape punishment if detected ? " Such an individual has passed, if indeed he has not always been in advance of, that period of hesitancy when inquiries are made after this manner : " Can I honestly give this contract to my friend who engages to fill it at the figures of the lowest bidder, and to liberally reward me if I will befriend him upon this occasion ? I have complied with the strict letter of the law. I have advertised for proposals. I have secured a fair competition. Neither the Government nor the Indians will experience loss if I accept the offer, and I shall be materially benefited thereby." He has passed, we say, beyond the childhood of his crimes when a whispering conscience can cause him to linger before taking an advancing dishonest step, and he is only checked in his course by a dread of worldly punishments. As chance favors him he becomes either the corrupt servant or the swindling guardian. The money of the Government and the stores of the Indians are alike subject to his avarice.

But where are the evidences of the past or present existence of frauds in the Indian service ? Upon what established facts are the insinuations contained in the few preceding pages based ? Pertinent questions and difficult to

be answered. The courts of law have not busied themselves in attempts to establish the crimes committed in
that Bureau. Agents are allowed to withdraw or are removed from their positions on suspicion of guilt, and are
not often subjected to searching investigations. They are
also frequently succeeded by others for political party considerations, after a brief tenure of office, before belief in
their ill conduct is generally established, and are never dis-
turbed in their retirement.

It would be very difficult to bring them to justice even
if seriously attempted. The system under which they
transact business is favorable to the concealment of official
corruption. Receiving large quantities of stores for distribution, they issue directly to the tribes, and support their
action by the signature or rather the pen mark of the chiefs.
Should they distribute only a portion of the supplies received, they could if they chose cover the pretended issue of
the entire quantity without perplexity, for the Indians in
their ignorance will usually receipt any paper presented to
them upon simple request. The latter know not the value
of the articles given them. They are unable in most instances to compute amounts, and few have any positive
knowledge of measurements and weights or the shares to
which they are entitled under the instructions of the Government. The agent too holds over them the rod which
will enforce acquiescence, since he is able to withhold supplies until they accede to his demands.

What better opportunity could a dishonest person wish,
or what greater temptation could a feeble-minded one have,
than is here presented ? With no one present who could
bear testimony against him except his confidential clerk,
he can deal out from his well filled store-house the whole
or a proportional part of the goods which should rightfully
be turned over to the tribe, and then can by simple arithmetical calculations, make his official return to the Depart-

ment in such manner as may best suit his purposes. The receipt rolls signed by the chiefs support his abstract of issues, and he has in his possession the evidences of a legally executed transaction, which cannot be opened for investigation, except upon very strong averments of fraud on the part of white people, none of whom have personal knowledge of the proceedings.

But what shall be done with the stores converted to private use? They may be disposed of in various ways. They may be secretly conveyed to a distant market or often sold in the vicinity. They may be used to cover a subsequent issue, and receipts for goods never delivered be passed for a consideration to a contractor. It might be more convenient to receipt in excess in the first instance; to take at the hands of the contractor furnishing supplies yearling cattle, instead of the heavy beef demanded by the Government, and deal out the same as fat oxen; also to take like action in regard to other articles. The shortage can be made up during the season and none will be aware of the frauds, excepting those participating in the profits; and made up thoroughly too without an entry on the page of profit and loss, or without a single submitted statement of gains and wastage in issues. It is a curious fact that contractors uniformly furnish good stores and that the transporter always delivers a complete and undamaged cargo. Unavoidable loss "by the act of God or the public enemy" seldom occurs. We have heard of complete destruction by fire, but an uncharitable public immediately charged the agent with arson.

When concealment is so easy of accomplishment, none but the most careless of blunderers would be in danger of exposure, unless the partners of their crimes should divulge the joint wickedness; and it is not therefore to be wondered at, that the courts should not be called upon to determine questions of guilt, nor that suspicion is so frequently framed upon a knowledge of actions which, trivial in themselves, are considered of questionable morality under the circumstances.

The prevailing belief of the hitherto wide spread corruption within the Indian Bureau is not based upon positive evidence, and yet it is as firmly impressed upon the public mind as a belief in the existence of the Indian himself. In high and in low places the opinion is openly proclaimed without contradiction. A western senator in his official place said but a few years since : "I believe that more than one half of all accounts that have been sent in for the last ten years from the Indian country have been fraudulent—more than half of the whole amount have been manufactured."

Said the Chairman of the Senate Committee on Indian Affairs, who warmly supported the peace policy of the late administration : "I believe there are voucher thieves still. There are men who still cheat in the value or number of the cattle they sell to the Government. There are men who still cheat in transportation contracts. So great a service as this, extending over so large a territory, is exceedingly difficult to purify effectually; but I believe there has been a purer administration in this respect during the past year or two than heretofore."

In the towns and small cities of the plains, the agent though eminently respectable, is supposed to hold a lucrative position simply because he has what are termed chances. He is called moderately economical if he can save from five to ten thousand dollars yearly out of his salary of fifteen hundred. The constant allusion to the Indian Ring and its reported swindling operations, is bewildering to the stranger, and he imagines its existence in some huge invisible Briareus which stretches its one hundred hands over the whole western country, manipulates all officers of the Indian Bureau, defrauds the Government and robs the natives.

But if this universal belief in corruption is not based upon positive evidence, there is much of a circumstantial nature to sustain it. The frequent and speedy transition from poverty to opulence, on the part of those engaged in the Indian service, offers the argument which many use to uphold their opinions ; and indeed one is forcibly impressed when, passing through some of the western cities, he ascertains the former occupation of those who wear soft raiment and live in luxurious palaces. The reports of strange proceedings which are spread from many of the agencies, the eagerness manifested to secure Indian contracts at figures below paying prices, the silence of those charged with guilt, and the boastful confessions of those who claim to have profited in some slippery speculation, the complaints of the Indians themselves who seem to have an established faith in the dishonesty of the whites who feed them, and perform their labors, all indicate that there are and have been grave abuses which require correction, and that the servants of the Government have and still are taking illegal advantages.

Whether these abuses are as grievous and common as the careless commentaries of the people of the West would lead one to suppose, may be doubted. That people are very imaginative. They are harsh and uncharitable in their criticisms of official action, and they are apt to misconstrue personal intention in private life. I would not affirm that this peculiarity has become a fixed trait of character, nor on the other hand that it is the result of a general misunderstanding of motives. The cause of its prevalence might be attributed to the unsettled condition of society, and the speculative spirit which pervades all classes of business. It might also be sought in a slightly diseased moral organism, which is prominently displayed in Indian matters. The West has not that high appreciation of the sacred rights of the natives which is manifested on the Atlantic coast. It has about the same idea of their virtues and vices which the east entertained a century ago. Ever since the formation of the earliest board for the direction of Indian affairs organized in Spain in fourteen hundred and ninety-three, to control commercial regulations with the natives of America, there has been an inclination to derive profit through Indian trade and management. Those who come in contact with the tribes experience a desire to share in their bounties or in some way reap the full advantages of the situation. Besides, the West, though rich in expectations and imaginary prospects, is very poor in reality. A large Indian appropriation is a golden egg which measurably relieves the pressure of poverty and assists to build up the waste places. Next to a prolonged war a vigorous peace policy is most beneficial in a pecuniary point of view. The temptation to serve the Government in its work of Indian civilization becomes, in the absence of other remunerative occupation, irresistible, and many citizens, who can command the means and influence, seek to participate in the labor. Competition to secure favor, so profitable in success, creates hostility between individuals, which gives rise to wholesale accusations and recriminations. It has been remarked that in some of the territories the most spotless character was subject to malignant attack. This is doubtless the opinion of the eminent and philanthropic gentlemen who composed the late Indian Board, and also of many of the sacrificing missionaries who have been most wickedly slandered. Careless in expression, rather heedless of evil report when it does not affect business interests, and then most eloquently vindictive ; liberal, hospitable, energetic and enterprising, the people who dwell upon the frontier or near to the Indian country, are inclined in some degree to build their statements of facts upon imaginative theories, and many of the stories of fraud which are repeated may be but the baseless fabrics of their visions.

If however this mass of floating rumor contains but an inconsiderable element of truth, the fact of its existence compels a painful inference. A sign of demoralization is betrayed by a people who originate and spread abroad unfounded accusations against a class of its citizens. It is more than probable that where many Indian frauds are charged there is an inclination to commit them when opportunities are favorable, especially when a charge of that character does not detract from the respectability of the proclaimed offender, as it does not seem to do in the west. Those who manufacture reports and those who busy themselves in disseminating them are very likely prepared to act as they accuse others of acting, when they may be surrounded by similar circumstances. That society is in an unhealthy state in regard to morals which confessedly believes and yet smiles at such rumors ; which can receive into its confidence at the termination of official transactions, the Indian agent or contractor, whose evil practices it has published with a thousand tongues. It shows by its conduct that it is influenced by a dishonest policy, or that its moral sentiments are somewhat blunted. Though sound it may be in its judgments of those matters which concern individual citizens alone, ready to condemn and ostracise any of its members who wilfully defraud or commit injury upon the whites, it not only throws the mantle of charity over those of its members whom it charges with robbing the Indian, and through him the Government, but receives them with favor and invests them with power. The conclusion is inevitable whether reports are true or false, that the West, far from being the valuable censor of business proceedings between the Government and the tribes which its position would enable it to assume, is either culpably interested in, or indifferent to, peculation in the Indian service.

This unfortunate condition of sentiment, so pernicious

to right conduct on the part of that large number of citizens who measure latitude of action by public opinion, and who engage in some capacity or other in the work of furnishing and distributing supplies, has been developed during many years of Indian mismanagement and abuse. It cannot be expected to correct itself while the opportunities which have allowed it to grow continue, not only because misappropriation is excused or tolerated, but for the further reason that those who reap the advantages exert sufficient influence to bend public opinion to their will. As long as the tribes occupy present local relations to the people of the West and are the recipients of large Government bounties which are dispensed under present existing regulations, contractors and freighters of Indian supplies will cheat or demoralize weak-minded agents, and will enter into combinations to effect, by promises of reward or division of spoils, the guilty coöperation of those who are more capable and who intend to honestly perform their duties. The only measure which can purify the service, in case it is continued under present existing rules, is the substitution of men of known integrity and capacity, of untiring industry, of moral courage and aggressive temperament, who will seek out and fearlessly expose attempts at corruption, in the place of the incompetent agents of the past.

The inspecting system adopted a few years since is a futile endeavor at purification or reform. Unless the inspectors can personally number the Indians who are fed at the agencies, unless they can personally determine the quality and quantity of supplies received, unless they can personally verify the pay-rolls and pass a skillful judgment on the value of the labor rendered, unless they can personally witness issues of stores to Indians, their inspections are but a formal and meaningless procedure. All this cannot be accomplished without constant presence and ceaseless vigilance. The numbers of the uncivilized tribes present at agencies vary at almost every issue, and sometimes large bands are absent therefrom and do not receive subsistence for a period of many successive weeks. The pay-rolls' always contain as many names as the law and appropriation allow, whatever may be the number of assistants and employés actually retained. The issue of stores may be cut short at any time, and the savings disposed of by an agent, before danger of detection can arise through an official verification of amounts on hand with reported amounts.

It might be suggested that an inspector could obtain information upon such matters other than that which his observation would furnish him. But should he consult the attachés of an agency, or the few citizens in the vicinity, he would find them wonderfully ignorant. He would not, if he understood the character of the Indians, place credit in the complaints which they might make, for they uniformly express themselves as dissatisfied. Their regard for veracity is very well displayed in the remark of a distinguished chief against whose people another tribe made complaint of unjust action : "All Indians lie. I lie myself, but that tribe greatly excels us in that accomplishment." In the majority of instances they are unable to report the amounts received with exactness, nor do they know to what they are entitled. The grain of truth which an inspector might glean from such a source, could not be separated from the abundance of falsehoods which would accompany it.

Even on the supposition that inspectors will escape the pernicious influences which surround them in their labors, it is doubtful if any system of inspection can be devised through which detection can be made certain, while the agencies maintain present relations to white population or while existing regulations govern responsibility. Purification is a more difficult task than preservation. The

10

attempt to bring honorable dealings out of long practiced fraud and deceit is always an undertaking of vast proportions, and it is doubly so as regards the Indian service, since watching will rarely be able to detect and bring to punishment. The honest, competent, fearless and aggressive agent is the one thing needful, and if he cannot be obtained, all reformatory trials of the present system will prove abortive. He is unquestionably in the market but does not hold himself at the price which Government offers. The annual fifteen hundred dollars would hardly influence him to bear the odium which now begins to be attached to the office in the public estimation, and to battle with those who would use him if possible for their pecuniary advantage. This risk of character, with its attendant labors which he must assume, is not we know taken into consideration in fixing compensation, and yet it is the source of great annoyance and perplexity. If the agent's reputation for probity is not firmly and widely established, a public press finds as a cause for Indian complaints and outbreaks, though without proof, his thefts or evil practices. If he turns from and exposes the offers of contractors, if he resists the blandishments of the corrupt, he will probably be called upon to meet bitter assaults upon both his private character and official actions. The business man of the frontier is a shrewd manipulator of reputations. Through his score of affidavit-men, as they are called, he is enabled to bear about with him in his pocket the record of his enemy's dishonor. Unless the director of a large agency is above suspicion, he will most likely be worsted in the contest and be sent into retirement humiliated and ostensibly disgraced. To subject one's self to such a risk, which in itself would retard many a conscientious and proud-spirited individual from assuming the position of an agent, is worthy of some recompense.

It is not safe to declare that increased salaries would

produce honest servants, but the proposition that they would draw into the field of labor men of a higher stamp might pass unchallenged. The latter is a result particularly desired for the success of the present policy, as it would be an advancement in the direction of integrity and efficiency. The tendency of Indian administration has for many years been toward open and shameless corruption. Could the tendency be checked and a start made in the opposite path, the Indian, if not benefited thereby, would in the public belief have less cause of complaint and less to excuse him for his practiced barbarities, while a most salutary influence would be shed upon public morals generally.

A great government should not be conducted upon the theory that its citizens will serve it from a sense of moral or religious obligation and without receiving adequate pecuniary reward. It cannot afford to accept cheap labor when skilled and enlightened industry is imperatively demanded. That policy which advocates retrenchment in wages, and supports its argument by the fact that it can fill public positions at very low rates, is hostile to a long continued successful management of public affairs. There are those in every community who, devoid of ability or even of a fair proportion of intelligence, are willing to attempt any official employment, whatever difficulties or perplexities may attend it, and receive as compensation any sum which may be offered. The frontier service of the Indian Bureau can be maintained at one-half the present rates of pay, and I am of the opinion that a complement of agents could be found, who would engage to perform the necessary duties without salaries, and would depend upon the so called emoluments for remuneration.

A government should be administered upon principles as strictly economical and business-like, as those which control a private corporation established for the accumulation of property. The latter seeks and obtains practical ability of the character desired, and pays for it according to its market value. It expects zeal, efficiency and integrity in the employé, and rewards him in proportion as he displays those qualities. The men can be discovered and hired who would make competent and zealous agents. The additional compensation which must be necessarily given to secure their services, is not worthy to be considered when attempting to make comparison between the benefits which would presumedly attend their labors, and the results which the agents of the past have accomplished, whether for evil or for good.

An honest administration of Indian affairs is also necessary to the settlement of a question of great importance in Indian management. The friends of a pacific Indian policy, who deprecate the employment of force and believe that persuasion and intercession, accompanied by justice and integrity of action on the part of the whites, would speedily bring about Indian civilization, will stoutly advocate their views until the test of experience has been applied. They continually cry out for reform and attribute past failures to the iniquitous proceedings of Government employés and contractors. It would be very satisfactory to the country at large, could honesty be substituted in the place of abuse, that the important question might be determined whether the crop of folly hitherto produced from government dealing, is the product of fraud and deceit only, or whether it does not partially grow out of the sentimental policy of peace so loudly applauded. That problem solved by experiment and set at rest, Government would be enabled to deal more understandingly with its time-honored wards, might save treasures, diminish crimes and accelerate Indian advancement.

CHAPTER VII.

CAN THE INDIAN BE CIVILIZED?

HAS the American Indian the capacity and inclination to adopt the customs, and receive the faith of the white man?

The Christian denominations of the country have entertained as false impressions upon this subject as our legislators. The belief that the Indian would readily perceive the benefits resulting from our practical civilization, and would gladly accept our habits of life, also that he would be firmly impressed and radically changed by listening to the simple teachings of Christ as conveyed by our missionaries, was formerly well nigh universal. The experience of two centuries has materially shaken that belief, although a large class of our most enlightened citizens still suppose that the Indian might easily and at rapid pace be conducted along that path of development which we have been so long treading, and might possibly overtake us in a brief period of time.

This erroneous opinion may be attributed to several causes. Omitting for the present all speculation regarding the capacity and inclination of the native race to follow the pursuits, and to receive the ideas and creeds of the whites, let us ask why this opinion has been so prevalent among our people.

The European and his descendants are apt to assume, that theirs is the only true civilization in existence, and upon the assumption is based in part the supposition, that other races will strive to attain it, could they be made to

understand its nature. They assume that the benefits and
personal comforts which it bestows, are so immeasurably
great in comparison with those to be derived from all other
forms, and especially from that low type which exists among
the Indian nations, and which they consider barbarism,
that its acceptance by those nations is certain as soon as
they can be brought to a knowledge of its character. They
assume that it is plain and can be readily understood and
grasped by all men. They further assume and believe that
the Christian religion, as professed and practiced by them,
is a simple faith, easy of comprehension by all classes of individuals, whatever their intellectual condition or previous
religious convictions. They forget that European civilization is the product of centuries of determined struggle, in
which the opposing mental, moral and religious convictions
peculiar to a portion of the world's inhabitants contended
for the mastery ; that some of the elements which entered
into it, and by which indeed it is still maintained and propelled, are the distinctive features, the special characteristics, of a single race of mankind.

It is questionable if any nation or people could understand the rudiments of that civilization unless it possessed
in a very marked degree that spirit of personality or of individualism which distinguished the old European tribes.
It is certain that it could not be forced upon any people
which did not have that element of character strongly represented. Our American civilization, which commends
itself to all, as we think, on account of its simplicity and
practicability, is in fact of very complex construction. We
who are born to it, who have received it as a heritage, who
are, according to the rules of the doctrine of heredity, possessed naturally of those qualities from which it springs
and which have been gradually developed through repeated centuries, cannot appreciate the difficulties which
for instance the Asiatic, whether cultivated or uncultured,

would encounter in an attempt to comprehend our institutions.

The intelligent moral practical individualism which pervades that civilization and which is now its great vitalizing principle, is the slow growth of time, and would even require much labor on our part before it could be thoroughly understood. We must pass through a long and tedious study before we ascertain the forces with which that individualism, as formerly existent, has been compelled to contend ; how it has been built up, and how it has been conditioned and modified. Of course it has had a retroactive effect and impressed itself upon the forces brought against it.

Examine this quality as it manifested itself in central Europe nearly two thousand years ago, when the intelligence from the south and east and the Christian religion were placed in conflict with it. It could not endure the restraint of regulated society and broke through all barriers of law.

When Christianity endeavored to calm it, it despised the doctrine of passive obedience and almost discarded the fundamental principles of that faith. The empire which attempted to place it under subjection was subdued and dismembered by its power. It was restless and impatient of restraint. Its highest delight was in absolute personal freedom—a freedom which might properly be denominated license.

The struggle between this quality and its modifying influences, intelligence and Christianity, continued sharp and severe. Through it all we trace gradual intellectual progress and moral improvement; but we find that this same power of individualism, though constantly changing in disposition, remained active and belligerent. At length the seemingly incongruous forces found their proper spheres and balances, and rapidly moved society forward to its present stage of advancement.

But what was the retro-active effect of this quality of
individualism upon Christianity and thought? It is this
action with which we are more particularly interested, that
we may discover if possible whether the ideas and religious
faith, which we consider so easy of comprehension and acceptance, are imbued with those distinctive peculiarities,
natural only to a certain class of mankind. Or to state
the proposition more strongly, whether they are the products of that class undergoing mental evolution in a particular direction. Individualism was the groundwork of
new theories in all the departments of knowledge. It
was the basis of new theological doctrines. As it received
Christianity, as it became intelligent, it forced independence
of thought into theology and the entire mental world. It
demanded the right to apply the test of individual reason
to whatever was presented for its acceptance, and even while
it contended for this right, it measured in its bigotry the
legitimate scope of all action and belief with the rule by
which it gauged its own. This zealous freedom-loving and
power-seeking characteristic of Europe which shattered
political systems, which compelled monarchy to abridge its
pretensions, which built up estate by force, was not content
to place limits upon conduct alone. It sought to impose restrictions upon thought and to regulate belief by prescribing creeds, so that Christianity created as severe conten-
tions as the theory and form of government. The faith
which came out of Judea and for three centuries was extended by reason and persuasion, which was so innocent in its
results upon the subjects of the Great Empire that its sup-
pression was deemed unnecessary, assumed, when it was impressed upon the barbarians of the north, a new, practical
and energetic form. It was not then the cause of peace
and good-will, but the excuse for wars and violence.

Out of the dark ages of superstition and intolerance
there proceeded a Christian faith unlike, to a great extent,

that proclaimed by the early Fathers. It was infused with the life and ideas of those who built it up from its simple foundations.

It partook of the character of our ancestors. Their interpretation of divine will depended entirely upon their impressions of duty, responsibility, and the highest excellence. This religion has progressed or been developed in each succeeding century, has been beautified and enriched by cultivation, and has kept pace with our advancing civilization. It exists among us as an intensely practical faith, shaped by educated conscience, and reflecting the best intelligence of our people.

The effect of this individualism upon thought in its largest signification was equally well marked. While wars were waged and force expended to repress and obtain freedom, the mental powers were employed to decide the absolute and relative rights of man. They were employed to ascertain what rights belong absolutely to the individual, and what duties arise from the social condition. The elements of society were analyzed and the necessities of its welfare and advancement sought. The result of this long and tedious study, attended by constant experiment, is manifested in our present customs, manners, and institutions. They are the products of centuries of earnest toil, in which enters that harvest of practical knowledge, gleaned from the extended research into the laws of the material universe, in which we have been engaged. Our political system, our domestic institutions, our habits of life, are but the perfected results attained by a race true to its early instincts, following its tendencies as if led by an inexorable fate, and working out its civilization and enlightenment by earnest practical labor, and entirely through a process of gradual development. Our religious beliefs, our laws for the government of society, and of political bodies, are all the outward manifestations of the

10*

true mental condition of the people.   Our social practices and observances are spontaneous.   Our customs, domestic arrangements, and all our modes of conducting affairs, whether individual or public, are natural products of certain mental characteristics, varied they may be by relation or circumstance.   Nothing has been borrowed from any source unless homogeneous and readily assimilated.

It is this civilization which has been and still is freely offered to our native race, and which that race is either unable or unwilling to accept.   Has it been refused on account of capacity or will ?   It is possible that both causes have been instrumental in its rejection and for obvious reasons.

An attempt to portray the character of the Indian and his mental and religious condition, would be deemed an arduous task.   Certainly we could not here enter upon a detailed analysis of those subjects.   But we might sufficiently cite the result of observation, and the effect of experiment, to raise grave doubts on the question, whether the Indian's ideas and mental capacities are such as to enable him to comprehend, and his habits and tendencies of that nature to make him wish to receive, the great boon which has been presented.

It must be recollected that this proposition does not involve the inquiry whether or not the Indian tribes are capable of improvement.   Examples may be cited wherein progress has been effected without extraneous aid.   The limited civilization of the village Indians of New Mexico, resulting from the cultivation of corn and cotton, and the practice of utilizing their labors to much advantage ; also from the discovery of the art of adobe making and placing the manufactured articles to practical uses, was an advance upon the estate of the nomadic tribes, which subsisted entirely upon the products of the chase.   Still it did not change domestic institutions or social relations, and was only an improvement in so far as it added to the comforts of life or furnished more easy and certain methods to obtain its necessaries. The civilization of Mexico, which, whatever its origin, was maintained by nations from the north, and which Prescott pronounced equal to that of England under Alfred, and in nature similar to that of Egypt, was masterly in its accomplishments. It did not consist however in individual regeneration. It was built upon force and upheld by cruelty and superstition. The smoke of the human hecatombs ascending from the altars of a savage priesthood, proclaimed its character. It would have drawn within its folds any barbarous tribes or people which might enter the geographical boundaries within which it held sway, and would have quickly subdued and localized them. They would have been placed under it, or at least have been compelled to accustom themselves to its influence, whether understood or not. But the civilization which we hold out is not forced. It is persuasive. It asks as conditions for its acceptance, certain individual virtues, and intelligence, and makes that acceptance dependent upon inclination. In the case of the Indian, moral transformation and mental growth, in a certain direction, are necessary to its reception ; and these modifications, it is expected, are speedily to be obtained by individual effort, induced by appeal and example.

The difficulties to be met with in attempting to civilize the Indians, while tribal influences remained in full force, were discussed in a former chapter. It was there affirmed, that the tribal relations retarded progress, as it perpetuated the barbarous customs in which they had their origin. In the present instance, we intend to remark upon the difficulty which must still be encountered, in the endeavor to engraft our modes of thought and habits of life, upon a nation radically dissimilar to ours, though unimpeded by any antagonistic social systems. Even with the severance of tribal institutions, a great labor must be performed by those who would bring our Indian population to the knowledge and enjoyment of the civilization which our race has worked out, and which is essentially its own.

The white man has misconceived his red brother, ever since the two first met upon the continent. Misjudging his mental powers and his moral qualities, he has viewed him as one having like sentiments and desires as himself, but wanting the knowledge necessary to improve his condition.

The agents of Louis XIII, who offered Christianity to the natives of Canada, and made the ceremony of baptism the only needful qualification of citizenship, were fully as well informed upon the nature of the Indian as the eastern philanthropist, who now occasionally visits the plains and expects to remodel tribal institutions through persuasive promises and gifts.

Said the Indian Commission a few years since, while in conference at Washington : "It is our opinion that if the present peace policy can be persisted in for four years longer, the Indian problem will be placed in a fair way of solution," and it gave as reasons why that policy had not been successful, "the laxity in the enforcement of the laws when the Indians were the complainants and the whites the aggressors," also that the agents and missionaries had been "defeated in their purposes by thieves and robbers who were allowed to live among the Indians." These abuses corrected and slight impediments removed, and the interesting nomad would, it is inferred, be seen clothed and in his right mind, engaged in agriculture and acquiring the virtues of the thrifty husbandman. Such expectations were unreasonable, and could not have been predicated upon a fair consideration of all circumstances.

What qualities then does this American Indian lack, that he is so little impressed by the efforts which have been put forth for his amelioration. He has the same physical properties, the same senses, the same elementary mental powers which we possess, but here the parallel ceases. Although equally if not more skilled in the use of the senses than the white man, he lacks the faculty of abstraction, and consequently his imagination, reason and understanding, are of a very low order. He is almost entirely destitute of the moral qualities, and his religious nature is of that kind which presumes the existence of a Supreme Being, simply to account for facts and occurrences beyond his comprehension. His conceptions of that Divinity are extremely vague and uncertain. It may be one and indivisible, or it may exist in many and antagonistic forms. Whether the Indian is more Monotheist, or Polytheist, or whether his belief is akin to Pantheism, is difficult to determine, and he could not probably furnish much enlightenment if questioned on those points. His Divinity has none of the attributes of goodness, for he, in his utter ignorance of virtues, is unable to imagine their existence. It is only propitiated by substantial material gifts, and may be persuaded to assist in enterprises of the most wicked character.

Like all savage people, the Indian has not the slightest conception of definite law as a rule of action. He is guided by his animal desires. He practices all forms of vice, and even to a great extent those crimes which are pronounced as against nature. He takes little thought except for the present, knows nothing of property in the abstract, and has not therefore any incentive to labor further than to supply immediate wants. Instead of making an effort for moral improvement he strives to strengthen his vicious propensities. He eats the raw liver of ferocious beasts to augment his ferocity, wounds and bruises his person to increase his animal courage, boasts in council of his brutalities, parades them as deeds of approved valor and as examples worthy of imitation.

The brief picture here presented is intended to portray the members of the wild tribes, and is not overdrawn, although they exhibit to us in their superstitious ceremonies and in their councils of state, and even in the hospitalities of their lodges, certain qualities which do not appear to harmonize with the character we have so quickly sketched. It is the manifestation of these traits, such as reverence for the Great Spirit, respect for the dead, affection for those within the family relation, hospitable reception of strangers, admiration for mental endowments, and an occasional display of cunning sagacity and rich imagery of language, which has made the Indian a psychological and metaphysical enigma to many. And indeed to the casual observer of Indian life and manners, our representations would appear paradoxical at best. How shall the seeming inconsistencies be reconciled?

The Indian possesses of course the natural instincts, the general characteristics of humanity, among which is an innate love for kindred and a desire for fellowship. The superstitious observances which attend his mode of worship, if such it can be denominated, the rite of burial, and indeed all religious ceremonies from the sun dance to the exorcism of evil spirits, have been handed down by tradition through countless generations. From whence they proceed, whether borrowed and adapted to circumstances, or whether of native birth and growth, the natural product of the Indian mind, endeavoring to account for existence and cause, cannot be ascertained. So analogous, however, are many of their ceremonies to those practiced in eastern Asia, many centuries ago, so similar are many of their traditions to those long since extant in the old world, that the conclusion is almost forced, that they are in substance of foreign origin. The slaughter of horses over the grave of a relative reminds one of the action of Achilles at the tomb of Patroclus. The act of piercing the ears of children is suggestive of the Jewish rite of circumcision. The conjurations of the medicine man assimilate the sorceries spoken of in ancient history, and the traditions and crude mythology of the Indians, contain much which might be ascribed to the Asiatic pagans.

But from whatever source their ceremonies may be derived, they have become the inheritance of the tribes and have been practiced successive years without variation. They are found to be, when examined, characteristic of those who maintain them, and are attended with cruelty or with a repulsive indelicacy shocking to moral sensibility. Reverence when analyzed becomes a superstitious dread of an unappeased vindictive Deity. The beautiful service of sepulture is an observance repellant to the civilized because of the bloody scenes which accompany it.

The Indian is sometimes called a statesman and an orator. His dignified bearing in council, the beautiful metaphors and rich imagery with which his efforts at oratory often abound, challenge admiration. Language is the embodiment of thought. It mirrors the mind, though it does not reveal intention nor morals. While, therefore, manifestations of the highest excellence which the red man has attained may be witnessed in the proceedings of their great tribal gatherings, no correct opinion of their moral condition can be gained. He is a keen observer of nature, and its objects supply him with figures to illustrate and impress his primitive ideas. Oratory, says a distinguished scholar, seems to have made but little advancement since the days of Homer. If it consists in simple illustration rather than in the employment of abstract terms, the statement is correct, for barbarous and semi-civilized nations excel in the first particular. With the Indian it is an art, the result of study and repeated practice. Few acquire it and they become the leading spirits of the tribe. The maiden speeches of the young chiefs about to assume control of the movements of their people, are generally miser-able failures. After a few years of trial some become fluent declaimers and fervent exhorters. Fortunately for their reputations, their ideas are few and simple, and they can by their labor, be frequently reproduced with increased adornment.

The efforts of years secure a dress which is rich and oftentimes brilliant. Still it must be remembered that before the speech obtains our criticism, it is embellished by the imagination of the poetical interpreter.

We think that a progress towards civilization has a tendency to weaken the charms of Indian oratory. The wild savage is more eloquent than his half-tamed brother. He who has seen him as he comes from the excitement of battle to name conditions of peace, when every word is vehemently uttered, when passion, strangely visible in his countenance, finds vent in words, and in his peerless gesticulation, will agree in this assertion. So also he might do the same who has observed him as he rises in council, flings back from off his shoulders his pictured buffalo robe, shakes back his waving hair, and with a haughtiness more befitting a conqueror, proclaims the fancied wrongs of his race, and defiantly refuses the requests of the Great Father's commissioners. But should the savage be followed from the council to the feast or the dance, the respect which his talents had inspired would be lost, because of the sudden transition from superior dignity of manner to abasement or degradation of deportment. Within the same hour he may be seen carrying himself with proud nobility as he indulges in flowing declamation, or with rude song keeping time to the beating of the tom-tom, while sitting in the dust and filth of camp.

Considering then fairly the character of the superstitious observances maintained by the Indians, also the nature of their mental productions, neither their devout and religious tendencies, nor their arts and accomplishments, are incompatible with that degree of savagery which is destitute of moral principle and the knowledge of abstract right. These deficiencies, together with that spirit of communism which is prevalent among all tribes, and which is due as well to an undeveloped idea in regard to property, as any desire for common ownership, make the reception and understanding of our American civilization very improbable.

Another defect of Indian character which, though it it has not been stated apart by itself, may nevertheless be inferred from what has been said, consists in inability to comprehend a Christian dogma, and even to gain a tangible idea of the simplest elements of the Christian religion. We mention this as an important fact, and thus independently, because it has been the opinion of the Government and public, that the reception of Christian doctrine is the stepping-stone to substantial improvement. Said the distinguished Indian Commission : "The religion of our blessed Saviour is believed to be the most effective agent for the civilization of any people." The establishment and maintenance of Christian missions among the tribes was therefore supposed to be a most necessary requirement, as the conversion of the heathen was the first demand of worldly progress.

We would not attempt to raise an objection to the sentiment expressed in the foregoing quotation, but only remark that the Christian religion, as received by the tribes, does not materially aid in subduing savage passions or in fixing settled habits. That obdurate portion of the Six Nations of New York, which has rejected all the appeals of the Episcopal Church for nearly two centuries, and which now mocks the religious ceremonies practiced by their converted relations, has kept pace with the latter in all respects. Those of the heathen class live in as good houses, cultivate farms equally as well, and are as obedient to civil law, have as much knowledge of the affairs of the world, and are as good citizens, as the latter. The truth is, that the Christian religion is the religion of civilized man. It is a progressive religion and has reached a stage beyond the grasp of the savage. As developed by our ancestors, it is, as we have already suggested, an intense, practical, individual faith, directing the practice of all those virtues which an advanced state of morals makes known.

The Indian has an accommodating disposition as regards a willingness to accept religious doctrine. Like the old Roman, an additional divinity is not objectionable. Many will readily profess Christianity if they believe that material benefits can be gained by so doing. They will reverently engage in prayerful confessions and intercessions, but let misfortune come during the period they are so engaged, let a fire sweep their camp and consume their property, they will, if left to themselves, immediately renounce their new faith. They are very utilitarian in their views, and demand substantial and immediate payment for time and labor expended in any form of worship. A few pounds of bacon will induce them to present their children for baptism, notwithstanding the rite has already been many times administered.

Their convictions, however, whatever may be their professions, cannot be very satisfactory. The doctrine of the atonement would involve them in inextricable perplexity should they attempt to consider it. A rule of duty could not enter the mind of one whose system of morals consisted in following the propensities of his nature. The Indians may practice the forms and give heed to the outward observances of the church, but their religion is in fact their own superstitions crammed into the shell of Christianity. For success in missionary labor among them, that type of Christianity which is attended with the largest share of external forms and ceremonies is the most efficient, and for that reason the efforts of the Roman Catholic church are crowned with more than ordinary prosperity. The Missionary Fathers of the West understand this and sometimes confess it.

While therefore we agree with the late Indian Commission, that Christianity is a wonderful element in civilization, we do not believe that it can be firmly engrafted on the Indian stock. It would produce fruits if properly applied to childhood for successive generations, but the adult Indian cannot accept it, even if he is inclined to do so, and there is no inclination on his part to accept it, unless he can be convinced by some process that he will thereby reap a worldly advantage. The Indian cannot at once grasp a moral truth nor receive a religious conviction, nor can he readily change his wild, roving, idle life and assume habits of industry. He will not and cannot revolutionize his nature, and any essential modifications, which outside teachings and influences shall bring about, will be the tardy results of generations of labor.

The history of experiment upon this continent confirms the views herein expressed. Two hundred years of labor for the amelioration of the red man, accompanied by a large expenditure of money and extending over a vast tract of country, has failed to firmly fix our civilization upon a single tribe. It will not suffice to attribute failure solely to the misdeeds and dishonesty of the whites, for much well directed effort can be discovered, which has also been barren of permanent results. The earlier enterprises of Christian denominations, both on the eastern and western coasts of America, and upheld in some instances by the fostering care of governments, promised well. The Puritan, Moravian, Episcopalian, Quaker, and the different orders of the Roman Catholic Church, were all zealously engaged in prosecuting missionary work. The French founded convents and colleges for the education of Indian children of both sexes. Many Jesuit Fathers gave the unremitting toil of years to bring their converts to the knowledge of civilized life. The work was commenced as early as sixteen hundred and thirty-six, and was pushed forward through many trials and discouragements. The Spanish priests had established eleven missions between the Gulf of California and the Rio Grande River, and claimed to have gathered into the fold eight thousand converts at the beginning of the seventeenth century ; and thirty-five thousand Christian Indians dwelt on the California coast fifty years ago, if Spanish accounts are correct. Eliot, Williams, and their successors in New England, the Moravians in Pennsylvania, the English Church in New York, the Roman Catholic church in Maryland, and so on down the continent until we find the Spanish again in Florida, and the French in Georgia and Louisiana, all engaged in the establishment of places of worship and schools for the youth, and nearly all inviting the adoption of the habits and customs of the whites by example and much practical instruction, should certainly have perfected, for the encouragement of posterity, a tribe or two of enlightened, industrious and self-sufficient Indians.

Turn where you will, however, and nothing of the kind can be found. Remove the agents, instructors, missionaries and white laborers, from a tribe, and it would relapse into barbarism, unless the same had been strongly infused with white blood. The California Indians have been gradually retrograding since the Spanish priests were withdrawn from their midst. The Pueblos have rapidly undergone mental deterioration since Mexico achieved its independence, and neglected its native race. A former generation of them acquired the rudimentary branches of education, but its offspring have entirely lost all such accomplishments.

I find in an old report of Sir William Johnston's his opinion of that small band of Hurons in the vicinity of Quebec. He says, in seventeen hundred and sixty-three : " The Hurons at Loretto are a civilized people." The one hundred and fifteen years which have passed since that report was rendered, have made more noticeable among them the blue eye, and fair hair of Normandy, but it has not made that civilization distinguished for thoroughness. The boy still delights in the practices of the forefathers, and is a clever master of the bow. Indian squalor and idleness are still noticeable features of the village. The Delawares became Christians, it is said, under the teachings of Moravian missionaries. They have made little if any progress then, since that long ago period, and Eliot's ten thousand converts served no purpose, except to adorn the page of history with the recital of a life nobly rendered.

All who have labored long and faithfully in the field of Indian missions occasionally give utterance to disappointment if not discouragement. The Jesuit Fathers often lamented that their toil was so lightly rewarded ; and now the Christian agent and instructor, who entered upon his duties with fond anticipations of a glorious harvest, frequently concludes that he is engaged in the cultivation of a desert. Our people, say they, display neither ability, industry nor gratitude. Unless constantly exhorted and compelled, they sink back into brutish indolence and besotted vice. The churches make no visible impression, the schools languish, and the cultivated fields are abandoned, unless the white man is present to perform the agricultural labor.

Feelings of the greatest depression often come to the most sanguine and earnest of those who have actively entered upon the work of Indian education, and yet for nearly three centuries self-sacrificing people have entirely given themselves up to this discouraging employment.

Their labors have not been in vain. The condition of the tribes longest subject to their influences varies materially from that state of barbarity which we depicted as belonging to those still unreclaimed. The influences combined with other causes, such as friendly intercourse with whites, and the slow acquisition of new ideas thereby, has elevated them very many degrees in the scale of humanity. Still these tribes have not passed through a natural process of growth. They have not been developed. The seed sown may have taken root, but the soil is not congenial, and the plant does not flourish.

We venture to affirm that notwithstanding the vast expenditure of money, by this and other governments, on behalf of the Indians, and the long continued labors of instructors among them in arts and agriculture, notwithstanding the constant appliances on the part of churches of the various methods of imparting a knowledge of Christianity and the useful arts, there is not to-day a single tribe upon the continent which could support itself, and retain the civilization already acquired, if left entirely to its own management and made to depend solely upon its own resources. We intend that the statement shall apply to all tribes, no matter to what extent they have been absorbed by the white race. Let any one of them as now existing, be deprived of the strong arm of Government, and of all instructors from without, and not be interfered with to its detriment by outside forces, and it will, we believe, commence to retrograde. The civilization which has been forced upon them is not natural. It requires constant encouragement, and careful nursing, to make it flourish on the stock in which it has been inserted.

It may be asked if tribes having acquired civilization have not been disbanded and the members of the same merged into the great body of our citizens. No tribe of any importance has ever been disbanded. A few scattered

bands living in proximity to or surrounded by white settlements, have been broken up and citizenship conferred upon
those members who could comply with certain conditions.
Civilization was not, however, promising in these instances,
but the circumstances which surround those individuals
will serve to keep them in the positions in which they
have been placed.

It might also be asked if the Indian raised under the
same influences and allowed the same educational advantages as the white man, would not be his equal, or at least
would not acquire permanent civilized habits, and the
white man's modes of thought. As regards equality it
might be answered that the half breed, brought up in the
Indian camp, is far superior mentally to the full bloods
who have been his constant companions; also that the half
breed youth can be taken from the barbarous associations
of camp, and soon established in the ways of the whites.
Regarding the question whether the Indian would not,
with advantages, gain permanent civilized habits, and the
white man's modes of thought, it might be said that there
have been but few exceptions to the rule that the Indian
educated in eastern schools and colleges cannot, or at least
does not, make any successful practical application of his
education. He seems to have the power to take in or
memorize the contents of books, but he cannot absorb and
assimilate them. He acquires a mass of disconnected facts
and lacks the ability to bring them into relationship or
harmony. His mind cannot digest them, so that he obtains therefrom very little mental nourishment. The
child selected from a tribe by some religious denomination
for the purpose of education, and placed in some noted institution of learning, is, when finally moulded, almost an
object of pity. Not only is his native language fearfully
mixed with the English, Latin, and Greek, and with any
other tongue to which he may have turned his attention,

but his ideas upon theological and philosophical subjects are also lamentably confused. College graduates of the Indian blood are frequently met in the Indian Territory, who are the possessors of fair libraries, but who dwell in filthy cabins and are as indolent, as far as regards the performance of practical labor, as their benighted neighbors. Many experiments were tried in the old colonial days. A large number of the Indians of Massachusetts spoke and wrote the English language. Harvard College has in some instances used all its endeavors to impress its culture upon the Indian mind, but met with absolute failure.

Still, notwithstanding past experience, the present generation of reformers expect by like expedients to revolutionize Indian character in a short term of years, and believe now as those of the past believed, that with the removal of evil white example, the task might be speedily accomplished. The churches still give liberally in men and money, to further this desirable object. Fifty-five years ago they were demanding of Congress an increase of appropriation to civilize and educate the red race, and to-day through their members the same demands are pressed.

In the adoption of the peace policy, it was believed that the proper and certain measures to bring about civilization had been inaugurated. Localization and a generous application of certain influences were to be attempted. The theory was not new, but had been long ago advocated by the New England colonies. After a short season of trial the success of the policy was thus declared by the Commissioner of Indian Affairs : " As a result the clouds of ignorance and superstition, in which many of this people were so long enveloped, have disappeared, and the light of a Christian civilization seems to have dawned upon their moral darkness, and opened up a brighter future." The commission of citizens appointed to coöperate with the administration in the management of Indian affairs said : " The reports of the Indian Bureau will be found to abound in facts going to prove, that the Indians as a race can be induced to work, are susceptible of civilization, and present a most interesting field for the introduction of christianity."

At this time the wild tribes had been collected at large reservations, where they were being fed, and where white men were employed to build for them cabins. Some members of the tribes had been induced to discard the blankets for the coats given them, and had begun to demand wagons and farming utensils. The transition was so marked and flattering, that to those engaged in Indian labor, it seemed that improvement would continue and that triumphant success would be speedily achieved. Eight years have passed, and the lesson of failure so often repeated is again presented for our instruction. That most stupendous system of public pauperism ever yet organized, has totally failed to advance in any respect our Indian population. Those very tribes upon whom it was brought to bear in all its force, are more troublesome, and no more humanized than they were before they became the recipients of the great bounty.

Philanthropists are greatly mistaken in supposing that the Indian who has thrown aside his blanket, who has cut his hair and received baptism, and dwells at his agency in a cabin, eating the rations furnished by Government, is permanently reclaimed, or that he is only slightly removed from the condition of our citizen agriculturist or laborer. In most instances there is but the semblance of an advanced state. Many of the wild and barbarous Sioux Indians of eighteen hundred and seventy-six, had been, two years previous to that time, engaged in tilling soil, were living in houses, had harnessed their horses to the wagon, and had acquired in part the English language.

Still there were members of the roving tribes, generally
11

men of advanced years, who could distinctly perceive that
the Indian must after a period of time, betake himself to
pastoral or agricultural pursuits.   They expressed themselves at the inauguration of the peace policy as anxious to
be permanently located and instructed.   They led their
tribes to reservations, labored with them in council, and
seemingly put forth great efforts to improve the condition
of their people.   When instructors were sent among them
they apparently strove earnestly to form other habits, and
to live in a manner befitting the new existence desired.
But the old life was too firmly fixed to be shaken off.
They were children groping in darkness, were unable to
catch new ideas and to practice constant industry.   As a
result of their endeavors they lost influence, and the
younger portion of the tribes fell away from them and only
visited the agencies to obtain the food which was there
freely distributed.   The conduct and representations of
these men deceived the officers of the Government, who
were engaged in applying its policy, and threw over their
earlier efforts a fictitious show of success.   This will explain
in part why the reports of a few years ago were so highly
colored.

The reasons which suggest themselves to the mind,
after full deliberation, to sustain an opinion that the Indian
is incapable of receiving our civilization, are so manifold
and convincing that the failure of all experiment which
has been undertaken, appears natural and not in the least
a matter of surprise.   That civilization is, as we have remarked, the result of many centuries of mental and moral
development in a uniform direction, and is the old European individualism conditioned and modified by practical education and by a religion which has ever been adapted
to social and domestic relations.   The system of laws, the
doctrine of morals, and the religious tenets which enter
into it, are based to a great extent upon the old Saxon belief

and practice of equality and life partnership of husband and the one wife ; for the character of the marriage tie has shaped our social customs and domestic institutions. Even if it had not reached a point beyond the mental grasp of the Indian, or indeed if he was mentally competent to fully comprehend its manifestations, why should it commend itself to him except on grounds of expediency ? Why should he wish to obtain it unless, because of his complicated relations with the white race, he might by so doing better his worldly estate ? Surely there could be no reason unconnected with the selfish idea that he could thereby gain the necessaries, or possibly the comforts, of life more readily. For, assuming that he is religious and is possessed of a system of morals (although hitherto, judging from our own received views of religion and morals, we have supposed that he has neither) they are so diametrically opposed to those which enter as elements into our civilization that he would not strive to practice the teachings and demands of that civilization from any sense of duty or conscientious convictions.

His religion and his morals allow action which we would deem infamous, which Christianity would mark as deadly sins, and which our moral sentiment would abhor. Construct for him then a house and induce him to live within it, give him our clothing and persuade him to wear it, assist him to yoke cattle to the plow and to cultivate the ground, finally teach him to harvest the crop and prepare it for food, and still nothing is accomplished as regards his improvement, except that he is being taught to lead an agricultural life instead of gaining a living from the chase. He is not civilized in the proper sense of the term, but has only changed his pursuits, and he has been prevailed upon to change them because advantageous to subsistence and comfort.

Let him proceed farther. Influence him to conform

outwardly in his social and domestic sphere to the requirements of our civilization. Prevail upon him to discard all
but a single wife and to be bound to that one by the Christian ceremony of marriage ; induce him to practice in his
household none but civilized observances; teach him the rudiments of our language; place him in church and persuade
him to take an active part in the services, and still he has
not been brought to a knowledge of civilization. He is
still an uncivilized man following the teachings of others,
and cannot advance a step without the aid of his instructors.
In fact, he would fall by the way unless constantly sustained by them. Look at him casually and it is hard to
detect the counterfeit, the skin has been so deftly fitted.
But interrogate him upon an abstract and well settled principle of right ; request his opinion upon some question of
morals to which his teachers have not furnished him with
a categorical reply ; ask him the reason of any law, custom
or observance, and he will be unable to make intelligent
answer.

The civilization of a people is nothing more nor less
than the mental, moral, and possibly religious condition
which that people has attained. Its proofs consist in the
outward manifestations of that condition, from which also
its character, quality, and extent may be determined.
Those visible demonstrations which may be seen in the
prevailing customs of domestic and social life, which may
be witnessed in all the appliances and expedients devised
and resorted to in order that the life may be made comfortable or enjoyable, which may be perceived in modes of
thought, as expressed in law, literature, and art, are but
the natural results of enlightened taste, perception, and
conviction. Our refined household is developed naturally
out of the Saxon home. Constitutional democracy is the
developed idea of the old Saxon individual liberty. American Christianity is the educated creed of a race believing

in individual responsibility, and unity of relation ; of a race whose better sentiments at the time of the acceptance of Christianity accorded with the Biblical doctrines of marriage, of parental government, of filial affection, and with the fundamental principles of Holy writ.

The Indian, too, has for many centuries, been undergoing a process of development. Those tribes which yet retain their nomadic habits, are far removed from the state of savagery which existed in pre-historic ages. The law of motion applies as well to the mental as to the material world. Cause is continually at work, producing effect, and results are discovered in new mental conditions. The peculiar characteristics of the mind are transmitted as well as physical lineaments, and there is a certain growth in that particular direction whither natural tendency influenced by surrounding circumstances invites.

That long imagined primitive state of simplicity, is now believed to have been an almost beastly state of barbarity, from which all races of mankind have in some degree elevated themselves. The red man has advanced slowly, but he has succeeded in building up and establishing domestic and social customs, a most ingenious consanguineous relationship, a system of ceremonials, expressive of long cherished superstitious beliefs, and in fine a mode of life as determined and fixed as that which prevails among white communities. To induce him to relinquish habits and observances, which are but the legitimate products of his mental faculties, brought in contact with the objective world, while following his propensities, in so far as circumstances would allow, and to assume those which are entirely foreign to his nature, as conditioned by thought and reflection, and which he can neither appreciate nor understand, is a change of so radical a character as would seem to require miraculous interposition to effect.

But we have, say the philanthropists, firmly impressed

upon a portion of the native race civilized habits, and it is zealously following civilized pursuits. We have succeeded in bringing it out of heathen darkness, and have implanted sound Christian doctrine.

It is admitted that the semblance of our civilization has been produced in certain instances, where the force of circumstances has compelled the Indians to rest in permanent and abridged localities, and to take up in a measure the labors of the agriculturist. But to what extent has he been regenerated ? Has natural deceit given way to an innate love for truth ? Has characteristic cruelty been displaced by the dictates of educated humanity ? Has the desire for retaliation been supplanted by a love for justice, license for the unchangeable forms of law ? Has ignorance and habitual indolence succumbed to intelligence and industry, and does zeal and activity mark the newly acquired efforts at reform ? Remove from those gardens the white laborers who have been so long engaged in their cultivation. Let the plants, which have been so carefully placed and tended, be left to themselves, and then ascertain how long they will remain unchoked by weeds—the natural products of the soil. Ascertain, then, how deeply rooted are the new beliefs and practices, and what length of time will be required to corrupt the ordinance of baptism, and the ceremony of the mass.

But, say these philanthropists, compare the conduct of some of these people with those of the whites who surround them and judge which answers best the demands of society.

We reply that it is not fair to conclude from the comparison of a well disposed Indian and a depraved white man, that the former excels or even equals the latter in civilization. The former follows example and endeavors thereby to attain to a higher plane of existence, while the latter purposely discards virtue, although he has a knowledge of its principles and wickedly pursues vice. If the former had the same intelligence, the same insight into truth and morals, which the latter possesses, he would soon rise in the scale of humanity, and become a social ornament in the western population. What then has been accomplished by all the labors which have been put forth to improve the native American race ? The question can be viewed from two stand-points, which are, what advantages has Government derived from those labors, and to what extent has civilization been pressed upon the Indians ? Considered from the first view, it might be briefly stated that Government has been profited by the conversion of many of the tribes from turbulent into peaceful communities, but has paid lavishly for the change.

The other aspect requires much study and reflection before it can be comprehended, and even then much unsatisfactory speculation must be indulged in, for we cannot definitely determine whether the progress which certain tribes have apparently made, is firmly fixed and will become the foundation of further advancement. However this may be, it must be admitted that the changes in Indian life and manners which have been effected, have proved the salvation of that race, for stern necessity decreed that it must either submit to them or to extermination.

But here another question arises when considering the cause of change, and that is whether progress has not been as much the result of circumstances, as of the expensive instruction furnished. This also will remain matter of opinion, as arguments, presumedly based upon both fact and theory, are not wanting to the advocates of either side of the issue. But in the present discussion, we might concede that improvement has been entirely due to the fostering care of the Government, and to the exertions of the teachers in arts, religion, and morals, for the inquiry con-

cerns the ability of the Indian to become a thoroughly
civilized member of the community, whatever influences
may surround him, and we wish now to arrive at some
conclusion as to the point in civilization which the most
gifted tribes have reached.

The Indian Bureau makes a classification of the tribes
as follows : civilized, semi-civilized, and wild. It places
those which are permanently settled in the first class,
those which are not yet supposed to be definitely located
and have not altogether abandoned the chase in the second
class, and those still wandering and subsisting on wild
game, in the third class. | In its opinion, a community
which had ceased to lead a nomadic and predatory life,
which had fixed its abode, and betaken itself to agricultural and pastoral pursuits, which in part practiced the
observances of Christian sects, and which refrained from
the commission of robbery and murder, would probably
be considered civilized.

The Indian Bureau illustrates its arguments for a continuation of past Government action, by a reference to
these and others more improved. Said the Commissioner
in his annual report of eighteen hundred and sixty-eight :
" Now, if the laws of God are immutable, the application
of similar causes to each of the other tribes under our jurisdiction must produce a like effect upon each. If the
Cherokees, Choctaws, Chickasaws, Creeks, and Seminoles
are civilized, and advancing in development, so will be the
Cheyennes, Arapahoes, Apaches, Kiowas, Comanches,
Sioux, and all our other tribes, if we will only use the
means, in their cases, that have been so wonderfully successful in the first named tribe."

This is simply begging the question of the possibility of
Indian civilization, and christianization, and accepting a
very narrow definition of the meaning of those conditions.
In truth, those tribes have only reached the beginning of

civilization,.however faithfully they may copy some of its practical manifestations. Behind the surface there lurk the inclinations and paganism of their forefathers, which circumstances have repressed but which instruction has not eradicated. Men there are among them, some white, a few red, and a few tinged with negro blood, who seem to fairly represent the intelligent American, though no independent opportunity has yet been offered them to show the true tendency of their mental operations. The great mass may be said to be in a transition state, without definite opinions or ideas upon a single abstract truth. It is the pauper element of the United States living to a certain extent upon Government bounty, whether bestowed as annuities, as money under treaties, or as subsistence.

The condition of the Cherokees has been alluded to in a former chapter, wherein it was shown that all their schools and public institutions were maintained without any pecuniary assistance from them, and it might be stated that the success of those institutions depended upon a continuance of aid. (Civilization as it exists among them is maintained by outside influence, and has not yet taken sufficient root to allow of the withdrawal of Government interference.

No one would be prepared to say, that by constant practice for a long term of years, the newly acquired pursuits and the forced systems of education would not become permanently fixed, should all foreign supervision be removed and even former situations be revived. Children raised to certain habits of life, are apt to retain them if influences are favorable, notwithstanding the nature of transmitted tendencies and character, and the qualities of the mind are conditioned by surrounding circumstances. After a few generations of careful training the Indian might not only conform of his own will to the observances

11*

which mark our social and domestic institutions, but might possibly have similar ideas, regarding external nature, might pursue the same processes of thought and indulge in the same mental reflections as those which characterize the descendant of the European. Not until this vague supposition becomes reality, will he become thoroughly indoctrinated with our civilization. Not until this wonderful transformation is effected, will he fight the battle of life energetically, vigorously and successfully, with his European neighbor, who pursues, as it were by instinct, what he must follow by another's guidance.

The civilization of the Indian is not yet in any particular an accomplished fact. The labor which has been expended in his interest, with all attendant circumstances, has in many instances produced this result, viz : the substitution of some of those customs through which we earn our daily bread, and make comfortable our settled homes, in place of the Indian's former mode of gaining subsistence, and as a consequence those rules and regulations which necessarily govern the new state have been in part accepted. He is tamed, he may be civilized, but he has not by any means acquired our civilization.

CHAPTER VIII.

HOW CAN THE INDIAN BE CONTROLLED AND IMPROVED ?

GOVERNMENT must still exercise a long-continued control over its Indians. That population is now increasing, and it has not materially decreased during the past two centuries. Its progress in civilization has been so tedious, that we may safely assume that many years must elapse before it will be competent to entirely care for itself, or satisfied to live harmoniously under our laws.

The question of Indian treatment has become more important than formerly, for the reason that, western territory far removed from white settlements, is no longer available, and consequently the aborigines must necessarily come in continued contact with our citizens. The latter cannot be restrained from mingling with the former while relations are peaceful, and they will demand and are entitled to protection in seasons of hostility. The proper means of Indian education and advancement is no longer therefore a problem for the philanthropist only, but it becomes one for the practical law-maker also, since through these means must the quiet and safety of the western settlements be sought. Henceforth the United States must labor to improve the Indian as well as to localize him, and abridge his territory. Under present circumstances it is of vital importance that his disposition and nature be so transformed, that he may be induced to quietly live in the neighborhood and peaceably follow the pursuits of the whites.

All former legislation and all past treaty proceedings
were to a great extent based upon the idea that civilization
could be speedily enforced by instructors under a carefully
restricted intercourse between the two races. The old
policy, in so far as it concerned Indian advancement, was
built upon the belief that tribes kept apart by themselves,
could in the course of a few years be induced through persuasion and material aid, to permanently adopt civilized
habits.

Jefferson's ideal Indian nation, Calhoun's northern and
southern reservations, were conceived in this belief. But
we have endeavored to show that our trade and intercourse
laws and the treaty system pursued, which practically excluded virtuous example, preserved tribal structures and
destroyed individual responsibility, have not been beneficial to the Indian and have in many respects been pernicious to the country. We have endeavored to show that the
large amounts of money expended in the execution of the
past policy of the Government, have yielded little fruit of
the desired nature, but on the contrary have encouraged
and produced wide-spread corruption among a portion of
our citizens. We have from the outset borne in mind the
fact, that the majority of that class who have labored to
educate and Christianize the Indians, attribute the meagre
results of their efforts to a laxity in the execution of the laws.
They approve the theory of the past policy of the Government. Keep faith with the red man, they constantly exclaim,
and remove from his association all evil disposed white people, and his speedy civilization is assured. It has been answered that circumstances did not permit the rigid enforcement of the laws, that it was impossible in the very nature
of things to faithfully execute, on our part, the treaty
promises made ; and we have also attempted to find the
difficulty which has been met, in the unwillingness of those
who have been invited to be taught, to receive the instruc-

tion persuasively extended, and their incapacity to understand or appreciate it.

The old idea, whether or not begotten in error, must be
abandoned because of the impracticability of even attempting to keep the races separated. Definitely established
Indian settlements in localities contiguous to white population is imperative, and instruction must be imparted under
such circumstances. In future a treaty or contract system
cannot be maintained. Many provisions of the statutes
for the regulation of trade and intercourse will become ob-
solete, and the members of the tribes must be made personally responsible to the criminal law of the country.

These modified relations were recognized, in part, by the
authorities several years since, when a determined effort
for civilization was undertaken by the inauguration of the
Peace Policy. Every red barbarian in the land was invited
to accept support from the Government, and to learn at
his leisure the blessings to be derived from permanent residence and agriculture. A radical and immediate change
in Indian life was expected, such as the new situation required ; but sufficient comment has been made on the system and its results to show that the scheme has disap-
pointed its founders and supporters. This experiment may
be considered as an extreme test of the possibility of effecting Indian civilization under the conditions of tribal seclusion and through mild persuasion. Unless some new
method of Indian control and treatment can be discovered,
the disturbances of past years will continue indefinitely.

The people demand that some system be devised, and
put in operation, by which our Indian population can be
permanently located, governed and improved, and that, too,
quickly, that the development of the country may be no
longer retarded, and that the safety of citizens may be no
longer put in jeopardy.

It is easier to criticise action than to discover expedients. It is much easier to theorize than to furnish suggestions suited to circumstances. Still the experience of the past helps to solve the questions of the future. We should form a correct opinion of the results necessary to be attained, and then enforce such action as will soonest bring them about. And not only should we ascertain the imperative claims of the near present, but should strive to gain an idea of the far distant relation of the two races to each other, from the study of experiment and natural tendency.

It is well known that no portion of the Indian population can much longer maintain itself after its old customs of life, for wild game can only be found in sufficient quantities for its subsistence in small sections of the country. It is well known that it is impossible to improve the Indian while in a nomadic state, and that in such condition he is a constant source of menace to pioneers, and to the frontier settlements. It is also well known that much of the country now rendered insecure and unremunerative because roamed over by irresponsible tribes, is sought by our citizens for occupation, and that it is desirable that routes of travel be opened through the same which can be safely journeyed over by the public. In fine, it is well understood that imperative necessity and the interests of both races demand, that the entire Indian population shall be permanently located, either individually by tribes or collectively, and that it be compelled to conform to the laws of the country. It might also be stated as a fact, that this population must be compelled to work for its food, which must in future be largely gained through agricultural toil, for neither charity, gratitude nor justice, requires the Government to feed it in idleness, and its own well-being and prosperity calls upon it to labor for its own maintenance and support.

The questions which arise for determination are these : By what process shall the tribes be localized ? Should they be placed upon a single large reservation, or upon scattered fragments of territory ?   How shall law be established over them, and how can they be made self-supporting ?   These are questions of primary importance, and each relates particularly to those bands still devoid of decidedly permanent habitation, although some of them may be in temporary occupancy of tracts of land.   The questions of control, of compulsory labor, and of improvement, are pertinent to every tribe within our borders.

The subjects must be looked at in their true aspects. No false sentiment based upon imaginary rights and wrongs incident to past treatment, should be allowed to have weight in the formation of opinions.   That old benevolent idea of original landed proprietorship should be entirely discarded, for whatever equity it may contain, more than the market value of the territory will doubtless be consumed in efforts for Indian amelioration.   Circumstances should be viewed as they actually exist, and the welfare of both races taken into consideration in framing decisions.

And first, what course should Government adopt towards those irresponsible tribes which are alternately in a state of pauperism or pupilage, and open hostility : which occupy at times large reservations, where they are subsisted in idleness, and then upon the return of summer renew their nomadic life, and set all laws at defiance ? Shall a system depending for its success upon the inclination or desire of the Indians themselves be still pursued ? Experience teaches that many thousands of dollars must be gratuitously expended for every man, woman, and child within such tribe, independent of all cost of the police regulations necessary to be maintained for a long term of years, before it can be flourishingly localized.   The crimes and murders which will be committed during the period, might also be placed at a high figure, but are too greatly subject to contingencies to be approximated.

Shall force then be used ?　Not unless a saving of blood and treasure can be expected, and the ultimate good of the Indian race thereby subserved.

A short time since it was announced "that it was cheaper to feed the Indians than to fight them." Be that as it may, the feeding process does not seem to diminish wars, nor has it apparently improved Indian disposition or estate. Force is now employed to resist attack, and is stayed when the enemy ceases to slaughter. The Government merely strives to defend itself against its rebellious children, instead of correcting them through any form of coercion. Is it not the duty of a kind parent or guardian, to exact by adequate compulsion correct action on the part of the child or ward ?　The welfare of the Indians—the wards of the Government—demands that they be permanently established in residence, and such is the interest of all parties concerned. Why not, then, if practicable, place them and keep them in proper localities ?

The doctrine of force seems at first sight harsh as well as extravagant, but it is necessary to put it in practice if entreaty is a failure, and it might be made to appear that the thorough application of that doctrine would prove humane and economical.

The sooner the Indian can be compelled to select his abode and be made to understand that it is definitely fixed, the sooner will he be induced to turn his attention to agricultural labor. A roving tribe, which has been fed and instructed in form at its agency during the cold season, but which moves its lodges, and deserts its cabins, for the purpose of pursuing the buffalo as soon as the weather becomes favorable, and indulging its wild nature, cares nothing for the instruction offered and cannot be induced to interest itself in any kind of manual toil. It will continue the same lawless and troublesome mass, as long as there is game to feed upon, or while the border inhabitants can be made to contribute to its support. But place that tribe under the care of a controlling force ; let it be made conscious that it is obliged to remain at the agency, and that should it break away therefrom, it would assuredly be driven back, and it might become interested in the place, desire to construct houses, and to grow fields of grain. The force should be adequate to the emergency, and instructions executed to the full letter. Better for the tribe that it pay the penalty of disobedience in blood, than that it be allowed to triumph over authority.

We have already commented upon the fact that the beginning of true social advancement, that the fundamental law of all civilization, of whatever character, consists in obedience, and self-imposed restraint. A knowledge of abstract individual rights, and a willingness to be governed by the regulations prescribing them, alone preserves well organized society.

Experience teaches that centuries pass before the barbarian, left to himself, learns to restrict action within proper limits. Experiment shows that the Indian race cannot be induced through persuasion, to practice this first necessity of lasting improvement. History demonstrates that tribes and nations can quickly learn self-restraint, through a present controlling external power. A forcible restraint upon the tribes, compelling them to remain within assigned boundaries, would impress upon them the primary lesson of obedience, of which they stand in so much need. The more such force is exerted to execute definite, just and simple regulations, the sooner will they be satisfied to conform to legal requirements.

While considering the value of a thorough police system, capable of restraining the wild tribes within definite boundaries, as an aid in correcting their wandering propensities, and enforcing a lesson of obedience, it might not be amiss to allude to the benefits which would result from

the establishment over them, after compulsory settlement,
and indeed over all the tribes, of a criminal code of laws.
A sense of individual responsibility, and consequently an
idea of relative rights and obligations, is quickly formed
when the commission of crime, or the infringement of
others' privileges, is followed by punishment. Personal accountability for offences to the law of the land without the
possibility of escape, makes peaceful subjects. The vi-
tality of all law depends upon its proper administration.
A penal statute is enacted to restrain the depraved class
of community, and lives only in the execution of its penalties. Far more advantageous for the welfare of a civilized people, that definite law be proclaimed, and fully
carried out, even if it does not answer its demands, than
that a wise system of legislation become dormant through
lack of proper enforcement. An unjust law, maintained
in letter and spirit, will do more for the improvement and
civilization of a semi-barbarous people, than just laws
feebly executed. The imperative needs of the whole Indian population within United States limits is a prescribed
rule of action, simple and just in its provisions, attended
by a power capable of compelling obedience to its requirements.

It is not necessary to impose at once our whole criminal
code, and indeed it might be the part of wisdom to withhold for a time such portions as could not be readily comprehended by the Indian mind, lest it give rise to confusion and groundless apprehension of insecurity. Those
plain prohibitions which the law has made to guard life and
liberty of person, and which forbid robbery and stealth,
require little interpretation to bring them within the
understanding of the uneducated. Let them be extended
over the tribes, and firmly impressed through virtuous
decisions and the rigid execution of the penalties adjudged,
and soon the license which now characterizes the conduct

of the Indian in his dealings with his fellow man, will be
measurably corrected, by a knowledge of and a regard for
the rights and privileges which belong to every individual.
Ten years passed under the corrective influences of our
courts, and their appliances, would free his mind from the
enthralment of ignorance and vice to a greater extent than
a century of persuasion and teaching.   Objections will be
made to a policy of forcible treatment on these grounds,
viz : That the Indian tribes are possessed of certain national attributes, and therefore their internal affairs cannot
be regulated by the Government ; that existing treaty obligations forbid any interference with those affairs, and that
it would be inhuman to put in operation any such system
of forced responsibility, since the tribes have been perse-
cuted, defrauded and in part demoralized, by our fault and
neglect, and since the means sought to be effected can be
accomplished through milder measures.   It is not intended
to again discuss the matter contained in these objections,
but only to show by a glance how untenable are arguments
based thereon.

Necessity controls action, whatever the obligations
created by past promises.   Conditions due to fallacious
judgment and erroneous treatment, which render impossible
the carrying out of previous intention or the fulfillment of
stipulated agreements, must be governed by existing circumstances.   The stern logic of facts pronounces the first objection indefensible.   The fiction which was once admitted,
that tribes possessed sovereignty as nations, did not in truth
create them dependent or independent powers.   Relieved
of our treaty embarrassments, we would deem them, and
without fear of contradiction, part of our subject population.   But notwithstanding those perplexing treaties
which declare our opinions on the question of sovereignty,
is it not undeniable that they are, as now circumstanced,
without that quality in any particular ?

The disposition of the second objection is much more difficult. The nation's faith is pledged to a line of conduct which cannot be carried out, and it has been so pledged because of lack of foresight regarding celerity of national development, and false impressions concerning the ability of the other party to the contract, to fill the situation which it was supposed he would occupy. Accepting this statement of the case, the objection might be met by the plea that the supreme and unwritten law which neutralizes all constitutions and statutes in cases of manifest necessity, which legalizes action taken to meet unexpected exigencies, now places the Indian tribes under the guardianship of the United States even without their expressed consent. The proposition seems wild upon first thought and somewhat dubious after mature reflection, but consider well the relation which this population holds to the Government, as shown by actual attitude, and does it not appear that from the very nature of the position it is amenable to its authority ? Suppose, by way of illustration, that some Indian of a small treaty tribe, injured in person or robbed by his associate, should appeal for the protection of life or for the restoration of property, would it or would it not be the duty of the United States to listen to the complaint ? Under its constitution and statutes it could not interfere. The aggrieved party must seek safety and protection within his own tribal organization, and there he is not able to obtain either. The law of nature and humanity would not turn a deaf ear to his entreaties. He is a subject of the United States to all intents and purposes, if not a citizen, and is entitled to the protection of its courts. Suppose that he is wronged by some member of a treaty tribe other than his own, how can he obtain redress for his grievances ? The declared law of the land gives him none. He must take punishment in his own hand and content himself with such retaliation as he may be able to inflict, else peaceably submit

to his injuries.   As well base moral reflections upon a lie,
as to excuse murder because of treaty stipulations founded
upon the fiction of independence.   The agreements which
could only exist upon a mistaken supposition of facts, are
opposed by public policy and are hostile to public morals.
It is the duty of the Government to protect the individual
members of the Indian population in the exercise of their
inalienable rights, and the execution of that duty necessitates the action of our courts under the guidance of a well
defined criminal code.

But a different answer may be found to the objection.
The facts are supposed to be these : The Government has
made certain admissions and promises in treaties which require it to recognize as Indian territory large tracts of land,
and forbid it to exercise any control over the internal affairs
of tribal communities.   The existence of these treaties is
universally deplored, but no escape therefrom can be discovered, unless through the consent of the tribes, without a
violation of the national faith.   It is admitted that those
tribes should be subject in all particulars to governmental
authority, and the inference that they are really so, is drawn
from the statute which disallows any further contract by
treaty.   The difficulties then, which oppose a change of
Indian treatment, arise from a construction of law based
on action committed through erroneous beliefs.

One exit from the perplexing situation which all would
approve, could it be wisely effected, would be an abolish-
ment of the treaties through a bargain with the tribes.
This, though a strange proceeding, as the latter must
agree by contract to give up the privileges which they
hold by treaty, would soon place the Indians in their
proper status.   But the trials made during the last few
years, are sufficient to convince a candid person of the
impossibility, or at least the impracticability of consum-
mating such a bargain, for at the present time millions of

dollars are demanded for a transfer of land, or the surrender of an imagined vested right, where formerly a few thousand would suffice. The country could not afford to indulge in the lavish and unjust expenditure which a purchase of this nature would involve.

If the object cannot be attained by contract, the only course remaining to be pursued is by an apparent ex-parte action under statute. We say *an apparent ex-parte action,* since the action could only be such in legal aspect and not in reality. Congress must sooner or later determine a remedy. The territory claimed by the Indians must be abridged, and control established over them, and if these necessary measures cannot be accomplished through reasonable purchase and consent, resort must be had to forcible expedients. To what extent can they be applied under strict legal principles ?

The tenure by which the tribes are in possession of land is really of the same character as that by which a private citizen holds his patented real estate. The patent is equivalent to a warranty deed, with full covenants, and such an instrument passes continued complete ownership. The estate belongs to the patentee and his heirs forever. So the tribes have been invested with real property, with power to hold the same for all time. They gain no greater title in law by reason of original occupancy, for their tenure, in such territory, is the same as that conveyed by treaty. Their title and that of the private citizens, in the land occupied by them respectively, does not differ in any particular. In either case the Government holds the ultimate fee, and can exercise the right of eminent domain. If public necessity demands portions of this estate, for highways or for permanent use and occupancy, it can, through the forms of law, take possession of the same, and cancel the holder's claim by paying an appraised valuation.

Analogous deductions follow the further application of

strict rules to facts. It must be remembered that Congress has found that the tribes are no longer in any respect sovereign, and therefore the nature of political relations with them has materially changed. One of the parties to the treaty stipulations has expired and left no successor. Expired too by its own act, since it freely relinquished whatever national attributes it ever possessed in those same stipulations. What becomes then of the treaties ? Do they live and can they be enforced? Admitting that the Government should, if possible, perform its promises, which they contain, how, we ask, can it leave the tribes to their own control?

The moment the latter lost their sovereignty they passed under United States laws. The members thereof at that time became subjects, and Congress could not constitutionally exempt them from the resulting legal accountability, even had it been disposed to do so. They are not children nor people of unsound mind. They formerly constituted nations with which the United States contracted by treaty. They did not fall from that estate into legal imbecility. Those stipulations which promised self-government, expired with nationality, and the members of the tribes are, by strict construction, responsible for their actions to United States authority. They are in theory answerable to the criminal law of the country, and it can and should be extended over them practically. While roving over an extensive territory they are able to elude justice, consequently they must be confined to such limits as will insure their liability to proper jurisdiction.

Similar conclusions might be reached upon any presentation of legally acknowledged facts. View the Indian treaties as past international compacts, or as the deceitful proofs of a deceitful and unnatural policy, their validity as binding unexecuted agreements, either in law or morals, may be seriously questioned.

So much of the remaining objection as asserts that the tribes have been demoralized by reason of the mistakes or negligence of Government, and that they can be quickly improved or effectively controlled by mild and persuasive measures, has been already sufficiently answered in preceding chapters. The conclusion that a system of forced responsibility could not be rightfully practiced would. if the views which have been advanced are correct, be of slight importance. The apparently humane idea that the Indian population is excused from accountability for criminal conduct, because of ignorance or because of wrongs received, is not in accordance with commonly accepted Biblical doctrine. The ignorance of man is a sin, if instruction freely offered for his enlightenment is refused. It will not preserve him from future punishment if he is guilty of wicked action nor will it justify retaliation. Surely that class of citizens which has the welfare of society at heart, and which believes that the decrees of Divine wisdom would not permit ignorance and moral obliquity to palliate offences, could not consistently oppose the establishment of a penal code of laws over our Indian tribes, upon the simple dictates of humanity.

But neither rigid legal conclusions nor the claims of expediency ought to prevail over the conscientious discharge of a duty when it can be fulfilled. Although the specific performance of Indian treaty agreements is manifestly impossible, they have some validity when considered as moral obligations. Those promises of the Government which affect territory and stipulate the continued payment of annuities, may be cancelled for a money consideration, and this mode of procedure appears to be the only honorable course which can under the circumstances be pursued. A fair appraisement of the market price of the land not needed for agricultural and grazing purposes, and a proper estimate of the present value of the annuities, should be made, and the sums adjudged should be appropriated and held in trust to be expended for the benefit and education of the tribes. The necessary legislation might then be passed to fully explain their actual status and to fix conditions for future control.

The Indian opposition with which a policy of enforced restraint would be obliged to contend, cannot be ascertained except by experiment. Opinions on this subject would vary widely, and all would be supported by unsatisfactory speculation. A fair presumption would lead to the supposition that the tribes still roaming would stoutly contest all attempts to keep them within the boundaries of small reservations, and that many of those already settled would resist the officers of the courts engaged in serving process. As regards settlement, much depends upon the extent to which the freedom of the individual is abridged. A measure which forbade the person simply to pass beyond certain narrow territorial limits would be an unnecessary check to liberty and calculated to provoke hostility. Combinations of individuals absenting themselves for lengthy periods, passing the time in wanderings and relying for subsistence upon the indulgence of their former hunting habits, is the proceeding which must be especially guarded against, since it defeats the purposes which are sought to be accomplished. This continues the natural characteristics of restlessness, vice and indolence, and retards any growth of interest in local habitation, and a permanent home. Occasional absence of individual Indians from their reservations, might not impede instruction nor work any injury, and they might esteem a permitted absence a privilege.

There is likewise an opportunity for the display of wisdom, when practically establishing the jurisdiction of courts of justice. Light offences might at first be overlooked and only those persons guilty of grave crimes and misdemeanors be subjected to arrest, trial and punishment.

12

This would bring the action of the courts within the intelligence of those liable to answer for their deeds, and they could therefore act understandingly.

With the exercise of prudence in management as regards such particulars, opposition, if not allowed to prevail at the outset, would soon become weak. The tribes will submit when they feel that a controlling force is exerted to accomplish a definite object and is not cruelly exercised, although it may abridge the freedom formerly practiced.

Inquiries regarding the means proper to be used to promote the education of the Indian population, when confined on reservations, are pertinent in this connection, since upon them will depend largely the vigor and endurance of its determination to resist the restraints advocated. If its necessary wants can in some manner be supplied, it will much sooner be disposed to accept the new situation, and if the comforts of life could also be obtained, a contented acquiescence might finally result. We intend to make but a few suggestions in this connection, and they will be of a general character.

Aid must be extended, but it should be of such a nature as to encourage, if not force, industry. Subjection to law will crush out all vestiges of tribal authority and assist to create individual responsibility. Some additional expedient should be resorted to to break up community of interest and to abolish tribal ceremonies. Then whatever exertions are put forth by the Government, they will be brought to bear directly upon the person, and in this way only can they be made effective. This indispensable requirement of public action should be kept steadily in mind. The agent should be vested with sufficient authority, and granted the requisite power, to enable him to practically discourage all forms of communism. Assistance should in all instances be extended to the individual, who should be made responsible for its uses or abuses. It must be supplied in a variety of forms. The Indian must be subsisted for a time, as well as furnished with domestic implements and educational resources, but conditions should accompany those gifts which are intended for consumption, or as appliances of labor, and attendance be compelled whenever instruction is imparted. The conditions meant are these : That work should be exacted of the person who receives food, and that he should not be allowed to retain such tools, agricultural equipments and household utensils as are provided for him, unless he properly applies them.

By the compulsory measure suggested, we would be understood to convey the idea of the necessity of obliging attendance at such simple educational institutions as must be put in operation to secure mental improvement.

This qualified bestowal of benefits, or rather these forced conditional gifts and advantages, are essential in order to effect the progress of the Indian. The visionary conception that he will voluntarily employ the means placed within his reach to enable him to take up and faithfully pursue a laborious occupation, conflicts, we maintain, with all the teachings of experiment. Instruction and material aid must not only be offered, but the intended recipient must be compelled, in some manner other than by peaceful argument and spoken encouragement, to take and profit by them. In placing restraint directly upon the individual, instead of reaching him through an intermediate tribal organization, the possibility of effecting desired results is created.

Of course the heads of families of a roving tribe must, after settlement, commence the cultivation of the soil, and definite portions of land must be assigned to them upon which they may erect their cabins and establish their homes. Let them understand that much of their food will depend upon their exertions in planting fields and tending crops, and that they will be unmolested in their occupations. Let them be practically instructed and furnished with implements as soon and as long as they are disposed to use them advantageously, otherwise to be deprived of them, and let stringent regulations be carried out, giving but meagre subsistence to the idle and permitting the industrious to reap the full benefits of their labors. Make labor an object by allowing its rewards to increase the comforts of those who expend it, beyond that of their less industrious neighbors by the full value of its proceeds. Assist those disposed to work to prepare comfortable dwellings, and supply them with the furniture and utensils necessary to proper domestic life, and finally let all appliances and means be resorted to which will strengthen the sense of individual importance, responsibility and reliance, whether by encouragement, compensation or punishment, according as conduct merits commendation or reproof.

While this most important lesson is being impressed, a practical understanding of a new mode of life is being rapidly acquired. Rapidly we say, although that word needs qualification. We mean as rapidly as Indian characteristics will permit, for it cannot be expected that natural improvidence and indolence can be mastered without a long and severe struggle. Yet such a course of treatment will produce dual results, each having the same tendency, and both necessary to be achieved before the Indian can be fitted to occupy his destined political position, which is that of citizenship. The first and most essential of these, although its importance seems hitherto to have been greatly overlooked, is a fixed individual accountability to authority, accompanied by a definite comprehension on the part of the person, of his duties and obligations and his legitimate relation to society. The second, and that which has been sought by the Government in all past dealing, is a practical knowledge on the part of the Indian of the habits and occupations which must be voluntarily observed and followed by him, before he shall cease to be a burden, and before he can be invested with political privileges. The former sustains the latter and insures its accomplishment. The latter cannot be permanently secured except through the existence of the former. Every step, therefore, gained towards both results is an advance in the direction of substantial progress.

The compulsory process which must be resorted to, in order to impress that other requisite of true advancement, should be considered. Owing to the indifference of parents in the matter of their children's education, and the absence of any kind of family government, it has been found impossible to secure the attendance of the Indian youth at the schools provided for them. The children, soon tired of restraint, withdraw, and mild inducements to correct the evil have thus far failed. Statistics yearly sent to Washington from the agencies, would make the statement appear erroneous, but it is believed that no portion of the official reports are more calculated to deceive than those which give the enumeration of the scholars yearly instructed. Our statement is true, if allowed general application, and is supported not only by naked fact, but is rendered probable by the very nature of circumstances.

The difficulty should be met in some way, for without the proper application of this measure, the Indian population cannot very soon reach that point in civilization which would suffer citizenship to be conferred. The unnatural mental development which it must undergo before it can rightfully demand the privilege, cannot be effected, except by impressing the minds of its children with wholesome instruction, and fixing upon them different habits than those which have governed their fathers. The great advantage to be gained in supplying the cabins of adults with utensils, furniture, and those articles which are commonly looked upon as household comforts, is that the young, becoming accustomed to their use, will consider them necessities in after years. The parent can be taught to plow, to sow, to reap, and to construct buildings, but cannot be made to unlearn the practices of his youth, and will, unless sustained and restrained, glide back into them. He would not be profited by the study of books, for his creed, opinions and twisted theories, cannot be supplanted. The child takes by inheritance, it is true, but he can be modeled. The course of natural tendency may be changed somewhat, and a second nature, as it were, fabricated. By such action, persevered in for a few generations, might the white and red races be gradually assimilated both in thought and belief. Schools should be maintained, and the children be compelled to attend. Parents must direct it, and the children be encouraged to yield a willing obedience. A rule established to accomplish the purpose, can only be successfully carried out through the instrumentality of the former, and their acquiescence and support must be secured through conditions affecting their interest or desires. The course of treatment herein recommended, should be extended as far as the same may be applicable to the tribes already definitely located. They also need to be taught the lesson of individual accountability and self-reliance. They require prescribed law, and more correct conceptions regarding the necessities and advantages of labor. Treaties should be annulled, a criminal code imposed, the rights of persons protected, and educational regulations carried out. In no other way can tribal influences be overcome, and independence of character established.

The success of such radical measures demands vigor, ability, and integrity of administration, and the results which it is believed would follow, are those which have been desired since the foundation of Government. The great Indian problem, simply stated, is this, and nothing more : How shall the Indian be converted into a law-abid-

ing, self-supporting member of society, and not how shall
tribal structures be preserved, or how shall Indian nations
be built up ? The measures suggested lay hold of the
individual, and bring him out of the darkness, which
tribal influences throw around him. They place his feet
in the path of true development. They allow him neither
to fall back, nor turn aside, and assisting him by advice
and encouragement, they bid him journey on and secure
his manhood.

A strong, efficient force would be required to fully in-
augurate these innovations in our system of Indian management. It might not be expedient to commence proceedings against all the tribes at one and the same time.
The necessary laws might be enacted, and they might be
put in operation among those bands which are hostile or
troublesome. These must be forcibly driven upon reservations, and there they should be forcibly held. While this
labor is being expended, the extra force required to carry
out the measures of control proposed, would be inconsiderable, and its maintenance would result in a saving of money,
because under the present policy the bands, when driven to
their agencies, where they are fed in idleness, deliberate
upon and mature projects for future hostilities, and having
perfected arrangements, go boldly forth to execute them.
Then they must be again met and compelled to promise
peace. Placed at their agencies under the vigilant eye of
an energetic police or military power, and disarmed of all
weapons of war, they would be obliged to check their passions and seek a change of employment. Not until then
are they prepared to listen to proposals for fixed abodes,
cultivated fields, and productive labor. Even if the yearly
expenditure thus incurred is in excess of amounts formerly
paid out, the course will prove economical in the end. If
the measures are pursued with persistent determination for
a short term of years, the tribe subjected to the action will

have reached the position of those already sufficiently advanced to be officially termed civilized, whereas under past treatment, millions of money and decades of years would be required to force it to that point.

Those tribes which are already localized and are ostensibly following agricultural pursuits, would not probably make any decided united opposition to the increase of restraint, which must necessarily follow the introduction of new features in our Indian policy. Part of them have ceased to be a threatening element of our population. An armed force is not required to hold them in check as at present situated, and should a change of treatment compel its establishment, public expense would be augmented thereby. Still, politic proceedings on the part of those engaged in exercising control might avert serious disturbances, although there would undoubtedly be many instances of individual enmity. The actual or near presence of a power able to maintain the peace and execute orders, would be a wise precaution against meditated danger, and that the prudent might with good reason predict trouble even with our most cultivated tribes, in many cases which must arise, is shown by the conduct of the Cherokees a few years ago when they defied the lawful writs of the United States Courts.

Evidently the force at the command of the Executive head of the Government is entirely inadequate to the full inauguration of an active Indian policy of restraint. Prudence and expediency might dictate that it be put in actual operation only among those tribes which threaten the rights and the lives of peaceable citizens, and possibly those still totally unreclaimed. On purely economical grounds, however, we believe that its complete and vigorous enforcement upon our entire Indian population, as quickly as adequate arrangements can be made, would prove beneficial. It must be applied and cannot be indefinitely deferred.

The relative local positions of the two races will not long permit a continuance of past proceedings. Much of the territory now covered by treaty stipulations must be cleared of its incumbrance. Tribal institutions cannot be perpetuated. The Indians must shortly come out from under their baneful influences and unwarrantable protection. They must be fitted by some process more speedy in the production of desired results than the present one, to engage in the struggle for the necessities of life through lawful occupation, else be overwhelmed by opposing agencies. The millions of dollars now annually expended in their behalf in measures of restraint, maintenance and education, might in so far as the money prepares them to become American citizens or indeed intelligent and virtuous subjects, be considered as almost wasted. That portion appropriated in support of the two last named measures may be regarded as the cost of a mistaken charity, or as tribute rather, exacted as the price of peace.

The yearly payment of the entire sum must be continued while the present system of management is pursued, without effecting any great degree of permanent good, and finally force, either for destruction or restraint, must be resorted to. That sum, increased by a small fraction thereof, would, we believe, if properly applied, be sufficient to establish and maintain the conditions of control we have named. Much of it would accrue from the fund created by the equitable extinguishment of treaty land title and of promised annuities, for which the Government would receive an equivalent, and which, sooner or later, it would be morally bound to pay. In reality therefore the gratuitous expenditure would not be greatly augmented. Each year of successful management would diminish the fear of outbreaks, and the force could be correspondingly decreased. Each year of successful management would also, it is believed, firmly impress upon the Indian more correct ideas

12*

of life and duties, and the cost of supporting him would be gradually lessened. Economy and the welfare of both races interested in the issue advise the full adoption of the policy.

Suspicions that a forcible course of treatment brought to bear upon the members of the tribes would produce any determined and united hostility on their part, cannot we say, be reasonably entertained, and yet should there exist a well grounded expectancy that such would be the case, the proper action should be applied, and the necessary preparations made to meet the anticipated emergency. It is worse than folly to continue the present system in all its features. It drains the treasury of the Government, and will do so indefinitely, without bringing about any of the results aimed at, not even preserving friendly relations.

The mistaken notion still prevails, that the Indian population should be concentrated upon one or possibly two large reservations. Sufficient has already been said upon the effect, as regards progress in civilization, produced by the removal of the eastern tribes to the territory west of the Mississippi River. It was maintained that their growth, mentally and morally considered, was retarded and not accelerated by the change, because it deprived them of the example and influence of regulated society. It was also maintained that the collection of 'such large bodies of Indians upon a centrally located and large tract of territory within the United States, would create further disturbances and a variety of legal conflicts, because of the attempt which was being made to erect by the treaty process, a quasi nationality, or at least a subject government of purely Indian constituency. It was affirmed that any such creation of the character designed, could not be constructed and operated, because it would be an anomalous political institution. We shall not therefore speak further of the erroneous practice still persisted in, of transferring bands of Indians from populous localities to places remote from those in which civilization has been established, nor of the dangers to be apprehended from the false measure of concentration, except as allusions to the benefits which it might be conceived would follow a contrary course of action may make it desirable.

After a careful consideration of the objects which it is important to accomplish, the impression that the reservations for the permanent occupation of the tribes should be in the neighborhood of white settlements, should be of very limited extent and many in number, is confirmed. This view would not be agreeable to the inhabitants of States and territories who dislike the proximity of Indians, but the good of the latter has been alone considered in reaching the above conclusions. Contiguous neighborhood would not only afford near example, but would render less difficult the administration of law. Trial by jury ought to be followed, as the constitution requires, and legal practices should conform to those universally existing throughout the country, both that the spirit of liberty might be maintained by common custom, and also that the courts might have precedent to guide action. In order to carry out such usages acceptably, judicial districts should contain a fair proportion of inhabitants capable of serving as jurors in trials. Legal innovations adopted to suit a particular class of the public are dangerous to the permanency of our institutions, and that such must be introduced in order to successfully apply the law to the majority of the Indian communities, might be presumed, if upon them alone is to depend indictment, and the discovery of facts constituting crime.

And here a question arises for consideration :—Whether the United States Courts should alone take cognizance of the crimes committed by Indians on their reservations, or whether the courts of States and territories in which the same may be located, should pass upon them. The former have no inherent common law jurisdiction, but only such as is conferred by statute, and should they exercise sole judicial control, a code of criminal law must be enacted by Congress, intended to apply specially to the Indian population, or at least Congress must declare the common law offences criminal, before its courts can take cognizance of the same. In the absence of treaties and statutes, expressly forbidding it, state courts could now exercise jurisdiction over all reservations, situated within State limits, and this right has been declared by several State legislatures. To obviate, then, the necessity of enacting a special code, applicable only to a small portion of our population, treaties might be annulled, and all prohibitory United States statutes repealed, and thereupon State and territorial courts could exercise the needed control. In such an event, Indian residence should be within organized counties, and in proximity to white inhabitants, who are capable of performing the duties of intelligent jurymen. It might be better, however, to vest in the district court of the United States the sole interpretation of the laws regulating Indian action, and then a simple code of criminal law, which might be comprehended by the Indian mind, could be put in operation, and the Government would continue to retain entire supervision of its wards, until they shall have acquired sufficient intelligence to understand our complex system of judicature and individual accountability. Even then, the tribes must be so located, that resort may be had to a body of citizens, to assist in the administration of justice, both as judges of facts involving questions of alleged offences, and as officers enforcing the mandates of the courts, for unreconstructed Indians would be entirely unreliable in those capacities.

Reservations of great extent are undesirable. If they

are larger than required to permit the accomplishment of the purposes of settlement, they are an evil. The custom of granting a section of territory, or even a tract containing many square miles of land, that the Indians may indulge their propensities to roam about, weakens the effect of civilizing influences. It also keeps a tribe in perpetual unrest, since periodical demands will be made by Government for those portions actually unoccupied, as the citizen, immigrant or corporation, may make request therefor. This both renders it impossible to fix in the mind of the Indian a feeling of security in his home, and shakes his belief in the public assurances of future permanency which are always given him, whenever abridgments of territorial limits are made. Whatever amount of land is needed to enable him to follow the pursuits to which he is called, should be allowed him at once, and nothing more. Even with that intent in view, he would probably receive more than a required share; for the American idea, that one hundred and sixty acres are indispensable to a white inhabitant seeking to support a family, is generally enlarged when the requirements of the red race are considered. It seems, then, to be the opinion, judging from past actions, that reservations should contain one hundred and sixty acres for each Indian, man, woman and child, or a square mile for each family domiciled. Five times this amount might prove a scanty quantity, if situated on those barren plains of the West, but if selected in a fertile section of country, where abundant crops would reward the husbandman's labor, it should be greatly diminished. The American farmer suffers more from too great possessions in land, which he poorly cultivates, than from a limited supply. The work which he performs, if wisely expended upon fifty acres, would yield more profitable returns than if thinly spread, as is too apt to be the case, over thrice that number. The soil of Belgium supports three hundred and fifty persons to the square mile, and it is estimated that the continent of Europe, already peopled in the ratio of seventy inhabitants to six hundred and forty acres, might with proper tillage, independently sustain a doubly increased population. No Indian family can prosperously cultivate nor make use of more land than the white settler, and not more than the well-known quarter section should be given it. Then the authorities can suffer it to remain in undisturbed possession of its home, and sincerely promise that it shall enjoy the benefits of durable improvements.

The dimensions of reservations should be determined by calculations based upon some such opinion regarding agricultural demands, according to the number of proposed occupants. Large tribes of Indians ought to be divided as to residence. Experience proves that small tribes are more susceptible of improvement than those which are numerous, after both have been located. An aggregate of one thousand or fifteen hundred souls, collected upon a single reservation, exacts the entire time and ability of the faithful agent and his corps of assistants. Small bodies are also more easily tranquilized and influenced in all respects than great ones. The attempt to collect large masses upon reservations in the north-west, and there control them efficiently, has resulted in disaster, because of continued agitation and turbulence, which were thereby rather provoked than allayed. Agents could do little more than feed them, and if a portion reached a well considered intention to locate and till the soil, the opposition was too strong to allow of its execution. Those reservations became nurseries for treasonable projects and criminal designs. Pampered indolence indulged in licentious debauchery, and all those vices in which depraved barbarous nature takes delight. The agent was at the mercy of his people. His safety consisted in the fact that he was the dispenser of Government bounties, and therefore profit insured his preservation.

We do not intend to enter with any more particularity into those measures of Indian policy which suggest themselves when considering the position and condition of the tribes, and the requisite means of necessary education. The main idea intended to be impressed is this :—that the Indian, unless assisted by an overpowering force, will not give up his old habits and follow peaceful pursuits; and that if the Government does not apply this power, there will be no radical improvement, until the force of circumstances effects the change. The methods of application may be various, and some of them much more practical in their natures than those hinted at in the foregoing pages. It is however of slight importance what details are pursued, provided they speedily, firmly, and without unnecessary harshness, fix in the mind of the Indian a sense of responsibility, and a strong feeling of individual reliance. These qualities secured, and the guardianship of Government can be allowed to terminate.

It is possible, and we have thought highly probable, that agricultural labor could not be induced, unless more stringent measures than those suggested should be adopted. And yet, a plan which should compel it, through the immediate action of a present force, would impose a condition of slavery. So also the establishment of more rigorous rules to inculcate moral precepts, and to make profitable educational privileges, might be advantageous. Still, as they should not act with needless unpleasantness upon those placed under them, but appeal, in so far as they can be made to do so, to inclinations and convictions produced by the new surroundings, they should be as mild as emergencies will allow.

Those fertile in expedients could work out numerous plans, by which to impart the many necessary branches of

education, after the condition of rest is attained, and tribal
customs are weakened.

The question of the future relationship of the white
and red races to each other, cannot be satisfactorily determined. Very likely, the idea that a large civilized Indian
nation might be created, and preserved, within the country,
has been entirely abandoned. That has given way to the
hope that Indian communities may be perpetuated, and
made similar, in action and intention, to white societies.
Speculation, however, based upon tendencies as shown in
the past, might lead to the belief that such a hope cannot
be realized.

We have in mind more particularly, that gradual absorption of the Indian stock, which has been in progress
since the discovery of America, and which is even more
noticeable in Mexico, and in some of the South American
provinces, than in the United States. But even with us,
it has been so rapidly progressing, as to raise a strong presumption, that the Indian race will, in a few generations, be
practically absorbed. In eighteen hundred and seventy-six,
the Commissioner of Indian Affairs reported, that nearly
one-sixth of the Indian population of the United States,
exclusive of Alaska, was made up of mixed bloods ; and
his figures show, that only about one half of the Cherokees,
Creeks, Choctaws, Chickasaws and Seminoles are of pure
extraction. These estimates are approximative, and really
enumerate the mixed bloods at too low a rate. At many
of the agencies, a large number of the half and quarter
breeds there dwelling seem to be almost entirely ignored.

We would not attempt to say, whether this amalgamating
tendency is natural, or is due more particularly to circumstances ; but simply state the fact that it exists, and that
there does not seem to be a sufficient antipathy of race to
prevent its continuance. If due to circumstances, the very
measures which have been devised to arrest its operation,

have apparently assisted it. It is not those tribes which have uninterruptedly lived in portions of thickly settled States, nor those of the far West which have been undomiciled, and therefore unaffected by law, which display, in the greatest degree, the complexion and lineaments of the whites ; but those which have dwelt for a long time upon the border of civilization, and have been subjected to the regulations of the Indian Bureau. More than eleven-twelfths of the New York Indian population is reported to be of pure Indian blood, and the wild tribes show a much greater race purity.

Undoubtedly, in localities where the two races intermingle, the extent to which amalgamation or intermarriage is practiced, depends largely upon the proportion of females in the white population. If the two sexes are numerically balanced, there is but little intermixture. Upon this theory we will base the assertion, that within a few generations of time, the New York Indians will exhibit more true representatives of the original stock than any of the wild tribes of the plains.

If the measures which have been attempted in order to prevent this social and domestic commingling, have not really aided it, they have been powerless to prevent it. Indeed, as the tribes are situated, it would be difficult to suggest a possible remedy. There are but few instances in history, where clans, tribes, or people, of a distinct stock, have been so partial to their own lineage or descent, as to be checked from affiliating with, and intermarrying among those of a different origin and nature, in case both are thrown into close neighborhood ; whether or not there is among either, disparity as regards the number of sex. Religious antagonism and fanatical opposition have proved greater restraints to admixture of blood than pride or love of race.

People of varying types unite and become as one, when

placed under the same system of laws, with equality of
freedom and political rights. The consequence of this
union is a new order of humanity, in which the characteristics pertaining to both branches of ancestors are to a certain extent displayed. The fusion of discordant social
elements among the nations of Europe has resulted in
homogeneous populations. How many different races,
how many diversified civilizations, how many hordes of
barbarians, have been combined to make up the present
kingdom of Italy. Each has brought its influence to bear
upon the national character, and has produced mental and
physical modifications—even though foreign blood has not
at any time been sufficiently taken, to destroy traditional
sentiments.

The gradual absorption of our Indian stock will assuredly continue, and it is probable, that it will be finally
merged in the great body of our white population. The
question whether the unity of the two races will produce
vigorous physical organisms, is still debatable ; and the
psychological inquiry, whether the product will be mentally and morally of an inferior order, is still unsettled in
the minds of many. Our own opinions upon the latter
subject are decided, and have already been advanced.
The cross will be an inferior being, both in mind and
morals, when viewed in the light of our civilization, or
rather, when measured by the rules prescribed by our civilization, as tests of nature and quality.

However much such an ultimate result is to be deplored, the effect will scarcely be perceptible upon our institutions, except in those sections of country where the
Indians shall have been collected in masses. They are
now in numbers, only as one to ninety of our entire white
population ; and indeed as one to twelve of our colored
population. In nineteen hundred, the ratio of Indians to
whites, even if the two races can be restrained from much

intermingling, will be about as one to one hundred and seventy-five.   Whatever view therefore, may be taken of this social problem, no decided effect can be produced upon our national character.   It is only in the event that Indians are collected in large bodies (which certainly, in so far as attempted, seems to have encouraged amalgamation,) that any danger is to be apprehended.   Should a course of action, having for its object the concentration of the tribes, be persistently and successfully prosecuted, we shall have, within the heart of the United States, an element which will there prolong social disorder for generations to come.   If scattered throughout the interior, its evil effects will, in a short time, be neutralized.

THE END.